MY

TRANSCENDENT

A Starling Novel

Also by
LESLEY LIVINGSTON

In this series

Starling

Descendant

The Wondrous Strange trilogy

Darklight

Tempestuous

Wondrous Strange

TRANSCENDENT

A Starling Novel

LESLEY LIVINGSTON

HARPER TEEN

An Imprint of HarperCollins*Publishers*

HarperTeen is an imprint of HarperCollins Publishers.

Transcendent: A Starling Novel
Copyright © 2015 by Lesley Livingston
www.epicreads.com

Library of Congress Cataloging-in-Publication Data
Livingston, Lesley.
    Transcendent : a Starling novel / Lesley Livingston. — First edition.
      pages cm
    Summary: "In this epic conclusion to the Starling trilogy, Mason
Starling has taken up the Spear of Odin and has begun the series of
events that marks the end of the world"— Provided by publisher.
    ISBN 978-0-06-206313-7
    [1. Supernatural—Fiction. 2. Mythology, Norse—Fiction. 3. End of
the world—Fiction.] I. Title.
PZ7.L7613Tr 2015   2014022031
[Fic]—dc23   CIP
                                                                     AC

Typography by Jane Archer
    14 15 16 17 18   CG/RRDH   10 9 8 7 6 5 4 3 2 1

First Edition

For Laura

"This is not right . . . ," Mason Starling murmured softly as she sank to her knees beside the crumpled form at the center of a swiftly widening circle of blood.

The stone tiles beneath her shuddered with earthquake tremors and her ears rang with the screams of the white-robed crowd gathered on the terrace swaying high above the streets of Manhattan—streets tangled in chaos, awash in a blood curse that had turned the city into a slumbering wasteland.

None of that mattered.

None of it even touched Mason in that moment.

"I am the chooser of the slain . . ." The words drifted like smoke from between her lips. "I did *not* choose this."

"Neither did I, sweetheart," Fennrys whispered. "Not this time . . ."

A gout of blood bubbled up and spilled from his mouth down the side of his face, shockingly red against the pallor that washed his skin white. It sparked fire and fury in Mason's heart and the roar of her denial was so loud in her head she thought her skull might burst.

A clap of thunder shattered the night.

The raven, perched on the spear Mason held, shrieked and her mind snapped back into focus as the bird launched itself into the stygian darkness of the stormy sky. She stared in horror at the Odin spear, clutched in her armored fist. With a cry of outrage, she threw it away from her. It clattered against the black marble altar where her brother Roth lay bound, bleeding, gasping, whispering apologies for the murder he'd done. A deed, past and gone, that fueled the Miasma curse spilling out over the city.

That could wait.

This . . . couldn't.

Mason lurched forward, reaching for the dark slender figure kneeling on the other side of Fennrys's blood-soaked body. She grabbed the Egyptian god of death by the lapels of his sleek designer suit and said, "Fix this."

"Mason—"

"*Fix him!*" she howled, cutting short Rafe's protestations. Her hands balled into fists and she hauled the god toward her until they were almost nose to nose. Her howl turned into a harsh, choking sob. "I'm begging you. . . ."

The muscles of Rafe's jaw twitched and his dark brows drew together in a fierce frown. "You know damn well there's only one way I can do that. And there is no guarantee that—"

"*Do* it."

Still the god hesitated. Mason could see the anguish in his

dark, timeless gaze. The thing that had just happened . . . it was wrong, and Rafe knew it. Fennrys had beaten the odds. He deserved a second chance and now, to have that chance stolen from him . . .

Mason shivered in the wind. The water from Calum Aristarchos's trident soaked the front of her chain-mail tunic, shockingly cold. It had taken only a moment of thoughtless reaction on Cal's part to form the weapon—transforming water from a weeping fountain, turning it hard as forged steel with his newfound, godlike powers. And only another moment more to pierce Fennrys's body with the lethal instrument.

It had all been a terrible mistake. Still, Cal would pay for it. Later.

Cal could wait.

Fennrys's breath had gone from shallow to a rasping gasp. A death rattle . . .

"Do it!" Mason snarled at Rafe.

The god squeezed his eyes shut.

"I'll *owe* you," she said.

His eyes snapped back open. And there was fire in their depths.

Hellfire.

Rafe, who was Anubis, growled low in the back of his throat and his shoulders hunched forward toward his ears. Suddenly, he threw his head back, his helmet of dreadlocks whipping around his face and his features blurred like inky smoke. In the blink of an eye, the stylish young man in the tailored suit was gone and a huge, sleek black wolf crouched on its haunches on the stone terrace, lips pulled back from long, white, *sharp* teeth bared in a vicious snarl. The wolf shook its head from side to side, ears flattened back against its skull. The muscles along its shoulders and spine rippled and Mason backed off, fighting the urge to wrap Fennrys's body in an embrace and shield him from the monstrous creature.

She looked down and saw Fenn's eyelids flutter and go still. The planes of his face went slack.

Then her view of him was blotted out by the dark shape of the wolf as it lunged, jaws opened wide . . . to sink his teeth deep into Fennrys's throat.

Fennrys was dying.

Again . . .

Only, the weird thing was, it actually felt different this time.

Real.

He could feel the warm breath cooling in his lungs.

Hear the rhythm of his heart, slowing . . .

There was peace.

Acceptance . . .

And then, just as his eyes were drifting closed for the last time, his fading vision captured a glimpse of something twisting in the depths of Mason Starling's sapphire-blue gaze. And all of it shattered into a thousand jagged shards of pain.

Of course. It was never gonna be that easy, was it?

The sudden, scorching agony that tore at his throat flooded down into this chest and up into his brain. His heart squeezed like a fist and his body arched like a bow, stretching away from the cold marble floor and the warm pool of blood. A sudden, overwhelming, gut-deep feeling crashed down on him like a load of bricks falling from a great height—a purely, potently physical sensation—something that Fennrys was pretty sure he shouldn't be feeling in his death throes.

Hunger.

A dark red ravenous wave washed over him, pounding him insensible. . . .

And then there was nothing more.

II

L ightning flashed overhead.

And again.

And one last time.

The glass barriers surrounding the terrace shattered and shards flew through the air like deadly arrows, propelled by gale-force winds. Chaos erupted as the gathered crowd of white-robed Eleusinians—most of them the parents or relatives of Gosforth Academy students—scattered, pushing and shoving to get back inside the Weather Room and running for the elevators and the emergency stairs as they abandoned their truncated ritual. They fled from the terrace, and the black marble altar where Mason's brother, Roth, lay bound and bleeding, fueling the curse that had cast all of the island of Manhattan in a death sleep.

Mason didn't care.

Let them run, she thought. *They are sheep. They don't matter.*

All that mattered was the Wolf.

The Fennrys Wolf, whose body writhed and contorted before her, his throat gripped in Anubis's lupine jaws. Mason watched, numb, as the horror of the moment stretched out to seeming infinity.

She felt hollow, transparent . . . a phantasm.

Anubis sank his long white fangs into Fenn's flesh, spilling even more of the precious blood from his body, and in that moment the world all around her went from bright white to dark red . . . and then faded to a gray, grainy static. She stood there, detached, distant.

Fennrys is going to live.

He had to. Anything else wasn't an option.

Mason was dimly aware of when Toby Fortier and Maddox, Fenn's fellow Janus Guard and friend, stepped out onto the terrace. She heard their voices—angry, frightened, demanding to know what the hell was going on—and she ignored them. She saw Maddox step in front of Daria Aristarchos to keep her from going anywhere, and Toby rush to where Heather Palmerston still knelt, crouched in a ball behind the altar near the gaping space where the glass barrier used to be. The fencing master used his black-bladed knife to free her from the cloth ropes that tied her hands and helped her stand. She was covered in sharp, tiny shards that tinkled as they fell from her hair and clothes, but she seemed unharmed. Mason knew she should have been happy about that. Or relieved. Or something. Heather was a friend—a good one—and she'd gone to the wall for Mason and had suffered for it.

But in that moment, all Mason could think about was Fennrys. Time seemed to stop and the universe spiraled out in a dark wave from the single, spotlight circle where she knelt beside him. Beside him . . . and the dark god who was, at her demand, doing his best to save Fenn's life. In the worst way imaginable. She closed her eyes, willing herself not to see how much blood had already spilled from Fenn's body. An eternity passed, and then she heard a shredded gasp escape Fennrys's lips.

Mason's eyes flew open and she saw Rafe falling back and away from the prone body beneath him. The ancient Egyptian god, his human shape still blurred around the edges, staggered to his feet. He wiped the back of one hand across his mouth, lips pulled back in a feral snarl, teeth crimson with blood.

When he turned his gaze on her, Mason saw that his eyes were completely black. They stared at each other for a long moment. Then Rafe shook his head, the pencil-thin dreadlocks falling forward to curtain his face, and called to someone in the Weather Room in a language Mason couldn't understand. Before she could gather her thoughts, the wolves of Rafe's pack padded out onto the terrace, and Rafe disappeared back inside, stumbling with exhaustion. The pack surrounded Fenn, and two of the wolves shimmered and blurred, shifting. Suddenly, there was a pair of hard-muscled young men standing in their place. Without a word, they bent down and picked up Fennrys by his arms and legs. His head lolled back and he struggled weakly as they carried him in Rafe's wake.

The Fennrys Wolf was alive.

Mason almost wept with relief as the fog in her brain suddenly dissipated. She scrambled to her feet and started to follow, but another of the wolves—the she-wolf with the white blaze on her forehead—suddenly shifted into her human form and stepped in front of Mason and didn't move aside.

Honora, the investment banker who moonlights as a werewolf, Mason thought, remembering what Rafe had told her. She wondered fleetingly if the "moonlighting" was a literal truth. She didn't, after all, know very much at all about these creatures and their existence. *Maybe you should have thought about that before you consigned Fennrys to share their fate.*

I didn't have a chance. I didn't have a choice.

Mason cleared her throat. "Honora, isn't it?" she asked.

The woman nodded. There wasn't a hair out of place in her sleek chignon coif, accented with a streak of silver that corresponded with the blaze on the forehead of her wolf-self, and her eyes, a shade of pale greenish-gold, flashed with sharp intelligence. She was slender but strong looking beneath a navy tailored suit and looked almost exactly the way Mason had pictured she would.

"Excuse me, Honora," Mason said, trying to keep her voice from cracking with strain. "I need to go see him—"

"No. You don't." Honora didn't move. "Not now. Let the pack deal with him. He's one of us now and that's not going to be an easy thing for that boy to handle."

"What do you mean?"

"What do you think I mean, Ms. Starling?"

Honora's eyes narrowed as she held Mason's gaze. Her voice was quiet, but it was firm. Mason realized that she might find understanding in this woman, but not sympathy. Honora knew what Mason had asked Rafe to do, and she most likely understood why. But it was apparent in that instant that she did not approve. Not even a little bit. Mason wondered under what circumstances Honora had made *her* bargain with Anubis.

"I *mean*, you just turned that boy into a monster," Honora continued. "Now you're going to have to step back and let us help him hold on to his humanity. If he can." Then she turned on the heels of her sensible-but-sexy black leather pumps and stalked after her pack, her god, and Fennrys.

Mason watched her go, and then turned to find that only a handful of people were left standing on that windswept square of stone perched high above the city: Toby and Heather, both of them eyeing her warily, as if worried about what she might do next, and Calum—transfigured, transformed, alien to Mason on almost every level now, and looking strangely adrift in the wake of the chaos.

Maddox stood before Daria Aristarchos—one hand held out in front of her and the spiked silver chain he wielded so expertly dangling from his other fist. The high priestess of the Eleusinian mysteries barely seemed to notice the Janus Guard. She seemed frozen, her gaze the only thing about her that moved as it flicked back and forth, rife with disbelief, shifting with suspicion, from Mason to the blood on the terrace, to the face of her son, Cal.

The son Daria had believed was dead.

That belief had been the catalyst that had triggered a

diabolically planned—but long dormant—revenge scheme and pushed Daria to conjure a blood curse, using Rothgar Starling, Mason's beloved brother, as fuel. Because Roth was a kin killer. He lay sprawled on top of the black marble surface of the terrible altar, senseless and twitching in agony. Behind him, Gwen Littlefield—slender, purple-haired, her face a mask of anguish—still stood with her hands pressed to the cold stone, pale fingers splayed wide, as the blood curse coursed from Roth through her . . . and out into the city.

Gwen was Daria's haruspex—a young, hapless sorceress the Elusinian priestess had trapped into serving as her seer—and the conduit for her terrible blood magick. Mason could feel the power emanating from the slight, fragile-looking girl. It rolled off her in waves.

Roth was incoherent, his arms and chest covered in long shallow cuts made by the sickle in Daria's fist. The wounds must have been painful, but they weren't life threatening. It was only the curse that seriously afflicted him.

Just as it afflicted the girl he shared the terrible connection with.

Mason stooped to pick up the long knife lying in the puddled blood and water at her feet—the one that Fennrys had dropped when Cal had stabbed him through the chest—and she stalked over to Daria. The priestess swept the elegantly curved blade she held up to ward off the furious young Valkyrie, but Mason just ducked past the blur of the sickle and smashed her armor-clad elbow against Daria's wrist. Then she grabbed her by the front of her priestess robes and brought her own knife up to press against Cal's mother's throat.

The silver blade in Daria's hand clattered to the stone tiles and she backed up as far as she could, stumbling over the hem of her robes and grabbing at the low stone buttress surrounding the terrace—the only barrier left to keep her from plummeting off the building now that the glass panels had been blown to smithereens.

The wind pushed at Mason's back.

"Mason!" Cal cried out in alarm.

She ignored him.

"Make this stop," she said, her voice shuddering through the air like thunder.

For a moment, Daria just looked at her as if she was speaking in tongues. Her gaze raked up and down over Mason's Valkyrie armor, and she shook her head in dazed disbelief. Or denial. Her sharp shoulders, draped in the white tunic of her priestess order, began to quake as though she was on the verge of either sobbing or laughing hysterically.

Mason shook her by the arm, hard. "The curse," she said. "Make it stop!"

Cal took a wary step toward them. "Mase—"

Mason shot him a look from beneath the brim of her helmet that stopped him in his tracks. Then she turned back to Daria. *"Now."*

"I can't . . . ," she said in a ragged croak.

A sickly, silver light twisted in the black depths of Daria's widely dilated eyes, and Mason realized that the priestess was still caught in the throes of the enchantment herself.

"Once begun, the Miasma will continue until the engine

that drives the curse is no more," Daria continued. "You want me to end it? That means breaking the link between your brother and my haruspex—a link that can only be broken by death."

Death . . .

The word knifed through Mason's brain, acid-sweet, seductive as Siren song.

Down below in the streets, amid the wrecked cars and the brownstone blocks on fire, she could *feel* death. All of them. Every single one. She could sense—distantly, but distinctly—the passing of each and every human life that was ending in the city that night. And those numbers were creeping steadily upward. It was like a thousand tiny wounds, cutting her up inside. Mason felt a blinding rush of rage filling her head. She heard herself snarling like an animal as she pressed the knife blade into the flesh of Daria's throat. The high priestess bent backward, hanging out over the empty space high above Rockefeller Plaza, real fear carving the planes of her face.

Through the haze of incandescent anger, Mason heard someone calling her name again, but it wasn't Cal this time. "Mason!" Toby Fortier, Mason's erstwhile coach, shouted. "Stand down! Drop that weapon, Starling!"

Her knee-jerk reflexes from hundreds of hours obeying the fencing master's barked commands almost made her do just that.

"Mason! *Do you hear me?*"

She did. But she ignored both him and the impulse to disengage, and instead tightened her grip around the weapon's hilt and pressed the blade tighter to Daria's throat.

"Mason—"

"It's too late!" Daria screeched. "It's *your* father, Mason, who pushed me to this! He would end us all—you, me, the world!—if I don't stop him. You . . . you don't want that! I know you don't. Help me. Defy him. We can build a paradise on Earth. Don't let your brother's noble sacrifice be in vain—"

Over the sound of Toby's yelling, and the howling wind, and the skirling words of Daria's desperate pleas, Mason suddenly heard another noise. A low, gentle moaning, it was a sound that was full of sorrow and love . . .

And good-bye.

It took her a moment to place the voice—an older version of the one she used to hear chattering shyly with Roth in the Gosforth school quad when they were children. Gwen Littlefield's voice. The voice of a child who had grown up to become a power in her own right, except for the fact that she'd been harnessed—and used and abused—by Daria Aristarchos.

Gwen . . .

Mason turned and glanced over her shoulder, just in time to see Gwen lean down over the altar stone. Somehow, through a sheer act of iron will, she had managed to take back a measure of control over her rigid, curse-afflicted body and had pried her hands off the stone altar. Her palms were bloodied, but she didn't seem to notice as she placed a long, lingering kiss on Roth's lips. He struggled against the effects of the curse to reach for her as well. In vain.

Gwen drew back, shook her head sharply, eyes suddenly clear-witted and sparkling with tears beneath the fringe of her purple hair. Then she spun and sprinted for the edge of the terrace, swifter than a gazelle. Mason watched, horrified, as Gwen opened her arms wide . . .

And threw herself off the tower, into the embrace of the night.

III

Gunnar Starling stood looking into the enormous smoked glass mirror hanging on the wall of the sitting room in the palatial midtown condominium, staring past his own reflection as if he could see hidden things moving beyond. Rory stood in the doorway of the room staring at his father, at the way the light from the flames in the fireplace was echoed by the golden glow in Gunnar Starling's left eye. The shadows that leaped up the wall behind Gunnar seemed more . . . animated than they perhaps should. And Rory could have sworn he smelled smoke that was different from just the apple-wood scent the flames usually gave off in the sleek designer fireplace. He could smell the acrid tang of melting metal. And . . . flesh. He could smell blood.

He closed his eyes and, for a brief disorienting moment, he thought he could hear screaming. He opened them again and the sound vanished, and he wondered if it was just the muted strains of the chaos far below in the streets of the city. But the balcony doors were closed against the fierce, freezing rain and driving winds. Lightning strobed against the angry darkness of thunderheads that were so low in the sky Rory felt that if he stepped outside and lifted his hand—his shining, *silver* hand—he could touch them.

He turned back to watch his father and saw that the mirror no longer reflected the room he stood in. Rather, the image enclosed in the heavy oak frame was both familiar and utterly alien. A white room, lit with red and purple light, and his sister standing in the middle of it. Only . . . she looked . . .

Fantastic.

And terrifying.

Rory had never thought of Mouse in either of those terms before. But seeing her standing there, a raven-winged helmet on her brow, clothed head to toe in shimmering silver chain mail and supple black leather, a midnight-blue cloak swept back from her shoulder and a tall, slender spear held in her fist . . .

"She's magnificent," Gunnar said, "isn't she?"

The paternal pride in his voice grated Rory's nerves raw. Magnificent? More magnificent than a son with a silver hand?

"Yeah." Rory tried to muster enough enthusiasm so as not to incur his father's displeasure. Gunnar doted on Mason and so Rory had to play nice. For now. "She's something, all right," he said. "Nice hat."

Gunnar sighed and turned away from the mirror, pegging his youngest son with a disconcerting stare. Even though Rory knew his father had sacrificed the physical sight in his left eye to the Norns for the gift of "other" sight, it was *that* eye that seemed to see him most clearly. The thread of twisting golden light shimmered for a moment in the depths of that eye, flickering and fading as Gunnar dropped his hand from the surface of the mirror and the image of Mason and her companions faded to shadows. Gunnar crossed the room and put a hand on his son's shoulder, drawing him over to the fireplace. The light of the flames reflecting on the elder Starling's strong, angular features and the pale silver lion's mane of his hair made him look as if he were a god of fire. The thunderstorm raged outside, and the floor-to-ceiling windows of the penthouse behind Gunnar only served to heighten the effect. Rory was struck by a moment of awe as he stood regarding the man whom he had loved and hated—and feared—all his life.

"Rory . . . you are my son. You are precious to me, even though I know that you, yourself, do not believe that. And because you are my son, I have in the past turned a blind eye to your . . . indiscretions." Before Rory could even fully form the thought in his own mind, Gunnar's lip twisted in the shadow of a grin. "And no," he said, "that is not a joke, present circumstances notwithstanding. Now that I have sacrificed one of my eyes to gain true vision, I *see* so many things."

He gestured to the figures in the mirror and Rory saw Roth lying flat on his back and staring up with roaming, sightless eyes. It looked like someone had taken a truncheon to him— he was all blood and gashes—and his face was drawn in an expression of agony that went deeper than physical pain. And even as Rory's gut twisted in horror at the sight something else inside of him whispered, *Good*.

"Your brother has betrayed me," Gunnar said. "But it is all to the purpose. He doesn't know it yet, but his struggle against his fate is what has brought him face-to-face with it. I see that now." He turned to Rory. "As I see you. I understand you a little better, I think. You are a survivor. And that is as it should be. That is *your* destiny."

Rory wanted more than survival. But he was smart enough not to say so. And Top Gunn did have a point. Survival was a pretty intrinsic step to achieving what he wanted. And that was . . . well, everything. The goods, the glory, the girls . . . He wanted the Heather Palmerstons of the world to worship him and the Calum Aristarchoses to bring him drinks and grovel abjectly for mercy when they were too slow—mercy that Rory would be typically reluctant to grant. Of course, he realized he was, essentially, reveling in the potential of megalomania. Whatever. For some reason, pretty much everyone he'd ever known had pegged Rory as a bad seed from the time he was a little kid. Who was he to defy expectations?

"You know why we do this. You understand this drive toward oblivion." Gunnar gazed at him with that unblinking half stare that Rory could feel penetrating to the back of his skull. "You know there must be an end so there can be a new beginning. We do this out of love, Rory. Love for this world and the desire to make it whole again in the face of all that humankind has wrought upon the most precious creation in the universe."

Love? Rory thought. He didn't even have to struggle to school his expression in the face of his father's ridiculous sentimentality. It was *so* laughable that he almost felt sorry for the old man. Still, he had to be careful. If he was going to survive what was to come, he was going to need Gunnar. Right up until the moment he met his destiny. Which, if Rory understood correctly, was to fulfill the great god Odin's role and be slaughtered in battle by—if what his father had said was true—Mason's new boyfriend.

Rory felt his brow knit in a frown as he attempted—not for the first time—to wrap his head around that. Around all of it. From everything he'd been told, his understanding of the Norse gods was this: Over the long years, when the beliefs of men drifted from them, the Aesir began to fade from existence. Balder had been the first to go, and that started the whole long, slow decline. The other gods and goddesses had followed. Not all of them, and not completely. More like, the *person* of Odin had fallen away, but the *power* remained, to be assumed in time by one who was deemed worthy, or strong enough. *Or maybe stupid enough,* Rory thought. He understood that was not the case for all the gods. Loki, stubborn and contrary to the end, had endured, willfully remaining chained in torment. Heimdall, too, had clung to his grim post as harbinger of the End of Days. More than harbinger, lately, according to the Norns. Instigator. And they should know—it was what *they* had done throughout history, after all: instigate. Only this time, with Gunnar Starling and his family, it seemed as though they might actually be successful.

"Something bothering you, son?" Gunnar asked.

Rory clenched and unclenched his silver fingers. The feel of his hand closing into that hammer of a fist comforted him.

Calmed him. "I just . . . I guess I'm still trying to understand how all this is happening. And why."

"The 'why' is that we have—thus far—been found worthy by the fates to carry out the sacred duties of our forefathers to their ultimate end. The 'how' is . . . well, magick."

"Yeah. I get that. I think. But—"

He broke off when his father suddenly gasped and grabbed for the left side of his face with both hands. Gunnar's head snapped back and he staggered a few steps, teeth clenched in what looked like excruciating pain.

"Dad?" Rory took a hesitant step toward him, reaching out with his still-human hand. "You okay . . . ?"

Gunnar leaned heavily on the back of one of the room's leather wingback chairs, heaving in ragged gasps. He dropped his hand and Rory saw that a red gleam had replaced the twist of gold in his eye. All the blood had drained from his face and he was deathly pale. "Did you feel that?" he asked.

Rory frowned. *Feel what?* Truthfully, all he felt was a sudden hollowness in his stomach, like a deep hunger pang.

"The void," Gunnar murmured. "There is an emptiness."

Maybe he *did* feel something.

"Something has happened. . . ."

As Rory watched, Gunnar's red-tinged gaze turned inward and a slow, terrifying grin spread over his face. He nodded in satisfaction.

"The little witch," he said. "The haruspex . . . She's ended herself. I guess she finally had enough of being a thrall. Daria must be terribly disappointed, but now we have our opportunity. We will have to move with some haste, though. They won't stay at her temple much longer, and the Miasma will lift soon. Are you strong enough to go out into the city?"

"Of course I am," Rory snapped. Who the hell did his father think he was? Sure, he'd had the crap massively kicked out of him and his arm destroyed only a few days earlier. But like the Bionic Man, he was better now. Better, stronger, faster . . . At his side, his silver fingers closed in on themselves.

"Hmm," his father grunted. "We shall see."

He turned back to the mirror on the wall and lifted his hand, placing his palm on the smooth surface, which wavered like a mirage and resolved to show Mason again. She no longer wore her Valkyrie garb, and she seemed to be arguing with Cal. There was something very different about *him,* too, Rory thought.

"I want you to go to them. Find them and provoke them into a fight. I have resources you can use to such an end. Mason must be goaded into fulfilling her role as the chooser of the slain. It is against her nature, but she *must* take on that mantle—it is vital. Without a third Odin son—without someone to take up the mantle of Thor—there will be no Ragnarok. As I have been made the vessel of the Allfather's power, so you and your brother carry the essences of Vali and Vidar, the children of Odin destined to rebuild the world. Mason was to be the third son. The sacrifice. She was to fulfill the role of Thor and lay down her life on the field alongside mine." Gunnar's brow creased in a dark frown, and lightning from the storm cast his features in a sudden, ugly grimace. "Her mother thwarted me in that. But now I have the chance to right her wrong. Mason as a Valkyrie will choose the third

Odin son, and it is my wish that she choose . . . him."

Gunnar nodded to the mirror and Rory began to sputter in outrage.

"Cal?" he squawked. "Him? You have got to be kidding! That guy's a total tool! Jeezus, Dad—anyone but him!"

Gunnar cast a grimly amused glance at his son. "Are you going to let petty high school jealousy get in the way of a glorious apocalypse?"

"Yes!" Rory exclaimed. "He's not Thor—he's a . . . a pompous jerkass!"

"Here's hoping he's a pompous jerkass who can hold his own in a fight," Gunnar said. "I seem to remember from attending your sister's fencing competitions that he can. Well then. As I say—you must draw them into conflict. And you must see to it that Cal's striving is the most valiant. Mason must see him as the best candidate to choose."

"That's not going to happen." Rory shook his head. "Not with that Fennrys dude around."

"Do not engage the Wolf," Gunnar said sternly. "Do not give him anything to fight. Frustrate his attempts and concentrate your efforts on the Aristarchos boy. See to it she chooses him and then, when the final wheel is set in motion, get out of the way and let destiny take its course. The Wolf *must* remain as he is, so that in the end, he and I may meet on the field. He will take my life, and then Roth will take his. The Aristarchos boy, wearing the mantle of the thunder god, will die alongside us both. Now, how sweet an irony is that? And how convenient that he's half god already."

"He's *what*?"

Now, how in hell did that *happen?* Rory wondered.

Gunnar ignored his outburst. "He is also the son of my greatest rival, and he's already marked by the draugr."

"And he's a total horn-dog," Rory said, ignoring the shudder that ran through him at the memory of that night in the Gosforth gym, when the draugr—Norse zombie warriors—had first attacked. "He's got the drooling hots for your daughter, you know!"

"Good!" Gunnar enthused and clapped Rory on the shoulder. "Then he might even appreciate it when Mason bestows on him the power of the Thunderer. For the brief time he'll have left to live, that is."

Great, Rory fumed silently. *So that pansy-ass pretty boy gets ramped up to Thor status, Roth gets to kill Mason's wolf-boy, and I'm like . . . what? The overlooked middle god?* What exactly was Vali's claim to fame in the legends anyway, besides outliving most everyone? *Oh, right . . . something about being born to be a brother killer in the old tales.*

At that thought, Rory shrugged inwardly and sighed.

"Fine. I can live with that," he muttered to himself. "And then Roth better watch his ass in our brave new world."

IV

The gale-force winds howling around the top of the skyscraper snatched Gwen Littlefield's body and spun her out into darkness. She arced in a trajectory that took her far away from the Rockefeller tower's terraced sides and then plummeted like a stone toward the plaza sixty-seven stories below, where Mason could just glimpse the golden statue of Prometheus, Titan hero of Greek myth and champion of humanity, carrying his stolen fire down from the heavens.

Somewhere in the dark skies above, the raven shrieked.

Heather screamed.

Mason turned away before she saw Gwen's body hit the ground.

But even still, she couldn't stop from *feeling* the girl's death in her Valkyrie's heart. It felt like someone punching her in the sternum—hard enough to crack her ribs—and Mason doubled over for an instant, awash in agony. She thought she would fall to the ground, but suddenly there were strong arms wrapped around her, someone holding her tightly in a fierce embrace. Mason sagged against the wall of chest muscles, behind which she could hear the thunderous beating of a heart. She could feel breath flowing in and out of lungs and it almost sounded to her like the ebb and flow of the ocean—a tidal rush of pounding surf.

Waves . . .

Water.

She pushed away and looked up into Calum's sea-green eyes.

"Get away from me, you son of a bitch!" Mason struggled to free herself from the vise of his embrace. When had Cal ever been that strong? Then again, when had she? With a convulsive shove, she straight-armed him away from her—hard enough to wind him as he staggered back and his shoulders slammed into stone parapet.

They were so high up that, in the far-off distance, Mason could see the wreckage of the Hell Gate Bridge, starkly illuminated by the work lights of the demolition crews that worked night and day to remove the shattered fragments of the bridge that had taken her to Asgard not three short days earlier. A lifetime.

An eternity.

Cal reached out a hand toward her. "Mase—"

She batted his arm away with a savagery that surprised him. She could see it in his eyes, but she didn't care. The echoes of Gwen Littlefield's death clawed at the insides of her skull, and inside the Weather Room she heard the heartbreaking cry of wolf-song. Mason spared Cal a venomous glare and, tearing the helmet from her head, hurled it at one of the tall windows. The impact left a spiderweb of cracks, radiating outward like Arachne's fabled tapestry—the one that had so angered the goddess Athena that she'd turned the weaver into a spider.

It's a bad idea to piss off goddesses, Mason thought.

Is that what you think you are?

She didn't know. She didn't know anything with any certainty anymore. She only knew she hurt. And she wasn't the only one. The sound of ragged screaming made her look back to see Roth rising up from the altar. The narcotic *kykeon* and the curse magicks still coursing through him made his movements wildly clumsy and dangerous as he careened toward the stone ledge from which the girl he loved had just launched herself into nothingness.

He cried out her name, the sound on his lips like a raw wound torn in the air, and lurched for the parapet. Toby and Maddox rushed forward and grabbed him by his bloodied arms to keep him from following in Gwen's wake. Roth was too messed up to fight them for long. The sudden severing of his psychic connection with Gwen—shocking in its permanency—hit him devastatingly hard. His knees buckled and he sagged against the other two men. But as the fencing instructor and the Janus Guard tried to lead him away from the edge of the abyss, Roth's glassy stare locked on to Daria and his face twisted into a mask of horror and hate, carved with the blade of a breaking heart. He lunged, and Mason thrust herself in front of Daria an instant before Roth could rip her throat out with his bare hands.

"No!" she shouted at him, forcing him back.

"Get off me, Mase!" he snarled.

"No . . . Roth," Mason pleaded. "No more blood!"

Her Valkyrie strength barely kept him from reaching Daria as he thrashed and lunged. Mason dug her fingers into his flesh and shook him by the shoulders until his teeth rattled to make him look at her. When Roth's mad-eyed stare finally seemed to focus on her face, Mason's throat closed tight with sorrow at what she saw there. Her next words rasped from her mouth in a whisper.

"No more blood," she said, turning him away from Daria. "Not even hers."

"Mase . . ."

"Please."

Roth reached up to grasp the sides of his sister's face and he leaned his forehead against hers. His skin was slick with sweat. And blood and tears.

"This has to end," he whispered.

"I know." She nodded her forehead against his. "But not like this. We are not killers, Roth. You're not a killer. No matter what she made you do . . . no matter what happened in the past. We are not our parents and we are *not* pawns in this sick stupid game of theirs. Don't you see? Gwen just proved that beyond every shadow of a doubt. She made a choice, and you have to honor that." She pulled her head back and looked into his bloodshot eyes. "You have to trust it. And her. And me."

Roth blinked at her dully for a moment. Then he laughed. His laughter was the harsh call of a carrion crow and it chilled her to the marrow.

"*Trust* you, little sister?" he asked.

He let go of her and backed off a few lurching steps.

"I *ended* you."

"Roth—"

"You're not supposed to exist!" he howled savagely, waving one arm wildly in her direction. "And yet, here you are. You're a freaking *Valkyrie*. That *happened*. In spite of everything we did." He stalked back and grabbed her by the back of her head, pulling her face so close to his she could feel his breath hot on her cheeks. "You think you have a say in this?" he hissed. "You don't. And you want me to *trust* you? You scare the shit out of me, Mason. How'm I supposed to trust that?"

He let go of her and Mason took a stumbling step back, away from the rage and pain and hollow-eyed horror in her brother's face. Roth had always been a rock for Mason. The opposite of her self-absorbed jackass of a brother, Rory.

Roth protected her. He looked out for her.

He murdered you . . .

Maybe he was right. Maybe she shouldn't exist.

No.

She shook her head. That wasn't Roth talking. And it hadn't been Roth acting, all those years ago. It had been the will of the woman that Mason had just stopped Roth from attacking. Part of her whispered that she should step aside. *Let him do it.*

She'd been about to do it herself only a few moments earlier, hadn't she?

"No." Mason shook her head again, partly to convince

herself. "I don't know, Roth. Maybe we can't truly trust each other ever again. But if that's the case, then we might as well just give up and admit it's all over."

Roth's expression went from savage to stricken. His hands dropped to his sides and his shoulders slumped. In the lull that followed, the glass door to the terrace opened and Honora poked her head out. She didn't look at Mason, just gestured to Toby and Maddox.

"We could use some extra muscle," she said. "Just to keep him from injuring himself."

The look in her eyes made Mason think she'd silently added the words "or us" to the end of that sentence. Toby glanced at Mason, hesitating, but she nodded for him to go. Maddox was already through the door and gone and Mason felt better knowing they would be there to help Fenn. She desperately wanted to go to him herself, but Honora's request for help clearly hadn't been extended to include her, and the last thing Fennrys needed was for Mason to start stirring things up with the creatures—*people, Mase; they're people*—who were trying to help him.

As the door swung closed behind the wolf-woman, Mason looked down at the shimmering, magickal armor that still clothed her, head to toe. The Odin spear lay on the ground at the foot of the altar, an ancient, brutal weapon. As she stared at it, she felt the wetness of a tear spilling down her face and reached up a hand to wipe it from her cheek. Her fingers came away stained crimson. Mason was weeping blood.

Huh, she thought, numb with exhaustion. *Must be a Valkyrie thing. . . .*

She heard Roth's sharp breath as he saw the blood on her fingertip.

"Please," she said. "I just . . . I can't. I really can't handle any more death."

There was a moment of silence, and then suddenly he was back across the terrace and she felt his arms go around her.

"Little sister," he murmured into her hair. "I'm so sorry. . . ."

She let him hold her for a moment. Then she pushed away from him.

"So am I," she said.

There would be time to sort out what had happened to them when they were children later. There would be time to deal with Daria and there *would* be a reckoning and maybe, just maybe, Mason would stand aside and let Roth deal with that however he saw fit. But right then, in that moment, Mason needed to keep it together.

She shook her head, willing back any more tears and walked over to the Odin spear. Holding her breath, she bent down swiftly to pick it up. It was heavy, but so perfectly balanced that it felt as though she could throw it a mile with barely any effort. She closed her eyes and searched for the small, walled space inside of her that still belonged wholly to Mason Starling, before any of the crazy had happened. It had to still be there, she knew.

I have to still be there.

Because if it wasn't—if *she* wasn't—then she really was lost and nothing she did from that point on would matter because the end result would be inevitable. And it would be the *end* result. The end of everything . . .

Fenn . . .

She thought of Fennrys and the night at his loft when he'd first given her the silver, swept-hilt rapier and how good and right and perfect it had felt in her hand. God, how she wanted her sword back. How she wanted everything to go back to the way it was that night. When she was just Mase and he was just Fenn and everything else just fell away. She felt a shiver in the air all around her and when she opened her eyes, the Odin spear was gone, or transformed, its essence and power once more cloaked in the shape of the sword held in her bare hand.

And suddenly Mason was Mason again. The armor of the Valkyrie was gone. But somewhere deep inside, she could feel the Valkyrie's rage, like the still-burning coals glowing silently beneath the ashes of a banked fire. Waiting to spark to life again . . .

So she could burn down the world.

V

Mason shook her long black hair back over her shoulders and sheathed the rapier in the scabbard that once again hung from the baldric slung across her torso. She was back in her jeans and boots, the shimmery short-sleeved top she'd worn that night leaving the bare skin of her arms chilly in the wind. She crouched down and picked up Fennrys's medallion from where it lay at her feet. The clasp on the braided leather cord—the one on which she'd had the medallion restrung especially for him—had been bitten through by Anubis. Mason shook the blood from the iron disk and shoved it in her pocket. Then she turned back to her brother, who stood watching her, his gaze steady and solemn. The fog of grief and drugs had cleared, leaving behind a glinting darkness, like black ice, in his eyes.

At least he looked like Roth again.

Quiet. In control. Dangerous . . .

Good.

She'd need for him to be all those things, going forward. Of that, she had no doubt.

"You know this is going to get a whole lot worse before it gets better, right?" Mason said.

Roth shrugged. "*If* it gets better. Yeah."

"I need to know what you know, Roth." She walked back over to him and stared up into his face. "I need to understand what's going on and what Dad and Rory have planned. And I need to know that you aren't a part of it."

"I'm not."

They locked eyes for a long moment and Mason saw something in her brother's gaze that she had never seen before. "Are you afraid, Roth?" she asked in a whisper.

He nodded.

"Of me."

"Yes." He put a hand on her shoulder. "You really do scare the hell out of me, Mase. Not gonna lie. But . . . that's not because of who you are."

"It's because of what I am."

He nodded again. "Yeah. Except I'm not stupid; I know that you didn't want any of this any more than I did. Any more than Gwen did. You're right. I have no reason *not* to trust you, Mason. And I guess it's high time you had a reason to trust me back."

Mason tilted her head and regarded him. "I always *have* trusted you, Roth."

"I know." A deep frown marred his forehead. "You probably shouldn't have."

She stared at her brother, not understanding, until Daria laughed bitterly.

"No," Cal's mother said, her eyes fixed on Roth. "*None* of us should have."

"I did what I had to," Roth said. "And I never meant harm."

"Tell that to my wolfhounds."

Wolfhounds? Mason thought. She opened her mouth to ask the question, but Roth just shot Daria a death glare and turned his back on her, gesturing for Mason to follow him toward the glass doors. In front of them, he stopped and turned her to face him.

"Listen to me," Roth said. "I might not always have acted in your best interests, Mase—and you need to know that— but you also need to believe me when I tell you now that I am so, *so* sorry for that."

He reached up and tucked a strand of loose hair behind her ear, for all the good it did—the wind just tore it from his fingers again and sent it whirling around her head with the rest of her midnight locks. Roth's fingers were ice-cold as they brushed the side of her face.

"And I will tell you everything I know," Roth continued. "I promise. But only once we're on the move."

"Move?"

"We can't stay here. Dad will have seen the lightning strikes. He'll know. He'll be coming."

The instant he said it, Mason knew he was right. She could almost picture her father's face as he realized that he'd triumphed—succeeded in turning his only daughter into a Valkyrie. A chooser of the slain. The very thought was something that Mason was struggling to understand. Her father.

Dad . . .

Mason willed back more tears. In their stead, she felt the cold spatter of a raindrop on her cheek. She lifted her face to the sky as a rumble of thunder rolled overhead and the heavy black clouds began to weep for her. She glanced over at Cal's mother where she stood with her white priestess robes flapping wetly like the sails of an abandoned boat. She lifted her chin and strove for defiance, but all Daria's arrogant elegance—the superior attitude she wore like a suit of armor—had turned brittle and cracked at the seams. Mason could see the woman beneath the facade for the first time and she wondered fleetingly about the girl she might have once been. The one who had so fiercely befriended Mason's own mother that, when Yelena Starling had died, Daria had begun to plot an unfathomable revenge against Gunnar Starling that had spanned decades.

Roth followed Mason's gaze. "That's another reason we have to get going," he said. "The Miasma will begin to dissipate before too long. I can feel it. Gwen . . ." His face twisted again. "Gwen's death was like a lance. The blood curse is emptying out of me. It'll take a while, but when that happens—when the fog walls surrounding Manhattan fall—they'll send the military in. Come on, everyone inside." He walked over to the glass doors and opened them, glaring at Daria with the promise of revenge written in his eyes. "Even you. Much as I'd rather leave you to face whatever fresh hell is coming down, I think we might actually need you before this is all over."

As Cal moved toward the open door, he shook his head and spoke for the first time in what seemed like forever to Mason. "It's going to be an unholy mess down on the streets when the city wakes up. There'll be widespread panic. And they'll probably quarantine the whole island and—"

He was interrupted by the sound of another anguished, ragged howl coming from somewhere inside the Weather Room. Mason felt the small hairs on the back of her neck stand up as the bone-chilling sound—the cry of an animal caught in a trap—distorted only a moment later, twisting into a human wail of agony.

Fennrys . . .

The cries subsided into low, guttural groans, and Mason squeezed her eyes shut. But all she could see was Rafe—the way he had looked with Fenn's blood staining his teeth. Heather came over and put a hand on Mason's shoulder.

"You should go to him," she said. "He sounds . . . not good."

Mason hesitated. Honora had told her to stay away. The pack would take care of him, she said. And Toby and Maddox were there. And . . . she was afraid.

"It's okay," Heather said, misinterpreting Mason's reluctance. She glanced at Cal and his mother, and then at Roth, who looked less likely to pitch forward onto his face than he had a few minutes earlier. "I think we've got it covered out here for the time being." She bent down to pick up the silver sickle that Daria Aristarchos had dropped and handed it to Roth, who gestured Daria through the doorway with it and followed her close behind. "And in spite of whatever that she-wolf in Prada might think? I'm betting that the one thing Fennrys needs right now, more than anything, is you. Go."

She gave Mason a brief hug and sent her through the door with a gentle shove. Another cry of rage and pain rent the air, and Mason turned and ran through the deserted hall in the direction of the Fennrys Wolf.

Calum watched her go to him, and it took everything he had to not run after her and beg her not to. He almost gave in to the urge until he felt Heather's eyes on him. Her stare was palpable, as if she'd laid a hand on his shoulder—steady, cool, unforgiving . . . but somehow not entirely unsympathetic. Typical, complicated Heather Palmerston. He went over to where she stood by the door, stopping before he walked straight past her and into the room where Mason was with Fennrys.

"Hey . . . ," he said.

Heather nodded silently in response. She stood there, arms crossed, no doubt waiting for him to say something else, but the words just seemed to ball up and stick in his throat.

Heather sighed. Her eyes were ringed with dark circles. The dried tracks of the tears she'd shed that night marred her cheeks and her gaze raked Cal head to foot. Again he could almost feel it, only this time, it wasn't cool. More like the heat of a harsh white searchlight.

"So," she said eventually, shaking her head when it became painfully obvious that he couldn't find anything else to say. Her stare flicked from Cal's face to his fist—the one that had manifested the trident he'd stabbed Fennrys with—and Cal knew what she was thinking. He felt a surge of guilt. "What the hell, Cal?"

"Yeah . . ." He tried to unclench his fingers, but they seemed cemented. He could still feel the cool, smooth surface of the weapon he'd created with this mind. "I know. It's . . ." He huffed in frustration. "I'm glad you're okay, Heather."

"I could say the same thing about you, I suppose." She lifted one shoulder in a shrug, and he noticed that she was shivering. "If I was sure that was actually the case."

Trust Heather to give it to you straight, he thought bitterly.

Like the time she'd flat-out told him they were breaking up—because Cal didn't love Heather. He'd always thought that he did, but it wasn't until *that* very moment that he'd realized that she was right. She was always right.

"You know you *killed* a guy, right?" she asked, her voice was low and uninflected. It cut like a sharp-edged knife.

"He's not—"

"He *would* be. He'd be dead if it wasn't for . . . what came next."

She closed her eyes for a moment as if seeing again the terrible instant when the dreadlocked young man Cal knew as Rafe had transformed into the huge black-furred wolf and sunk his teeth into Fennrys's neck. When she opened them again, it was to look back at Cal, a deep wariness in her gaze.

"I'm still having a bit of an issue mentally framing just what, exactly, it was that that guy did," she said. "But *you* . . . I know what you did. Maybe not how, but I've got the what part down. I just can't figure out *why*, you know?"

"I didn't mean to."

"Yes you did, Cal."

"Okay. Yeah." Cal shook his head and huffed in frustration. "I did. I thought he was going to hurt Mason."

"So you . . . manifested, conjured, what*ever* you did and however you did it . . . you made the biggest, sharpest pitchfork I've ever seen—out of *water,* with your *mind*—and then you stabbed Fennrys *through the heart* with it. That's not stopping someone. That's ending someone."

Inside the Weather Room, another piteous howl shivered in the air like a warning siren. Cal wondered if Mason realized now, for *real*, who was the monster and who was the man. The scars on his face tingled and he winced. Heather was still staring at him. He couldn't tell if it was with pity or hate.

I don't care. It doesn't matter. I don't need her.

He had everything he needed in the next room. In Mason. And once she realized that—and that she and Fennrys could never be together now—she'd come to him. Standing between Cal and the doorway to that potential future, Heather smiled sadly, as if she'd read his thoughts.

"Never gonna happen, sweetie," she said. "Frankly, I'll be surprised if she doesn't put that spear she has right through your chest when she gets back. Just to show you what it felt like when you did the same thing to the guy she loves."

Cal winced. "Jeezus, Heather. You really can be a bitch

sometimes. You know that?"

"And you can be so blind." She shook her head. "I really hate to say this, Cal, but I think maybe there's a whole lot more of your mother in you than you'd care to believe."

"Shut your mouth—"

"Open your eyes!" Heather almost shouted at him.

She took a deep breath and closed her own eyes for a moment. When she looked at him again, he was shocked by just how much love for him he could still see, filling her gaze. It didn't make any sense, but he was starting to figure out that "sense" and "love" had very little to do with each other in his world. A wave of bitterness at the absolute, utter unfairness of his situation crashed over him.

"What's *happened* to you, Aristarchos?" Heather asked, a note of pleading in her voice. "Really. I'm trying to understand."

"I don't know how you could," Cal said. "We're not the same. We never have been."

"What's that supposed to mean?"

He shrugged. "Maybe that's why I couldn't ever really love you, Heather. It's not your fault. You're only human."

He hadn't really meant to say it like that. Like an insult. But that's how it sounded—even to his own ears—and from the look on Heather's face, he knew that's how it had sounded to her, too. She blinked and took a step back from him and her gaze became suddenly shuttered. Instead of crying or yelling or even looking at him with hurt in her eyes, Heather Palmerston just laughed at him.

"Yeah," she said. "I guess I am. Thank god—or *gods*, I

guess—for small favors." Then she turned and walked past him through the door, tossing her hair over her proudly squared shoulders and leaving Cal standing there feeling like *he* was the lesser being.

VI

"Fennrys?"

No. No no no . . . not Fennrys.

Not this. This wasn't him.

This is not . . . I am not . . .

"Fenn?"

The pain was excruciating. A bonfire lit from within. He could feel the thready fibers of every single muscle in his body searing as if flooded with a virulent toxin. His blood wasn't blood; it was flame. It burned him as it coursed through his veins. The were-transformation had triggered something, awoken something deep inside him, and Fennrys didn't know what it was. All he knew was that it was hungry.

The great holes torn in his chest by Calum's trident throbbed with distant, detached hurt, already healing, flesh and lung and heart all knitting themselves back together. But the deep bite wounds on the sides of his throat were like constellations of agony—each puncture a miniature starburst of searing pain—and he could feel the strange, dark, transformative magick of the ancient Death god's bite flowing outward from those points. Taking him. Stripping him of his humanity. Struggling against his other nature. But what that other nature was, Fennrys himself didn't even fully comprehend in that moment. He was dead—had died—and he could feel those shades and shadows starkly now with a wolf's heightened senses wrapping around him like the heavy, gold-furred pelt he now wore as his skin. And he feared that his previous death had somehow warped Anubis's were-curse. Tainted it and twisted it, shaping it in a way that it was never meant to be shaped.

He could smell the fear clinging to the other members of Rafe's pack. It was intoxicating. It fueled his hunger and he lunged, longing to tear the fear from them with his teeth and swallow it in great raw chunks. But the slender silver chain Maddox had looped around his throat kept him from doing that. The silver burned like acid. In spite of the pain he still struggled, thrashing and scrabbling with long claws at the stone floor, and the sweat that dripped from Maddox's brow onto Fennrys's muzzle as the Janus Guard fought to keep him leashed would, he thought, taste so much better if it was blood.

No. No no no . . . not my thoughts.

Maddox was his friend. The pack was there to help.

He was not a killer.

Yes you are.

And so much more than that.

In the back of his throat, Fennrys could suddenly taste . . . *the sea?* Salt spray, ocean tang. Cold and ice-fog sharp. Beneath him, he could feel waves rolling, as if he lay on the deck of a ship. He could hear the snapping of sails in the frigid north wind. He could taste it in his mouth, and deeper than that—in his heart.

Like a memory.

Or a premonition.

What in all the hells in all the worlds is happening to me? he wondered. And the answer came back to him: *You're becoming the monster you always knew you were.*

Yes, he was. A monster. A beast. And now he was—could be—a faster, stronger, thousand-times-more-dangerous one. A brutal, four-legged weapon. Mindless bloodlust fogged his mind with gray and black and red. His flanks heaved, shoveling breath in and out of his lungs like a forge bellows, hot air surging through his quivering nostrils. He felt the human heart that was still beating in his chest—the one that Ammit the Soul Eater had, in her blindness, decided to let him keep—swell and transform, its shape, and its purpose, altered.

"Fennrys?"

That voice again. His heart lurched, twisted. Changed back . . . remembered its *real* purpose. Remembered the things it had been filled with before the trident had pierced it. Before the love that had filled it had flowed out onto the ground in a pool of his blood. Before the white feather had turned red.

He remembered.

And his body began shifting in the other direction.

Smells dulled, sights dimmed.

Hands. Not paws. Not claws . . .

His wolf's eyes looked down and saw the flesh of his arms

rippling beneath his fair human skin. His wolf's voice cried out against it. So close. The chains of his frail, mortal, human shell were stretched to breaking. Waves of yearning slammed through his mind like the pounding of a riptide.

So close.

To what?

The sensations were slipping away. The prize, the goal . . .

What goal?

. . . it had been there. In his grasp. Within reach of his snapping teeth.

I don't understand.

"Fenn." That voice. "It's me. It's Mason."

Wolf-song choked into an aching sob, deep in his throat. And Fennrys collapsed back into a golden-furred heap on the cold marble floor.

"I'm here . . ."

He wondered if he should be comforted by that. He was weak. Wounded.

Vulnerable.

"You're going to be fine. You'll be okay."

Anything but, really . . .

And *that*, he realized, was his new reality. Because of her.

"Stop!" Mason shouted at Maddox as he hauled on a chain, struggling to keep a massive, golden-furred wolf under control. "Stop it! You're hurting him!"

She squeezed past the milling dark shapes of the other lupines, ignoring the snapping jaws, and shouldered her way past Rafe. He reached out and grabbed her by the arm, yanking her back as the beast suddenly lunged for Mason, howling and snarling, teeth like long, white knives dripping saliva. There was a profound, savage hurt burning in the creature's eyes. Pain and madness and a self-awareness that no animal should possess. Mason drew back in confusion. She turned to look up into the face of the ancient Egyptian werewolf god.

"What's wrong with him?" she asked.

"You are joking, right?" Rafe said in a voice tight with anger.

"No!"

Mason twisted out of his grip and looked back at the Fennrys Wolf where he hunched in the corner, muscles coiled and ready to spring if she came within reach again. She read in the beast's eyes then that, given a chance, it would rip her throat out. Maddox tightened his grip on the chain, but his eyes were focused on her.

"Why is he like that?" Mason asked Rafe. "*You're* not like that! They aren't. . . ."

She gestured to the other wolves, who moved with almost one mind, constantly shifting and flanking the yellow wolf, keeping it at bay and surrounded. The air around Fennrys rippled with enchantment and it was as if, for a moment, she was seeing double. The wolf and the man occupying the same space at the same time. Then there was another rippling and the wolf was alone again, howling and writhing.

"It's different every time," Rafe said quietly. "Although . . . it's never quite like this."

Mason knew that he was angry with her. She could hear it in his voice.

She didn't care. She had forced Rafe to turn Fennrys into a creature like the rest of his pack. A werewolf. A monster. But *alive*. Strong. Strong enough to heal from the terrible, mortal wounds that Cal had inflicted with—of all things—a trident.

"Damn near unkillable" was how the ancient Egyptian god of the dead had once described his pack to Mason. And she had remembered those words when Fennrys had been damn near dead. She'd done what she'd done because Fenn had needed her to do it.

No.

That wasn't what Fenn had needed, a voice in her head corrected her.

That was what you *needed.*

Mason flinched at the flat accusatory tone of her own conscience. But she couldn't deny that what that voice in her head said was true. Fennrys? He'd been okay. She'd seen it in his eyes as he gazed up into her face. She'd seen there in that moment the peace that had been missing ever since she had first met him. The contentment. The willingness to let it all go and move on, finally. At last.

He'd looked at her with love and she . . . *she* hadn't been able to do it.

She hadn't been able to let him go.

His dying heart, his fading spirit, the strange, lovely smile that framed what would have been his last breath . . . those weren't things she was prepared to live without.

Suddenly, there was another twisting of the air all around him and Fennrys was Fennrys again—human and furious and fighting mad—and then, just as suddenly, he was a wolf.

His shape was morphing and fluid and he looked almost as though he was trapped at the heart of a thundercloud. The air in the room where it touched him roiled and twisted with dark energy.

"What's happening?" Mason asked Rafe.

"He's fighting it."

"Can he *do* that?"

"I've never seen anyone who has." The ancient god frowned deeply. "Not like this. I just made that boy the next nearest thing to a demigod and I don't want to blow my own horn, but what I did—what *you* asked me to do—is serious magick. It's not the kind of thing you sort of shrug off."

Fennrys heaved his shoulders in what looked, indeed, like a furious shrug and the shadows on the wall behind him rippled out like smoke. The chain rattled and the muscles under Fenn's T-shirt and jeans—which kept disappearing and reappearing, mirage-like—bunched and stretched taut.

"You know," Rafe said. "Like *that.*"

"He's not taking this lying down!" Maddox shouted as Fennrys lunged again, almost tearing the silver chain from the Janus Guard's hands. "Can't we hit him on the head or something?"

"With what?" Rafe snapped, shoving Mason back out of the way as Fennrys lunged for her. "Another werewolf? That's the only thing that might hurt him, but I don't think that's gonna help."

"Can't you get in there and do something?" Mason asked frantically. "Aren't you, like, the alpha of the pack or whatever?"

"Yeah—I *tried* that! All I did was make things worse. Look at him." Rafe waved his hand at the great golden beast. "It doesn't get any more alpha than *that,* and right now? I'm probably his second-least favorite person around."

Mason glanced back at the werewolf god, wondering exactly what he'd meant by that. *Second*-least favorite? Fennrys shifted again and started yelling in his human voice—a litany of swear words that impressed even Toby, from the look on his face—and then, with another shift, the Wolf was back.

Somebody had to do *something* . . .

Mason shouldered past Rafe and knelt on the floor just past the reach of the chained wolf's snapping jaws. "Fennrys?" she called softly.

The great, golden-furred wolf's ears flicked toward her. His nose lifted in her direction, quivering, and he bared his teeth. The marble floor vibrated with the sound of his deep growl.

"Mason!" Rafe hissed. "Don't be stupid. Please—"

"Just tell the pack to back off," Mason said, keeping her voice low and even. "He can't hurt me. You know that."

Rafe shook his head. "I don't know that at *all.*"

Truthfully, neither did she. But it was worth a shot. Fennrys was either going to tear himself apart, or tear somebody else apart if she didn't help him. Mason closed her eyes and became very still for a moment. It was hard, now that she was back to being Mason. Hard to reach for the sword sheathed at her hip. But she did, and the blade slid loose from the sheath and morphed into a long, lethal spear. Somewhere, a raven shrieked. There was a cascade of shimmering light, and when

Mason looked down, she saw that she was once again clothed in the shining armor of one of Odin's shield maidens.

It's not so very different from suiting up for a fencing competition, she told herself.

She could almost imagine that the silvery chain mail tunic was actually her lamé—the conductive overjacket—she wore in a bout, and the winged helm felt almost like the protective headgear she'd worn almost every day of her life for the past several years.

She heard Maddox draw a tense breath and tried to smile at him in a way that would make her Valkyrie manifestation less . . . scary. For everyone, herself included. Judging from the uniform facial expressions all around the room, she was utterly unsuccessful in the attempt.

Less "encouraging smile" and probably more "battle grimace," she guessed.

At the sight of her in full Valkyrie raiment, the Wolf that had been Fennrys began snapping and snarling again, teeth bared, ears back. Mason huffed in frustration and clamped down as best as she could on her own feelings of rising, red rage. She leaned the Odin spear against a wall and reached up to lift the winged helmet off her head. Then she stripped off her armored gloves and, not knowing what else to do, held out her hand, knuckles forward, as if she was approaching a strange dog tied up outside a coffee shop.

Maddox managed to crack a half smile as Fennrys tilted his wolf's head at her, and she felt a bit ridiculous. In the deep depths of his gaze, she could see that Fennrys did, too. Knowing him as well as she did, and seeing his all-too-human expression radiating from the eyes of an animal, was almost comical. It would have been—if she could get beyond the tragedy of the moment when she realized what she'd just done. Fenn whined at her and lifted one huge front paw in her direction.

Mason felt a shaky sob bubble up in her chest, and she sank to her knees and threw her arms around his neck, burying her face in the fur of his ruff. She felt Maddox loosen the chain around the wolf's neck and she reached over to pull the thing off of him, tossing it to the floor and hugging Fennrys, trying to soothe the panting, terrified animal he'd suddenly become.

Behind her, she heard Rafe quietly tell his pack to back off.

She sensed Maddox standing and moving cautiously away from Fenn, and she stayed as still as she could, wrapped in her armor, Fennrys wrapped in her arms, and willed them all to leave the two of them alone. When finally she could sense that the curtained alcove was empty, she loosened her grip on the thick gold fur, and did her best to help the Fennrys Wolf come back home.

Back to himself . . . and back to her.

VII

When Mason Starling was a child, she'd died.

The experience had left her with a few . . . issues. Catastrophic claustrophobia, for one. Several years of therapy had done little before she'd packed it in and decided that she would cope in her own way, without hypnosis or drugs or those interminable couch sessions where one kindly old gent—very old school—had told Mason that, whenever she felt the walls closing in, all she had to do was shut her eyes and, in her mind, go to her "Safe Harbor." She'd thought, at the time, it was the most idiotic thing anyone had ever said to her.

My Safe Harbor . . .

She wondered if Fenn had a Safe Harbor—if such a thing was even remotely possible for someone like him—but she decided to try and find out. Of course, she didn't have any pharmaceuticals or any idea how to hypnotize him, and she was pretty sure he wouldn't go lie down on one of the Weather Room's white leather couches.

But she had his medallion. She had magick.

Mason retrieved the spear and, now that she and Fenn were alone, willed it and herself back into "civvies." She sheathed the spear-turned-sword and, reaching into the pocket of her jeans, pulled out Fennrys's Janus medallion. She unraveled the braided leather cord and stretched it out as long as it would go, so that she could tie it around the thick yellow ruff of fur that circled Fennrys's wolf neck. Then she shoved aside any trace of her roiling, raging, recently manifested Valkyrie in order to concentrate on what Fennrys had told her about the magick.

Make it happen in your mind.

Find your Safe Harbor, Fenn, she urged silently, pushing her will into the medallion. "Find it," she whispered, even as she tried to find her own. *Find your Safe Harbor . . .*

The sudden lack of rain sounds was the first thing Mason noticed.

And the faint smell of dust.

Old wood . . . and metal . . . the distant sound of traffic and a feeling of space, even though she sensed she was indoors. She opened her eyes and felt everything just . . . fall away. Her mouth stretched wide in a smile of pure joy and she turned in a slow circle, the flirty skirt she wore whispering around her thighs as she moved and the heels of her shoes tapping lightly on the bare concrete floor. The dim, empty warehouse she stood in stretched off into shadowy corners, cobwebby and deserted, and Mason thought she had never seen a place so beautiful in her life.

Without hesitation, she walked over to the ancient-looking freight elevator in the corner of the derelict space and stepped inside. She pulled the door grating shut with a screech and flipped the lever on the antiquated brass operator panel. As the mechanism began to groan and the cab started to chug upward, Mason smiled and lifted a finger to the dust-covered glass plate on the wall that held the elevator's mechanical certificate. She drew a heart in the gray dust. And her initials and Fenn's inside the heart.

She was, she thought, probably blushing furiously by the time the elevator stopped on the second floor. She brushed off her fingertip and heaved aside the grate, stepping out into the secret, stylish loft that belonged to the Fennrys Wolf. As usual, when he knew Mason was coming over, he'd done her the courtesy of opening all the windows, and the sheer curtains along the long brick wall billowed gently in the breeze that carried the faint night sounds of the city.

On the far side of the living room, his back to her as he faced the smoked glass wall that hid his extensive collection of weaponry, stood the Fennrys Wolf. She could see his reflection—his eyes were closed and his face was relaxed—as he stood with one hand pressed against the glass. Mason stayed where she was in the foyer, reluctant to disturb his reverie, and took the opportunity to indulge herself a little. Her gaze drank in the shape of his silhouette—the lines of his back and shoulders, the way his waist tapered to narrow hips and long, strong legs—and she marveled at the easy, casual grace he held himself with, even in unguarded moments.

Without opening his eyes, she saw him start to smile in the reflection. "Hello, sweetheart," he murmured. "Fancy meeting you here. . . ."

She waited as he turned and slowly crossed the floor toward her. She met him in front of the hall closet, which was open, and her gaze slid to the collection of leather jackets hanging there. She reached out and lifted the one that had a sleeve shredded by the claws of some beast or other Fenn had fought in his past as a Janus Guard; she remembered the first time she'd seen it and the leap in logic—ridiculous at the time—she'd made. She grinned mischievously.

"See?" she said. "I *knew* you were a werewolf."

He threw back his head and laughed.

It was such a strange thing to see that, for a moment, it jarred her a bit. But then she realized that she felt the same way. Just . . . happy. Mason smiled at Fennrys and stepped past him, walking across the room over to the window that overlooked the High Line park, the green oasis built on a forgotten elevated train line that snaked through the stone canyons of Manhattan's Lower West Side. She leaned out into the cool night air and saw a great yellow wolf with the pale blue eyes padding along the park pathway where she and Fennrys had spent night after blissful night sparring and strolling and kissing. In the sumac tree above the wolf's head, a large black raven perched, watching it with unblinking eyes.

Mason felt Fenn's arms circle around her and she drew back inside. There was a fire crackling now in the cavernous hearth and she wondered if he'd conjured it, or if *she* had, unwittingly, with a thought. Not that it mattered. Not that she cared. She wondered for a brief moment if she could stay here with him forever, in their shared Safe Harbor.

"You brought me here?" Fenn asked her quietly.

"I guess so." She leaned back against him. "I just wanted to help."

"You might have to stop doing that at some point, Mase." His breath teased the hair at the back of her neck.

"Why?"

"You're here, helping me now, because you already helped me before. You know." He drew her hair aside, kissing the bare skin just below her ear. "With the whole werewolf thing."

"I . . . didn't really mean for that to happen."

"Are you sure?"

She turned around in his arms and looked up. "I just wanted to save you."

"You made a deal with a death god and he turned me into a monster. . . ." In contrast to his grim words Fenn smiled that odd, awkward, wonderful smile of his and leaned down to murmur a kiss into the hollow space just above her collarbone. "Just to keep me alive. I'm not sure that falls under the heading of 'saving.'"

Mason tilted her head back and lost herself to the sensation of his mouth on her skin. "Are you saying I should have let you die?" she asked, her voice breathy in her own ears. "Again?"

Fenn lifted his head and there was a calm serenity to his gaze as he looked down at her. The firelight reflecting on the side of his face turned his skin to molten gold, casting the other side into deep shadow. He looked like a renaissance painting of some classical hero, rendered in darkness and light, balanced between the two extremes. A study in contrast. He reached up to run a finger down the side of her face. His touch was feather-light as he tilted her face up and kissed her lips.

"Don't you think there's a time to walk away, Mase?" he whispered. "That there comes a point when you just have to let go?"

"Of you?" She shook her head, a small movement, but she meant it. Adamantly. "Not ever."

"Even if none of this is real?" he asked, but then she was kissing him again and, from the way his arms went around her and he pulled her toward him, it was clear he didn't care what the answer was. He kissed her so fiercely she felt the intake of his breath drawing all of the air up from the depth of her lungs. His hands tangled in her hair as if he would bind himself to her physically and Mason melted utterly into the heat of his embrace.

When she felt almost as if she was on the very edge of a good old-fashioned swoon, she drew back and gulped at the air. Fenn's chest quivered as he gasped himself and began, again, to laugh. Quietly this time, his head back and eyes closed. When he opened them again, she saw her face reflected in their depths and barely recognized herself. Her blue eyes sparkled and her cheeks were flushed and rounded with a smile that was wider than any she'd ever seen herself wear in real life.

Have I ever been this happy?

As she looked up into his eyes, she thought she saw what might have been the very same feeling reflected there.

Has he?

She opened her mouth to tell him how she felt. And *more* than that.

Now I can tell him. I can finally tell him that I—

"Mase?" Fennrys suddenly twisted his head to one side. He cocked his head, listening. "Do you hear . . ."

She did. The sound of the antiquated lift gears creaking and grinding into motion as the elevator cab began to rise up from the first floor. Which was, in itself, odd because Mason was sure she had left the door grate open and the cab stopped at the second floor when she'd first arrived.

Well, what do you want from a dream-vision? Logic?

"Were you expecting anyone?"

"No," he said, "but that might be because I don't really believe I'm here *to* expect anyone. You?"

"Unh-uh." She shook her head.

Fennrys took her hand and together they crossed the floor to where the old freight elevator was creaking and clanking its way to a stop. Fenn reached out and heaved the door grate open and stepped inside. Mason followed him, and was immediately struck by the disconcerting sense that the inside of the elevator was . . . *elsewhere.*

The air in the rustic, dusty, wood and metal compartment of the lift felt bracing and breezy. Laced with the smell of pine needles and nearby fresh, cold water. And . . . apple blossoms. She could feel sunlight on her shoulders where there wasn't any illumination but the single, dim incandescent bulb overhead, and there was a sense of vast space, even though she should have felt claustrophobic.

But . . . beyond that, the lift was empty.

Fennrys turned in a full circle, his head still tilted, listening. The frown on his face was one of concentration, though, not worry or dread. When something right behind her caught his eye, Mason turned to look. Fennrys was peering intently at the framed glass plate bolted to the wall of the cab that held the elevator's worn and yellowing mechanical certificate. The heart, circling the initials MS and TFW that Mason had drawn on the dust-coated surface was plainly visible in the dim light.

Busted, she thought, blushing.

Fenn's expression softened into one of wonderment as he took a step toward the wall, forcing Mason to back up so that her spine was up against the operator panel. He reached a hand over her shoulder, toward the glass and, with the side of his fist, wiped the dust away. Obliterating the cartoon heart.

Mason felt her own heart clench.

Then Fenn punched the glass, hard enough to make it shatter.

The chime of broken glass falling was like the sound of silver bells. . . .

The elevator, and the loft all around them, shimmered into darkness and disappeared. The cold pale walls of the Weather Room resolved back into focus as Mason opened her eyes. She was kneeling on the marble floor, Fennrys's head pillowed in her lap. The Wolf was gone—for the moment—and he wore his human shape once more. The iron medallion hung from the long leather cord around his neck, a faint glow dancing over its surface markings that faded as she watched. She put a hand on Fenn's tousled blond hair and felt the warmth radiating from his forehead. He stirred and sat up, running a hand over his face. His blue gaze was clear again, he was in control. But she could see that the Wolf was still there, buried deep, but quiet. She felt the same thing about her Valkyrie—the bloodred urge was like the glowing embers beneath the ashes of a banked fire or the fluttering of raven's wings in a distant tree. It was manageable.

"Are you okay?" she asked quietly.

Fennrys nodded. He glanced down at the medallion where it lay on his chest, and then back up at her. "How?"

"I just . . . wished for you to find your—um—Safe Harbor. . . ." She felt herself blushing. *Stupid touchy-feely therapist jargon.*

"Safe Harbor, huh?" He grinned wanly. "You, my loft, a nice cozy fire . . . sounds about right."

"I didn't actually know that I'd go there *with* you," she said.

"Maybe it wouldn't have felt as safe without you."

He didn't quite sound convinced, Mase thought. "It was something one of my shrinks told me to do when I was a kid. It never worked for me before now, but . . . I didn't know what else to do. I guess the medallion made the difference this time. Or something."

Or maybe you just never had a safe place to go to before you had Fennrys.

"It's okay. You did great, Mase."

He forced the grin into a smile, but it was a tight smile.

Not the strange, awkward smile he usually bestowed on her that made the soles of her feet tingle with warmth.

"Thank you."

A noise from behind them made them both look up and Mason turned around to see Maddox standing there, coiling up the silver chain now that the danger seemed to have passed.

Mason turned back to Fennrys. "In the elevator . . . why did you punch the glass?"

"I don't know." Fenn frowned, his gaze focusing inward. "There was . . . something. Something I was supposed to remember." He shook his head. "It's gone now."

"Oh," Mason said. "I just thought it might have been the heart. I thought you might have been mad or something. . . ."

"What heart?"

Mason blinked at him. He hadn't seen her doodle on the dusty glass? Even by the dim light of the elevator cab's single bulb, it had been there, plain as day. She wondered if they'd had the same experience after all. Maybe the details were different. Or maybe his safe, happy place didn't include a heart with his initials and hers written inside.

"It's nothing." Mason shook her head and forced herself to smile. "It's not important."

"If you two are feeling up to it," Maddox interrupted with delicate urgency, "we should probably get a move on it, yeah? Storm's getting worse. So are the tremors. And I, for one, don't want to be stuck in that elevator shaft if the power goes out or the nasties come knocking." As Fennrys stalked past him, Maddox grabbed his arm and Mason heard him murmur, "Are you . . . ?"

"Good as I'm going to be for the foreseeable future," Fenn said tersely. "Yeah."

"Right. . . ." Maddox didn't sound so sure. "I'll go muster the troops, then."

VIII

66 "**H**eather?" Toby called as he came around the corner, obviously looking for her. She put a finger to the corner of her eye, just to make sure there were no tears showing, and turned around.

"Hey, Coach," she said.

"You okay?"

"You mean, am I still human? I guess so. Seems like I might be the only one." She shrugged one shoulder, meaning for it to be a casual gesture, but it turned into a shudder and Heather hugged her elbows tight, realizing suddenly that she might very well be in shock.

Toby led her to one of the white leather chaises and sat her down. He kicked away a low table, spilling the contents of the silver dish full of rotted fruit that sat on it, and knelt in front of her. She raised an eyebrow at him as he turned over the palm of her right hand as if he was about to tell her fortune.

Instead, he put two fingers on the pulse point of her wrist and went very still for a few moments. Heather could feel her heartbeat rattling, quick and light, against Toby's blunt fingertips.

After a moment, he looked up at her. "Yup. Still human. And probably less shocky than you should be. But I want you to sit here quietly for a few minutes, okay? I know that none of this can have been very easy for you."

"For *me*?" Heather snorted. "You're kidding, right?"

"Yeah. Well. It's been a bit of a day for all of us, I guess," he muttered. "Some more than others."

"It's bad. Isn't it? The whole Mason thing." Heather nodded her chin in that direction. "I mean . . . she's . . . wow. Scary. I mean, smokin' outfit and all but, she looked so . . . different. Even more different than Cal and, y'know, *that*? I can't even."

"I can't even, either," Toby said, half a grin tugging at his mouth.

"It wasn't supposed to happen, was it?" Heather asked. "Mason, I mean."

"No. No, it wasn't."

"What are you going to do?"

Toby was silent for a moment. "Whatever I have to."

"Good luck with that."

"Yeah. If it comes to that . . . I'll need more than luck. We all will."

Heather sat there, not knowing what else to say, until the guy she'd heard the others refer to as Maddox came around the corner.

"Hey." He nodded briefly at Heather and addressed Toby in a low voice. "Looks like she's managed to get him under control. For the time being, at least. So we should all get clear of this place ASAP. While we still can."

"Agreed," Toby said. "I don't want to be caught hanging around anywhere Gunnar Starling might be headed right now."

Heather shivered. *Neither do I,* she thought, remembering what had happened on the train. She glanced over at Toby and did a double take. All of a sudden, he looked as if he'd been up for three days straight. There were deep shadows under his eyes and the beard scruff along the line of his jaw blurred the edges of what was normally a precision-trimmed goatee. His omnipresent travel mug full of coffee was missing in action and she wondered if the fencing coach wasn't maybe going through major caffeine withdrawal. It was, she realized, a weird thing to think just then. But she wondered if anything in her life would ever be un-weird again.

Especially when someone like Toby kept saying things to her like: "Do you still have the protection rune I gave you?"

Heather sighed, accepted the weirdness, and nodded.

"Good," Toby said. "That'll repel the Miasma curse when we're on the ground, and it should help keep you safe from whatever's coming. Saf*er*, at least."

"What about the rest of you?" she asked.

"The rest of us are . . . immune, through various means." Toby shrugged.

"Right. What's *your* deal?" she asked Maddox, who was both disarmingly cute and distractingly competent in the way he handled himself. "Demigod? Demon?"

"Human, thanks." He grinned at her. "But I have an impressive constitution. Eat right, don't smoke, wear a talisman chock-full of really useful Faerie magick . . . you know. All that virtuous stuff. Makes me hard to curse."

"Handy," Heather muttered.

"Plus I have over a hundred years' worth of martial arts training under my belt and that, in itself, tends to give one a bit of a leg up. I'm a firm believer in using every possible advantage to cover one's arse."

Suddenly Heather remembered her own possible advantage—the little crossbow, with the gold and leaden bolts that a mysterious . . . *someone* had given her on a subway train—and she ran and found her purse where it still lay on the floor near the elevators. She slung it across her body and turned to see Mason walking toward her.

"Yo, Starling." Heather waved casually. "How's it hangin'?"

Mason laughed wearily. "Oh, y'know. Typical Friday night. Werewolves, Valkyries, earthquakes, blood curses, and the End of Days . . . I expect a plague of locusts any minute now. You?"

"Weirdly the same." Heather grinned. "So. Where've you *really* been these last couple of days?"

"Would you believe me if I said Asgard?"

"I kinda think I wouldn't believe you if you *didn't*," Heather said. She glanced in the direction Mason had come from. "How's super-bad hot blond doing?"

"Okay, for now. Under control. Rafe says it's never

happened like that to one of his . . . uh . . ."

"Victims?"

"Pack." Mason shivered and hugged herself.

"Right." Heather nodded. "So—this Rafe guy—is like . . . *what* again?"

"Anubis."

"Lord of the Egyptian underworld."

"Ex, yeah." Mason nodded. "And—added bonus feature—god of werewolves."

"The textbooks never mentioned that." Heather noted dryly.

"I know." Mason laughed briefly and without much mirth. "Weird, huh?"

"Makes sense." Heather shrugged. "Look at all those tomb paintings of the guy."

"Yup. Pretty werewolf-y."

"And so . . ." Heather hesitated. "After, y'know . . . Fenn is . . . ?"

"Not dead."

"Right. And that's good. Right?"

Mason just looked at her.

"I mean, of *course* that's good."

Suddenly, there was another tremendous shuddering beneath their feet.

"It's been doing that for days," Heather said. "The whole city. Ever since the train bridge thing. It's like the world is cracking open."

"Maybe it is," Mason murmured.

"Come on," Heather said. "Let's get out of here."

Together, they went back to join the rest of the crew.

"Toby thinks we should head back to Gos because it's the only safe house in Manhattan," Roth was saying when Heather and Mason joined the others. Most of the shallow cuts on his arms seemed to be healing, fading with the breaking of the blood curse. "And I agree. It's protected ground."

"If that's the case, then why were we attacked in the gym?" Cal asked. "How could that happen if the Academy is protected like you say?"

"My guess is because the facility was brand-new." Toby shrugged. "So the draugr were able to climb the walls, cross over the roof to get access to the oak in the courtyard and bring that down—a kind of battering ram to breach the gym walls."

Daria nodded tightly in agreement, pushing her hands compulsively through the mess of her hair, over and over again, as if trying to physically regain control of herself. "It was the only section of the quadrangle that was vulnerable that way," she said. "The founding families hadn't had time yet to come together to install their integrated protection spells on it."

"I guess they didn't see this coming," Mason said, trying to control the urge to walk up to the Elusinian priestess and punch her in the face.

"Oh, they did." Toby snorted. "For the last thousand years they've seen this coming. Just, you know . . . maybe not *this* week."

"Then it's still not safe—"

"Yes. It is," Daria interrupted her. "The board reinstated

the defensive spell work later that night. It's secure. And probably the only square city block in all of Manhattan that would have remained immune to the Sleeper's Fog."

"All right, then," Mason nodded. "Gosforth it is."

IX

Gwen Littlefield's body was gone.

Shards of glass from the shattered Observation Deck barriers littered the plaza pavement, glinting like slivers of ice in the pooling rainwater. Over near the great golden statue of Prometheus, a section of the concrete was cracked and buckled inward, like a small impact crater. The cracks that spiderwebbed out were stained a dark crimson. Mason's steps faltered and she turned and looked back up at the Rockefeller tower. High above them was the terrace where the black marble altar still stood. And this was the place, she knew, where Gwen had fallen.

But her body was nowhere to be seen.

It was strange. Worrying. But seeing Roth standing there, staring down at nothing but a blood stain, Mason was grateful beyond words. She couldn't imagine what it would have done to her brother to have seen his love, broken to pieces. Mason reached out a hand and touched his shoulder.

"There's nothing we can do here," she said quietly. "Come on. We have to—"

"Mason!" Cal shouted suddenly. "Look out!"

He hurtled toward her, crashing his shoulder into her and sending her flying. She tumbled painfully to the ground and heard herself cursing as the palms of her hands scraped along the sidewalk. When she lurched back up to her feet, Mason rounded on Cal, fists raised, in the instant before she realized that he'd probably just saved her life.

The thing that had slammed out of the sky was so hideous that her brain found it difficult to put into words. A tornado of black, oily-feathered wings, with wildly tangled hair and gnarled feet ending in talons, the creature uttered an ear-splitting screech as it clutched at the empty space where Mason had been standing only a moment before.

Madly flapping its wings, the monstrous thing launched itself into the air again, generating gusts of rancid air. Mason and the others choked on the stench, reeling back. Roth threw an arm over his face and Cal retched violently. The creature landed on the statue of Prometheus, and perched there on the golden ball of fire in the statue's hand like an overgrown mutant vulture. It glared down at Mason and her companions, black bloodshot eyes staring out of the face of an old woman, only twisted and stretched over bones too sharply angled with a protruding nose that was long and beaky. Mason saw that, beneath the huge, ratty wings, the creature's body was a horrifying hybrid of bird and human, with scrawny arms and legs that sprouted feathers in places. The thing's bony torso was covered in a tattered and filthy tunic that appeared to be stained with blood.

"Wow," Mason heard Heather mutter nervously. "Midtown's starting to look like one big Halloween party."

"Harpy," Toby grunted.

"Thanks, Toby," she said. "I never would have guessed . . ."

Mason put a hand on the hilt of her sword, loosening it in its sheath, but she didn't draw it. The thought of cloaking herself in her Valkyrie raiment again was terrifying to Mason. Even if, deep down, it was also just the tiniest bit thrilling.

"Dial it down, Starling." Toby rolled a warning eye at her and then at Fennrys, who had begun to growl low in the back of his throat. "Let's keep the ravens and wolves out of it for now, yeah? If you've gotta fight, fight human."

"Right. Yeah." She glanced at Fennrys. He nodded, and she took her hand off her weapon.

"Good," Toby said and took a step forward, putting himself in between Mason and the Harpy. "Aello," he greeted the creature, a note of wary politeness in his voice. "Long time no see."

Again, Mason found herself blinking in surprise where Toby was concerned. She exchanged a glance with Heather and could see she was feeling the same way.

"Where?" Aello croaked at the fencing master in a voice like ground glass and thumbtacks. "Where is the broken soul? We claim her essence. The suicides are ours—mine and my sisters'."

"Gwen *wasn't* a suicide." Roth stepped forward, his voice cracking on the word. "She was a sacrifice."

"Quibble, mortal," Aello hawked and spat into the fountain pool beneath her. "We claim her."

Roth's fists clenched, but Aello had already turned from him and was scanning the faces of the others standing there in a tense knot. Her rheumy gaze sharpened when she spotted Rafe.

"Ah. *You* . . . ," Aello croaked at the ancient Egyptian god. Then she turned back to address Toby, her head tilting bird-like in Rafe's direction. "Did the death dog take away the broken soul? It is not his to claim. We will have it back."

"If I'd been of a mind to claim her soul, vulture, there wouldn't be a damned thing on this Earth you could do to stop me," Rafe snarled back. But then Mason saw him take a breath to calm himself. He rolled a shoulder and tugged the sleeve of his jacket straight. "But it just so happens that I didn't." He waved a hand dismissively. "Not my fault somebody else in this town was more on the ball than you three pestilential feather dusters. That must sting, yeah? Losing out on claiming a powerhouse essence like that . . . I imagine that little haruspex would have kept you three fed and watered for an age or two."

Mason remembered from her Gosforth myth classes that the Harpies were tormenters in the netherworld, feeding on the lost souls of those who'd taken their own lives. Which Gwen had *technically* done, even though she'd done it to break a curse and set Mason's brother—not to mention the entire city of Manhattan—free. But Mason also figured that the Greek mythological monstrosity crouched above her really didn't give a crap about the details. While Rafe held the creature's attention, Mason looked up to see two other winged figures hovering high in the night sky. She tugged on Toby's sleeve and pointed upward.

"Yeah," he murmured. "I see 'em. Stay alert, kiddo—they move pretty fast."

Mason nodded and shook out her shoulders, rolling her head from side to side like she would if she was getting ready for a competition bout. Toby shifted away from her then, stepping casually a few paces closer to the fountain's edge, giving himself room to swing a knife if it came to that.

"Are you okay if we have to fight?" Fennrys whispered in her ear, suddenly standing beside her.

Mason hadn't noticed him move, hadn't even heard him, but suddenly he was there. His breath was warm on her neck and all she wanted to do in that moment was turn her head just enough so that she could kiss him.

Probably not the best time, she thought, and nodded silently, not trusting herself to speak. Her hand dropped to her hip to rest on her sword hilt again, before she remembered that it wasn't her sword anymore. She wondered for a brief moment what would happen if she were to actually use the Odin spear as a weapon . . . and decided that it would probably be a really terrible idea.

Fennrys seemed to think so, too. He dropped his own hand lightly on top of hers, loosening her fingers. She looked up at him over her shoulder. He was pale and the muscles of his neck stood out, taut with tension. There was a sheen of sweat on his brow and his pupils were so large that the pale blue irises of his eyes looked like thin rings of ice surrounding bottomless black pools. She was close enough to count the stubble on his jaw and longed to run her fingers over the roughness of it.

Seriously. Not *really the time, Mase.*

With his free hand, Fenn reached for his own long-bladed knife—the one he kept in a sheath strapped to his leg—and, wrapping his arm around her back, eased its hilt into Mason's other palm. "Toby's right. And Rafe was right. Let's not play with our Asgard toys unless we absolutely have to. Okay?"

She nodded and let go of the sword hilt. "Okay."

Good point. How many times *could* she haul out the Valkyrie before she became that permanently? And Fennrys? What about the monster she'd unleashed inside him? Okay, granted, their mutual visit to Fenn's Safe Harbor seemed to have taken the edge off the uncontrollable rage urges they'd both been experiencing, for the moment, but she wondered how long that would last. She was already starting to feel like she was spoiling for a fight and, if that was the case for her, how much worse would it be for Fenn, who saw fighting as his purpose in life? Especially now, with the added pressure of his lupine instincts? When did the instinct take over completely?

Her fingers closed convulsively around the hilt of the knife Fennrys had handed her, and then she made herself relax them into an easy, ready grip—the way Fenn had taught her to hold a blade—and smiled at him.

"That's my girl," Fenn murmured with a grin. "Stay loose."

His fingers squeezed hers briefly and he moved away from her again.

His girl . . .

She desperately hoped he still felt that way and wasn't just saying that.

Mason watched Fennrys move to take up a subtly protective stance in front of Heather, who gave him a look but didn't protest. The knuckles of her hand, clutching a little silver sickle she'd taken from the Weather Room, were white with tension and she shifted nervously from foot to foot. Mason could totally sympathize. She remembered how she'd felt on that afternoon with Fennrys, at the Boat Basin Café, waiting for a boatload of draugr to attack.

Scared shitless.

She vividly recalled the suddenly overcast day, thick fog on the Hudson River rolling in, bringing with it fire and steel and chaos. Monsters in boats, monsters in the water, monsters in the sky . . .

Wait a minute.

Something twigged in the back of Mason's brain.

Right. Now I remember. . . .

The café. That's where she'd seen the Harpies before. Winged, shadowy shapes falling from the sky like meteorites during the chaos of that attack, they had swooped down from out of the roiling storm clouds and torn through the ranks of the undead Norse warriors, helping to even the odds.

"Wait!" Mason strode forward, ignoring Toby as he glanced sideways at her from under a raised eyebrow. She lifted her voice and spoke directly to the Harpy perched on the statue, thinking that maybe there was a way they could talk themselves out of this situation without having to resort to fighting. "You helped us once before—"

"Mason . . ." Rafe's voice held a note of warning.

Heeding that much at least, Mason stopped walking and spoke to the ancient Egyptian werewolf god over her shoulder without taking her eyes off the ancient Greek bird-woman goddess in front of her. "They killed a bunch of draugr when Fennrys and I were attacked down at the Boat Basin," she explained. "We might not have made it out of there alive if they hadn't."

"Huh," Toby grunted, unconsciously flipping the carbon-bladed knife he handled so expertly over and over in his hand, like a magician's prop. "So *that's* what happened. News reports were pretty confused about that whole thing."

"Uh. Yeah." Mason grimaced, remembering. "It was kind of chaos. Mostly screaming and running. *Any*way . . ." She turned back to the Harpy. "You must see that we're not your enemies, then, right? We really haven't stolen anything away from you. And you did help us—"

"*Help* you?" The Harpy threw her head back, shrieking with laughter that sounded like fingernails down a chalkboard. "Little Chooser, we did not help you. We will not help you. We merely understand that wherever *you* go, carrion is sure to follow."

"What?" Mason backed off a step, startled.

"You fill our bellies nicely." The creature smirked, oozing cruel sardonic amusement. "For *that* . . . we thank you in abundance!"

The Harpy smacked her thin lips. Suddenly Mason thought she might be physically ill. Was *that* what she was? A walking train wreck? A disaster waiting to happen, leaving a feast for Harpies in her wake?

"Stow it, Aello." Toby snorted in disdain, pulling Mason out of her horrified mental tailspin. "Mason's not your meal ticket and this isn't ancient Thrace. Stuff yourselves full of all the draugr you want. Hell, I think we even left a couple of centaur corpses a few blocks over—bon appétit—but heed me. You and your sisters don't get a free pass to belly up to the Manhattan mortal buffet. Not while I'm here to say otherwise."

He glanced around at the rest of his companions and his eyes momentarily locked with Mason's. His gaze, she suddenly realized, was filled with what seemed like thousands of years of dealing with this kind of situation. She was struck by the fact that she'd never noticed that weight of experience there before. But then he winked at her and turned back to the Harpy.

"Not while *any* of us is," he said.

"You're a consort of war, old man." Aello's face twisted into a grotesque sneer. "And a hypocrite. You've spread banquets of human limbs and viscera on more battlefields than we have toes to count upon down through the ages. You're not one to talk."

Mason stepped up beside him. "Toby . . . what does she mean?"

"Later, Mase."

"But—"

"I said later," the fencing master snapped.

His glance flicked back over to her for another brief instant, attention diverted for just long enough, and this time Aello was waiting for it. The Harpy was off her perch and almost on top of them in a flash. The mistake she made, though, was in going for the one member of their group who appeared to be the most vulnerable. Heather. Only the Harpy found herself brought up short in the most painful way as she slammed unexpectedly up against an invisible barrier almost a foot away from her intended target. As Heather screamed and covered her head, a flash of golden light bloomed out in front of her like ripples on the surface of a lake and the Harpy was thrown back through the air. The look of surprise on Heather's face was almost comical as the other two Harpies circling high overhead suddenly folded in their wings and dropped like stones out of the sky.

Toby spun and whipped his dagger at Aello, but she'd already launched herself higher into the air. The beating of her huge wings slammed rancid gusts of wind at them. Mason staggered back and swept her arm in front of her, slashing with the blade Fennrys had given her. It was a wild move—unplanned and instinctive—but she felt the edge of the blade bite flesh as one of the Harpies dove at her. Mason heard the creature's outraged cry of pain and threw herself out of the way of the grasping talons. She tucked into a shoulder roll, spun on one knee and, lurching to her feet, used her momentum to follow up the slash with a leg-powered thrust.

Again the knife made its mark.

Another scream of frustrated fury and the Harpy veered off, howling at her in what Mason perceived was probably very nasty ancient Greek invective.

Mason flicked her knife to shed some of the thick blood

smeared on the blade and turned to see how the others were doing. Heather was standing tall again, sickle held high and ready to fend off an attacker, but the bird-women seemed to have reconsidered the ease with which the willowy blond girl could be taken down. Instead, Aello's sisters had gone for Rafe's wolf pack—with some success—and two of the werewolves were lying on the ground, bleeding from long parallel gashes. Roth and the ancient god ran to cover them, one with a massive hunting knife in his hand, and the other with a shimmering bronze blade.

Over on the other side of the patio, Maddox's silver chain sang through the air. But the Harpies possessed agility that was, naturally, superhuman, and they evaded him without much difficulty. Cal had pulled a solid wall of water up out of the fountain and was using it to shield his mother, who was proving to be a pretty useless burden, without any handy curses to whip up.

The three bird-women attacked with ruthless speed and efficiency, riding updrafts between the buildings that Mason couldn't even perceive and swooping down in strafing arcs that kept everyone ducking for cover. But then Aello made the mistake of taking a dive at Fennrys.

She was maybe ten feet away when—instead of ducking—Fennrys launched himself into a leap that took the Harpy utterly by surprise. He slammed into her midair and twisted as they fell so that the vile creature was beneath him and took the brunt of the impact on her back, right between her ragged wings. Fennrys pinned Aello to the ground with a knee on her bony rib cage. His lips peeled back in a terrifying snarl as the Harpy squirmed and squealed beneath him. Mason heard a low animal growl and saw Fenn's eyes begin to gleam with an eldritch light, heralding his transformation from human to wolf.

She ran forward, screaming, "Fenn! No!"

But before she could reach him, a brilliant silver light flashed in the air in front of her and a voice, clear and bell-like rang out in the air.

"Enough!"

The sound of the word bloomed out like the shockwave from a detonation and stopped Mason in her tracks, forcing her back a few steps. When the afterglow from the brightness faded, she looked up to see a silver-haired woman, hovering in the air on iridescent wings above where Fennrys and Aello grappled in the street. A gust of wet wind swept over the courtyard, rain droplets shattering into rainbow prisms. Aello squawked like an aggrieved crow and flapped away as Fennrys hunched against the sudden torrent, his eyes still smoldering with pale blue light.

He was breathing heavily and the corners of his mouth were still lifted in a feral snarl as he visibly struggled to regain control of himself. It looked as if it took every ounce of strength he had not to lunge at the majestic, ethereal figure gazing down at him, a deep frown marring her lovely brow. When finally it seemed as if he had mastered his wolfish impulses, the silver-haired woman turned to glare at the Harpies.

"Enough, Aello," she said. "All of you. Enough fighting."

"We come only to claim the haruspex—"

"*I* claimed the haruspex."

The magnificent, iridescent wings twitched, scattering rainbow flashes into the dark air all around her, and suddenly Mason knew who this was. Iris, Greek goddess of the rainbow, messenger of the gods and conduit between the Beyond Realms and humanity. She was the one who had taken Fennrys across the River Lethe to help him escape from Helheim.

"It was I who took Gwendolyn Littlefield away."

"But she is a suicide!" Aello squawked. "She belongs to us!"

"She was a *sacrifice*," Iris said, and bestowed a sorrowful glance on Roth, who'd said the very same thing only moments earlier. "And she was deserving of a rest worthy of her actions. I carried her into Elysium."

"You took her across the River Lethe?" Fennrys asked quietly, having regained control of himself.

Iris nodded, the sorrow bending into a sad smile on her face.

Roth took a step forward. "What?" He looked back and forth between Iris and Fennrys. "What does that mean?"

"It means that she lives her afterlife in the vales of the blissful dead," Daria Aristarchos said in a hoarse voice. "And the trials of this life have been forgotten."

Roth's expression crumpled. *"Forgotten?"*

"Do not grieve." Iris held up one long-fingered hand to forestall Roth's cry of protest. "She has no memories of her life. But she has no memories of her *death*, either. Her shade is happy. And you may carry the memories of your time together for her. Be at peace, as she is."

"Peace?" Roth spat the word. "You mean like the kind of

peace my father wants? When everything I've ever known and loved is dead and gone? I'm already way ahead of you." He turned and kicked an overturned table out of his way as he stalked back to kneel beside the empty circle of shattered concrete, his heart just as empty. Just as shattered.

X

As Mason's brother walked past him, Fennrys had to turn away from the stark pain of Roth's expression. He could feel Mason's eyes fixed upon him, almost as if heat emanated from her gaze.

See? she seemed to be silently asking him. *Do you see now why I did what I did? I would have lost you the same way and I couldn't let that happen. Would you have?*

"As for you, Fennrys Wolf," Iris said, turning to address him in a cool, disapproving tone. "I did not think to look upon you again. And certainly not so soon."

He looked up at her. "I believe I expressed a similar sentiment last time we met," he said drily.

Her keen glance pinned him to the spot where he stood. "You no longer balance upon the edge of the knife, I see," she said.

"That's a matter of opinion." Fennrys felt his jaw muscles

tighten. "*I* just happen to think that maybe the knife's gotten a whole lot sharper."

Iris's gaze drifted over to Mason, who had taken a step forward.

"I know you," Mason said to the shining, winged woman. "I mean . . . I've seen you before. In the gym, the night of the storm. The night this all began. You were there, above the branches of the old oak when it crashed through the window. The rainbow window."

"I was." Iris inclined her head gracefully. "Your mother asked me to bring Fennrys to you, Mason Starling. So that he could protect you. Keep you safe."

Fennrys felt his lip twist in the shadow of a sneer. "Yeah," he muttered. "I don't know *what* she was thinking."

"I do," Iris said, rebuking him. Although her tone softened a bit as she said, "She sought to bring light out of darkness. She still does. She still believes in you. Both of you."

At the mention of her mother, a wash of emotion surged over Mason's face. Fennrys remembered what he'd said to her after he and Rafe had rescued her from Asgard, and from Heimdall the Aesir guardian god. The one who'd impersonated Hel, the goddess that Yelena Starling had become, in order to dupe Mason into taking up the Odin spear. Fenn had told Mason that, when the time came, they would return to the Beyond Realms to look for her mother. Now he didn't know if either of them would live long enough for the opportunity to arise.

He felt in that moment as if that was just another way that he was letting Mason down. Silently, he watched as she bit her lip and turned away from Iris, her eyes downcast, and all he wanted to do was take her in his arms and tell her that everything was going to be okay. But he couldn't. Mostly because he couldn't bring himself to believe that.

"*You must, Fennrys Wolf,*" Iris's voice was soft in his mind. Her words for him alone. "*You* must *believe. There is a wolf in the heart of every warrior. Yours is stronger, hungrier. But it remains, still, for the warrior to decide the wolf's prey. Trust those that believe in you and believe in those that trust you.*"

"*Like you, Lady Iris?*" Fenn asked silently.

"*No!*" She laughed gently in his head. "*No . . . I* still half *expect you to be the ruin of the world. But what am I to you or you to me when the day is done? I cannot help you, but I will not hinder you. And I do hope happiness finds you, someday. Keep faith. Keep friends . . .*"

"Farewell."

With that, Iris fanned her bright, impossible wings and rose higher into the dusky red air, calling aloud—and sternly—for her Harpy sisters to attend on her. They screeched reluctantly and Fennrys half expected one of them to launch into one last strafing run. But just then he felt a strange sensation in the pit of his stomach—a rumbling that wasn't hunger—and the ground beneath his boots began to tremble. At first Fenn thought it was yet another earthquake, but it felt different this time. Rhythmic . . .

He glanced around, trying to assess where the next threat was about to come from, but the plaza on all sides was eerily quiet. Sepulchral. Suddenly, with a burst of panicked screeching, Aello and her sisters did finally take to the skies again. In the wink of an eye, the Harpies scattered, vanishing between skyscrapers like a flock of crows startled by an eagle diving into their midst. A moment later, Fenn saw why. The thunderclouds suddenly lit up above their heads and half a dozen, blue-white comets punched through the cloud cover, blinding bright, streaking down toward the Rockefeller Plaza. The enormous ice balls, glittering and jagged, impacted at the far end of the courtyard like hailstones on steroids and began, impossibly, to unfold—limbs and heads jutting out from glacier-like torsos.

Maddox grunted in recognition. "Frost giants," he said, when Fennrys shot him a questioning look. "I've heard of these guys."

"How do we kill them?" Fenn asked.

"How should I know?" Maddox said. "I said I've *heard* of them. I haven't killed one yet!"

"Where the hell did they come from?"

Maddox chewed on the inside of his cheek and shrugged. "Uh . . . north?"

"You're an idiot."

"What?" Maddox grinned. "They're not Faerie, they're Norse. That's your end of the stick, boyo."

"Thanks to the Fae, I didn't exactly grow up in a Norse household like I was supposed to, you know," Fenn complained as the monstrous creatures heaved themselves to standing on massive ice-pillar legs. "I don't know all the Viking myths and—"

"Google it later!" Mason shouted, running, as she grabbed

Fennrys by the wrist and hauled him behind a concrete barrier. "Now? *Move!*"

A fraction of an instant later, a giant ice fist slammed down in the place where he'd been standing. Ice pellets and snow-crusted bits of rock sprayed the terrace like shrapnel.

"Seven hells!" Fennrys swore, rapidly assessing the situation. "Those things have this end of the courtyard boxed in. If we stay stuck down here for too long, it'll be like shooting fish in a barrel."

"Punching," Mason corrected him as one of the creatures slammed its fist into a stone pillar, sending huge chunks of rock flying. "*Punching* fish in a barrel."

"Yeah." Fenn snorted. "They'll pulverize us either way." He glanced around to see Maddox crouched behind the outdoor bar, his silver chain weapon ready. "Madd! Cover me. . . ."

Maddox nodded, popped up, and whipped his chain at the neck of one of the ice giants. The barbs bit like a mountain climber's grapple hook and he hauled with all his strength, pulling the thing off balance. Mason grabbed a nearby fire extinguisher and darted forward to bash great chunks of ice off the side of the thing's head. She did it without morphing into her Valkyrie gear—just yelling like a banshee, brave and crazy, charging into danger when she could have just kept her head down.

Good god, I love that girl, Fennrys thought as he ran, determined to find a way to tell her that again. And maybe one day hear her say words like those back to him.

★ ★ ★

Mason watched as Fenn made a break for the stairs leading up out of the courtyard, then she leaped into the fray with a fire extinguisher. Less than five seconds later, Fennrys was back.

The blow from the Frost Giant sent him flying through the air, and he slammed into the red marble wall behind the Rockefeller's famous fountain. The stone cracked with a sound like a shotgun blast and Fennrys fell face-first into the pool beneath the Prometheus statue's unblinking glare.

Mason screamed his name and dropped the fire extinguisher.

"You take cover!" Rafe yelled, sprinting toward her in his man-god shape, bronze sword in his hand, long white fangs exposed and gleaming. "He'll be fine!"

Mason ducked frantically back behind the barrier as a swarm of airborne icicles knifed through the space where her head had been a moment before.

Right, she thought. *Rafe said his wolves were "damn near unkillable."*

She really hoped he hadn't been exaggerating.

And a few seconds later, Fennrys lifted his head, his fierce eyes staring out from beneath a fringe of dripping-wet hair, and snarled at the icy abomination lumbering toward him. Maddox and Rafe rushed to engage the creature, to give Fenn a moment of breathing space. But suddenly, the Frost Giant—and its fellows—stopped in its tracks and dipped its massive head as if in deference. A strange, hollow silence descended on the sunken courtyard, as if the eye of a storm had settled over them, walling away howling winds.

And into that eerie stillness, Rory Starling swaggered down the stairs.

He wore a long dark leather coat that Mason recognized as belonging to their father, black leather gloves, black jeans, and thick-soled boots that echoed like hard slaps on the pavement. The only thing needed to complete the supervillain look was a pair of mirrored sunglasses.

"Somebody's in a party mood tonight," Roth said drily, stepping up beside her as she shifted out from behind the barrier. "Dad give you the keys to the Bentley or something, Ror?"

"Well, if it isn't little Mousie and my big, bad brother," Rory sneered. Then he laughed, and it was an ugly sound. "Dad gave me more than car keys, Roth. And you know it. Hey, listen—I owe you a little something from our last conversation."

"Let me guess," Roth murmured. "Pain?"

"I owe you *pain*!"

Mason sighed. "He doesn't disappoint."

"Just once, I wish he would."

"What happened between you two?" she asked.

"We had a little chat. It didn't go well. You know how he holds a grudge."

At Rory's command, the mammoth ice creatures started forward again, heaving large heavy tables and chairs in Mason and Roth's direction and wreaking messy, dangerous havoc.

Mason caught a flash of movement out the corner of her eye and turned to see Toby and Cal, along with Heather and Daria, darting toward them in a tight group. Their movements were covered by Maddox and Rafe, who worked in tandem with chain and sword to harry one of the Frost Giants and drive it back, with only minimal success. Mostly, it just looked as though they were annoying the hulking creature with their swift, darting feints. But Mason knew that if it managed to connect with one of its ponderous blows, that would be it. Every time one of the massive ice fists landed, chunks of concrete flew like missiles.

And Rory threw back his head and laughed.

"Guys? I have a bad feeling about this," Heather said, crouching down beside Mason and nodding at Rory. "Judging by the *last* time I saw your douche brother, he should be whimpering for his mommy by now." She shook her head. "*That* guy? Looks like he's having way too much fun."

"Yeah. We should definitely spoil that fun," Fennrys snarled, dripping wet and scorchingly furious. "Hey, Aqualad!" Fennrys barked at Cal. "I could use a lift. . . ."

"No problem, Teen Wolf," Cal said and flung out both hands toward the Prometheus fountain—almost as if in supplication to the Titan god—and the water in the pool beneath suddenly gathered in a wave that surged up and over the terrace, gathering beneath Fennrys, who bunched his legs under himself and braced against the water's sudden density. Cal made a hurling motion with his hands and the solid column of water flung Fenn through the air like a hydraulic catapult. Mason and the others watched in awe as he transformed, mid-air, into the huge golden wolf with teeth and claws that were far more effective than any weapon he might wield.

At least, they should have been.

Mason sucked in a horrified breath as the Fennrys Wolf opened his jaws wide and clamped down just above the wrist of her brother's outflung arm, expecting to see Rory's hand sever in a spray of blood and shattered bone. Instead, she heard the Wolf yelp in pain as Rory threw back his head and howled with laughter. In gleeful madness, he flung Fennrys to the ground like a rag doll, then brought his gloved fist down in a vicious arc toward the top of the lupine's skull.

If he'd moved just a fraction faster, he would have done it, too.

But the Wolf twisted frantically and rolled to the side, the swiftness of animal instincts far superior to his adversary's human reaction time, and Rory's leather-clad knuckles only made contact with the patio stones.

What's happened to him? Mason wondered, horrified.

Rory lunged again and picked up the golden wolf scrambling at his feet by the scruff of the neck—one-handed—and hurled him into the outdoor patio bar that had been shuttered. The metal slats covering the bottle shelves caved in with the blow and the Wolf howled in excruciating pain.

Heather murmured, *"Holy . . ."*

"Roth!" Mason turned to him, frantic. "What the *hell* has happened to Rory?"

"Witchmechs," he hissed. "Those bloody dark dwarves didn't just give him a new hand to replace the one that Fennrys shattered . . . they gave him a new hand meant for Tyr."

Mason blinked, stunned for a moment. "Tyr—the Norse *god*, Tyr?—the *wolfsbane* god?"

"Yeah. That one," Roth spat. "That hand is made of silver

and it's full of big-time magick."

"Shit," Toby swore. "Fennrys! Fall back!" he called out. "Fall *back*! He'll kill you!"

The Fennrys Wolf yelped in pain again as another blow from Rory sent him sprawling across the terrace. Mason couldn't see any other options. She reached for the hilt of her sword . . .

"Don't." Rafe's voice cut through the chaos as the god vaulted the stone barrier and dropped lightly to the ground beside her. His expression was deadly serious.

"Fennrys is getting his ass kicked out there, Rafe!" she said. "For us!"

"I noticed." He pegged her with a pointed stare. "Doesn't matter. Whatever you do, you *cannot* risk manifesting as a Valkyrie in the middle of a pitched battle, Mason."

"Why?" she pleaded. *"Why* can't I use all this power to do something good?"

"Because in a fight, the temptation—the chance that you'll give in to the urge to choose—is too great." There was compassion in Rafe's eyes, but there was also steel. "I know you're tough, Mason, and I know you're brave and you're strong . . . but trust me. The Valkyrie? She's stronger. Her only *purpose* is to choose. Under normal circumstances, she—*you*—would simply choose the most valiant of the combatants on the field. Whoever that is . . . dies a glorious death, goes to join the Einherjar in Valhalla. Only, in this case—in *your* case—there's a bonus round." The death god's eyes were black, hard, and glittering as obsidian. "In this case . . . the touch of the Odin spear transforms the chosen warrior into the third Odin son, whose prophesied destiny, according to the Norns, is to lead the Einherjar *out* of Valhalla, alongside your two brothers."

"And when that happens?" she asked, knowing full well the answer.

"Ragnarok."

"So what am I supposed to do? Sit here and wait for Rory to finish pulverizing Fennrys?" she demanded. "He's one of yours now, Rafe. Don't you care?"

Her eyes filled with hot tears of frustration. The circle of Frost Giants made certain that none of the wolves could reach the newest member of their pack. Cal was looking dangerously tapped out, and Toby and Maddox were woefully outmatched by Rory's ice thugs.

Her friends, all fighting gamely, were going to lose.

And Fennrys was going to die if they didn't do something.

He leaped again and Rory swung his fist in a roundhouse blow that caught the Wolf on the shoulder and sent him tumbling out of control across the unforgiving concrete. He smashed into another shuttered outdoor servery, and again the metal slats crumpled jaggedly inward on impact. Mason felt a hand on her shoulder and turned.

"Listen to me," Daria said. "I can get us out of here if I can call forth the Firebringer . . ." She paused, gasping for breath. "But I need . . . a spark."

"What are you talking about?" Roth demanded.

"You Vikings weren't the only ones weaving magicks into city landmarks back in the day," she said, referring, no doubt, to the Hell Gate Bridge.

Mason followed her gaze and looked up at the golden

Promethean effigy above the Rockefeller Plaza fountain. It was big, impressive, and carrying fire. It might just be what they needed to fight all that rampaging ice. . . .

"Do it," she said.

"I told you . . . I need a spark." Daria's shoulders slumped and Mason saw that she was pale and shaking.

"She's tapped out from the Miasma." Rafe frowned. "She needs a power source to act like a pilot light. A talisman or something—anybody got anything like that kicking around?"

"The medallion around Fennrys's neck would probably work," Mason said, "except it's around Fennrys's neck."

Roth grunted in frustration. "If I had any of Dad's stash of runegold on me, that would probably work," he said. "But I don't."

"Stash of *what*?" Mason looked at him.

"Acorns—golden ones—carved with runes," Roth explained. "The Norns gave them to Gunnar and they channel magick. I only just found out that Rory was peddling runegold magick like drugs to some of the meathead jocks at Columbia—"

"Wait," Heather said. She reached into her pocket and pulled out a small golden orb. "You mean this thing?" The acorn in the palm of her hand glowed with a warm, gentle light in the darkness.

"Uh . . . yeah." Roth blinked at it. "That's exactly what I mean. That's got a protection rune on it." He glanced at her sharply. "Is *that* what's been shielding you? Where did you get it?"

"In a Cracker Jack box," Heather snapped. "None of your business. Will it work as a spark?"

Roth hesitated. "Yeah, but . . ."

"But what?"

"I'd have to carve off this rune and replace it with another. You'll be vulnerable. To all of this." He circled a hand in the air. "The Frost Giants, the Miasma. It's still powerful enough that it'll probably turn you into one of them." He nodded his chin at the Sleepers strewn about the courtyard.

"Do it." Heather thrust out the acorn.

"Heather—no." Cal shook his head, reaching out to grab for her wrist. "It's too risky. You need that to keep you safe."

"Tell you what," Heather countered. "How about *you* keep me safe."

At the far end of the plaza, the Frost Giants were roaming mindlessly, committing random acts of wanton destruction. The courtyard looked like a war zone. The Fennrys Wolf was cornered, hemmed in by Rory, who stood there hurling taunts and waiting for the golden-furred beast to charge at him again.

Rafe's other wolves were nowhere to be seen and Mason knew the ancient god wasn't about to call them back, just so he could sacrifice his pack on their behalf. She could hardly blame him. She'd already asked an awful lot of a being who, for all intents and purposes, had very little to do with the burgeoning mess her family had conjured. Well, hers . . . and Calum's. She glanced over to where Cal was crouched beside his mother and saw that the fire had returned to Daria's eyes. They were fixed on the younger of the Starling boys and there was hate in Daria's gaze. Pure and potent. Mason looked back at Rory and realized, in that instant, just how much he looked like pictures she'd seen of their father when he was young.

Heather offered up the acorn once more. "Mrs. A, *can* you use this?"

Daria nodded.

"Then do it."

Cal's mother looked at Roth, who looked at Mason, who nodded curtly. He reached over and carefully plucked the little gleaming nut from Heather's palm. He used the razor-sharp edge of his hunting knife to pare off the marking on the acorn, replacing it with another. To Mason's untrained eye, the runes just looked like random scratches. But they were obviously much more. The moment the protective rune was gone, before Roth was even done carving the second mark in its place, Heather's eyes had rolled up into her head and she'd slumped over, unconscious in Cal's arms.

Daria barely glanced at her. "We'll have to leave the girl now. She'll only slow us down."

"Mom?" Cal said tightly. "The 'girl' has a name. It's Heather. You know that, because I dated her for about two years. She just gave us a fighting chance to get out of this mess alive and we are not leaving her behind. I'll carry her the whole way if I have to."

"You're not back together, are you?" Cal's mother frowned at him in displeasure.

"Heather is a friend," Cal said. His jaw muscles tightened and his scars twitched a bit. "You don't leave friends behind and you don't forget them. At least, you try not to."

It was, Mason thought, a sentiment very close to something she herself had said to Cal back on Roosevelt Island to get him to come back into Manhattan with her.

"I never thought that girl was right for you," Daria muttered.

"Again. Her name is *Heather*. And I don't care what you think." He stood there, holding Heather cradled in his strong arms like she weighed the same as an empty set of clothes would have.

Daria lost the staring contest and her gaze slid away. "Fine," she said, shaking back her disheveled hair. "Do what you have to do. Just . . ." She held out her hand to Roth. "Give me the runegold. And give me some room."

She closed her eyes and spoke a handful of low, passionately voiced words. Then she gestured to her head and heart and down to the earth with the acorn . . . and the others suddenly felt compelled to give her the room she'd asked for—because all of the breathable oxygen in a ten-foot radius vanished—sucked into the incantation Daria cast with the runegold spark, leaving them all breathless—and a pressure wave bloomed out an instant later. When she opened her eyes, they were black.

"Take it." She held out the acorn, the rune pulsing red on its golden surface, to Cal. "Give the Spark to the Firebringer and bid him wake!"

Mason watched as Cal gently put Heather on the ground, vaulted over the concrete barrier, and sprinted toward the fountain. Without stopping, he ran out *over* the surface of the water—which turned suddenly solid beneath him, rising up like a series of glassy steps in a sweeping curve—toward the statue's hand that held the ball of gilded flame. Cal sprinted up the steps and dropped the carved acorn in among that frozen-in-time burst of sun fire and shouted, "Prometheus! Wake up, brother!"

Then he got the hell out of the way.

"Well now, there's something you don't see every day," Mason said.

Her mouth went dry with fear, as the flame in the golden god's hand suddenly flared like rocket fuel set alight and Prometheus's massive feet splashed into the fountain as the statue's muscles rippled and the ancient Greek Titan stood tall and cast a searchlight gaze around at the courtyard.

Toby and Maddox came pounding back to join the rest of the group when the cluster of Frost Giants they'd been staving off seemed to suddenly realize that they had company on a similar scale. When a ball of blue-gold fire slammed into the ground at one of the Giant's icy feet, roaring up to flash melt the creature into a column of water that held its shape in the blast of heat for only a moment before turning incorporeal and drenching the ground in a tidal surge. The creature's companions roared, howling like the bitterest north winds, and rushed toward the golden colossus.

"Hey!" Rory shouted, outraged that his glacial brutes were suddenly on the defensive. He turned from Fennrys and stalked toward the Firebringer, picking up scattered debris and hurling it with his magically enhanced hand.

"Right . . . ," Rafe said, backing away from the clashing, elemental goliaths. "I think that's our cue to exit . . ."

"Not without Fennrys," Mason said.

"Mase!" Roth hissed at her, but she ignored him, crouching low and using the courtyard dividers and columns for cover. "Dammit!" Roth swore and sprinted after her. Rory saw her coming and launched a wild, roundhouse punch at her head, but Mason was smaller, faster. She ducked and wove around him without breaking stride.

And Rory didn't get a chance to follow, because suddenly Roth was on him. He took Rory out in a devastating football tackle that sent them both sprawling, and Mason kept right on running—straight for the column Fennrys leaned against, panting with pain, his wolf's tongue lolling out, and his yellow flanks heaving like bellows. His head drooped in exhaustion and there was blood on his fur—deep cuts along his back and left hip from where Rory had slammed him against the servery shutters and the buckled metal had cut into his hide. But even as Mason skidded to a stop and knelt down to try to help him, she saw that the injuries were already beginning to heal. And after a few moments, his breathing normalized and his head lifted.

The Wolf looked at her, wary, his lips lifting away from long white fangs in a warning snarl. Mason swallowed her fear and held out a hand. The great beast's nose snuffled at her knuckles, wet and quivering, and she reached past his muzzle to wrap her fingers around the Janus medallion hanging around his muscled neck. For a brief moment, Mason felt as if she was somewhere else. There was pale, pearly light reflecting off water, the slap of waves, and a sharp tang on the wind . . . and the Wolf sitting beside her on a long, empty bench . . . she could feel the thick fur of his pelt beneath her hand. But when she turned, she saw that her hand rested on the shoulder of someone wearing a heavy woolen cloak, damp with rain or mist, face obscured by a deep hood and clutching a bundle in rag-wrapped hands.

"Fennrys . . . ?" Mason said, her voice muted by sudden fog.

The shoulder under her hand heaved and Mason felt as if the bench beneath her bucked and shuddered. She snapped sharply back out of the moment of dream-vision and found herself kneeling once more on the cold concrete of the Rockefeller Plaza café courtyard. Fennrys—human again, pale and tense, but seemingly unhurt—was crouched there in front of her, his eyes still the gleaming, silvery blue of his Wolf self. Mason only had a moment to spare, she knew, but she took the time to rest her hand against Fenn's cheek and wait while he closed his eyes and fought, visibly, to shut the cage door on the beast inside himself once more.

When he opened his eyes again, she said, "We have to go."

He nodded, wordlessly, and together they stood. Fennrys had one arm wrapped tightly around his torso and his breathing was labored. Mason wondered how many ribs he'd broken in the fight, and whether they'd heal in time for the next round. She moved to get an arm underneath him, but he backed away from her, holding up a hand.

"Mase . . . no," he said through gritted teeth. "I can manage."

"Okay," she said, backing up and letting him stand on his own. "Follow me."

Fenn nodded, and she led him toward a corner staircase at a run. Before they ascended, Mason risked a brief glance over her shoulder and saw Rory on the ground with Roth standing over him. Roth had his broad-bladed hunting knife gripped tightly in his fist, raised and ready to strike. From somewhere high above, Mason thought she heard the harsh cry of a raven. Roth seemed to hear it too. He hesitated and glanced skyward. Then he lifted the knife again . . . and swore venomously. The hand that held the blade wavered and dropped and, instead, Roth delivered a single swift kick from his heavy motorcycle boot to the side of Rory's head.

His face twisted in an angry glower, Roth took off running. As he headed back toward the others, he signaled Mason to meet up with them topside. She waved one hand in understanding and, without a second look back at Rory, screaming in pain and fury on the ground, took the stairs three at a time, Fennrys following close behind.

Rory scrambled up the shallow steps that led through the channel gardens and out toward Fifth Avenue. He never made it so far as the street. The figure in the black, billowing coat and wide-brimmed hat striding toward him stopped him in his tracks and made him want to turn and run back in the other direction, regardless of the mayhem being wrought there by two opposing literal forces of nature.

But he knew that would be the absolute worst thing he could do.

Even beneath the shadow cast by the brim of his black fedora, Rory could see the serpentine golden gleam twisting in the depths of his father's left eye. For the first time in his life, Rory couldn't lie with his usual glib ease and get away with it. Not now that his father had drunk from the Well of Mimir. Silently, Rory cursed the Norns and held his ground. He stood there waiting so his father could ream him out.

God, he thought. *It's like report card day in sixth grade all over again.*

"What part of 'do not engage the Fennrys Wolf' did I not make absolutely clear to you?" Gunnar said by way of greeting, his monocular glance raking over the sleeve of Rory's leather coat, in the same way that Fennrys's teeth and claws had, shredding the sleeve, but not Rory's arm.

Rory barely kept from rolling his eyes. What did his father *not* get about that guy? About the fact that he was going down and it was going to be Rory who would be responsible for making that happen?

"I know, I know." He tried his best to sound contrite and went for the pity play. "It's just . . . that son of a bitch took my *hand*, Dad."

"And I gave you a new one," Gunnar snapped. "Please, tell me. Exactly what is it that displeases you about that gift? Because I'll be more than happy to take it back."

"No!" Rory had to stop himself from hiding his fist behind his back. "No. It won't happen again. I promise."

"I take promises very seriously," Gunnar said.

"Yeah. No kidding."

Gunnar raised an eyebrow and stalked past Rory to lean on the railing overlooking the courtyard where Prometheus was slamming one Frost Giant over the head with the arm of another Frost Giant. Rory still hadn't quite figured out exactly how his father had summoned the glacial creatures, but he knew that, ever since Gunnar had drunk the water of Mimir, the spirit of Odin was growing ever stronger within him. Rory wondered what, if anything, could actually defeat his father now. The thought of Fennrys accomplishing that prophesied task filled him with vague stirrings of envy.

But then, Fennrys wouldn't live much past that accomplishment, would he? And that thought, above all, put a spring in Rory's step as he joined his father to watch the Giant bout going on below for a moment before he continued on in his quest to turn his beloved little sister into a weapon of mass destruction.

XI

The weather was worsening. The sky overhead was a sickly, yellow-tinged pewter, hazed over from the Miasma and smoke from scattered fires, and dulled by dark, angry clouds. It was impossible to tell that the sun was even up, let alone where it was in the sky, but Mason judged that it must have been mid to late morning by the time they'd finally made it up the clogged and chaotic yellow cab wasteland of the Avenue of the Americas to West Fifty-Seventh Street. They were soaked and shivering, and the wind buffeted the group with a special malevolence, the fierce gusts having little effect on the Miasma mist that still swirled in dark, sparkling eddies.

Every half block or so, the group would stumble out of a bank of mist and into one of the walking Sleepers—those who had not fully succumbed to the death sleep, or someone who was beginning to wake up—and the farther north they went, the more somnambulists they encountered. The curse, it seemed, was dissipating. If too slowly. And there were bodies—ones on the ground that would not wake up. Not even when the mist was gone for good.

A gust of ice pellets peppered Mason's face and she threw a hand up to block them as she hunched her shoulders forward, wishing she was wearing something a bit more weather appropriate. She was almost tempted to draw the Odin spear again from its glamoured sheath at her hip, just so that she would have the protection of all that armor and leather against the elements.

Sure. That's the only *reason,* she chastised herself silently, frighteningly aware of the seductive call of the spear, and how it beckoned her in seething whispers, even as she walked through the jumbled mess of the streets of her broken city.

As they passed the hulking, dark red sandstone edifice of the Fifth Avenue Presbyterian Church, Mason noticed that Roth silently kept pace beside her. He looked straight ahead until she finally asked him a question.

"Roth . . ." Mason kept her voice lower so that the others wouldn't hear them as they walked. "What did Cal's mother mean back on the terrace? About not trusting you? About her wolfhounds?"

Roth's head dropped a little and for a moment, Mason thought that he wasn't going to tell her. But then he turned to her and said, "It was me."

"What was?"

"The night you were with Fennrys. On the High Line." His gaze was dark, his eyes full of secrets and shadows.

Under other circumstances, Mason probably would have

blushed furiously to know that her brother was aware of her after-hours trysts with Fennrys. Instead, she just said, "Which time?"

"The time I sent the hounds after you."

Mason's heart sank a little. But she realized she'd known. The minute Daria had brought up the dogs, she'd known. Maybe she'd always known that something between her and Roth had never been quite right. He'd always been so protective of her—even more so, in his own way, than their father—and it occurred to her in that moment that maybe all that overprotectiveness was really just overcompensation. She looked sideways at him as they walked, not really knowing what to say.

Roth sighed raggedly. "I've been working with Daria for years," he said. "You know that now. I used to ride out to her place on Long Island and stow my Harley in one of the out-buildings on her estate that housed the kennels where she kept her dogs. Purebred wolfhounds. I had a key."

"Oh, Roth. You *didn't* . . ."

"Yeah," he said. "I did. I brought them into Manhattan, augmented their natural tracking skills with rune magick, and sent them out into the city to find you. To find him."

"I almost died that night," she said quietly. "Again."

"I know." Roth grimaced. "That wasn't my intention. All I wanted was for you to stay away from the Fennrys Wolf."

"How did you even know I was with him?" she asked. "How did you know anything about him at all?"

"It was Gwen."

Oh. Right. Mason heard the brittle hurt in Roth's voice.

"She'd had visions for a while about what was to come, but they were vague and all tangled up until that night of the storm. Then all of a sudden, boom. Crystal-clear images of you and . . . this guy. Gwen called him a harbinger at the time." Roth shrugged. "A forerunner to Ragnarok. The thing I've been told all my life was the destiny of the Starlings to help bring about . . . and the thing I've been actively trying to stop for just as long. From what Gwen had told me, I knew that he could handle pretty much anything I could throw at him."

"And so you threw Daria's *wolfhounds* at him?"

"Yeah." Roth scrubbed a hand over his face. "Hindsight? Probably not the best idea. I just wanted you to stay away from him and I figured the best way to make that happen was to scare the hell out of you. I went on a hunting trip once with Daria and her dogs in the Adirondacks," Roth continued, somewhat reluctantly, "and I watched those dogs take down a bull moose. They scared the hell out of me. I figured they'd do the same thing to you."

"Scare the hell out me?" Mason asked. "Or take me down?"

"Scare you." Roth shook his head adamantly. "That's all. I knew you were with him that night. I just didn't know where, and I was worried that I was running out of time. When I set them loose, I knew they'd find you eventually."

Mason recalled with frightening clarity how the dogs had hunted them in the darkness—baying eerily as they tracked her and Fennrys down on the High Line.

"Fennrys had to destroy those dogs, Roth," Mason said, the spark of anger in her chest flaring into a flame. "You *knew* he would."

"I *didn't* know that." Roth frowned. "But even if I had, I still would have done it, knowing what I knew then. Hell. What I know *now*! I didn't have any choice. I needed to scare you, Mase. I needed to scare *him*."

And he had, she thought. Very effectively and on both counts.

She remembered the harshness in Fenn's voice as he'd yelled at her for not running fast enough—or far enough—away from him as he'd fought the wolfhounds. It wasn't until after that she'd understood that anger had been born of fear—fear for her safety, and Fennrys's very real terror that he was the one putting Mason in danger. She thought about how they'd argued, and how she'd turned and walked away from him. Almost for good.

And what if you had? she thought. *None of this would have happened. If that night on the High Line had been your last night with Fennrys, a lot of lives would have been saved. If I'd stayed dead in the first place . . . If the draugr had won . . . If I hadn't come back from Asgard . . .*

Mason had a sudden flash of insight. "And the Hell Gate?" she asked. "The explosion . . . that was you too. Wasn't it?"

Roth looked surprised that she'd drawn that conclusion, but there was a dreadful logic to it.

Reluctantly, he nodded. "I found out that Fennrys had already found his way to Wards Island after he left Gosforth that night after the draugr attacked."

"Gwen tell you that?"

"Uh, no . . . A troll."

Mason blinked up at her big brother.

"His name is Thrud. He's lived under the Hell Gate since they finished building it in 1916—I put him on my payroll some time ago and told him to let me know if anything out of the ordinary ever happened in and around the Hell Gate."

"Out of the ordinary?"

"I'd say that a guy in Gosforth sweats and army boots wielding a Viking sword and running from a couple of centaurs trying to plug him full of crossbow bolts definitely qualified." Roth shrugged. "I've known since I was a kid that Bifrost and the Hell Gate were one and the same, and I knew that, if what Thrud told me about had already been drawn that way once, he'd manage to find his way there again. I thought 'better safe than sorry.' So I had the troll rig the whole middle span with explosives."

"And when you found out *I'd* crossed over," Mason said, "you thought the only way to stop Ragnarok was to keep me from coming back."

"Yeah. So I blew the bridge." Roth glanced at his sister, a grim smile tugging at the corner of his mouth. "And any chance at an inheritance if Gunnar ever finds out it was me."

She shook her head, almost appreciating the bitter humor of the situation. "Wow, big bro," she said, "is there going to come a time in our lives when you're going to *stop* trying to kill me?"

"Mase . . ."

His grin crumpled and the expression that replaced it on

his face made her wish that she'd not made the joke. She knew Roth loved her and that he always had. With a love so fiercely protective that it might have even been rooted in the events of that terrible day that neither of them had even known about until that night. But he was still willing to sacrifice her—and Fennrys, and probably anybody else he deemed necessary—if he thought that they posed a threat. Okay—Ragnarok was, she had to admit, a pretty huge deal and Roth going against the supposed destiny of the Starling clan to thwart the end of the world was, she also had to admit, pretty admirable.

She wished she thought she had it in her to do the same.

But I don't.

I'm seventeen. I've barely even started my life.

I might be . . . No. I am in love.

And if thwarting the end of the world means giving up that life or that love, or—infinitely worse—sacrificing her love's life?

Not gonna happen.

And, once again, Rafe's words to her and Fennrys from that night in Central Park echoed in her mind. *"To hell with destiny,"* the ancient god had said. Right after he'd told them, *"Prophecies don't always come true. And even when they do, it's usually in all the ways you never expected they would. So there's always hope. Loopholes. A way around destiny."*

Roth may have been all about trying to thwart destiny, but in doing so . . . it seemed that all he was doing was playing right into its nasty, gnarly, blood-soaked hands. Rafe, on the other hand, was right. You didn't try to thwart destiny. Or play along with it.

"To hell with destiny," Mason muttered.

Right. It's a nice sentiment, but I somehow don't think it's as easy as that.

"Roth?" she said. "Back there in the courtyard . . . were you going to kill Rory?"

He chewed on the inside of his cheek for a moment and seemed to be seriously considering that. Then he nodded and said, "Yeah. I was."

"I . . . oh." Mason had half expected him to deny it.

He glanced at her sideways. "I didn't."

She nodded. "I know. Why not?"

"Because . . . I couldn't." His brow darkened in a frown. "Because I *can't*." His fingers flexed on the knife he still carried and she knew. As much as he'd wanted to, Roth hadn't been able to make himself plunge the knife into Rory's heart—even though that was what every fiber of his being had cried out for.

Of course you couldn't, Mason mused silently, hearing the remembered cry of the raven in her head. It had been her raven—her Valkyrie's raven—and Roth would do no such thing. Three Odin sons. That's what the prophecy said. Roth could no more kill Rory than he could kill himself.

Not until I make my choice.

She shook her head grimly. "You know . . . more and more it just feels to me like we're heading straight toward Ragnarok without even *trying* to fight it."

"What makes you say that?"

She rolled an eye at her brother. "Didn't we just manage to arrange a battle between Fire and Ice Giants back there?" she said. "Isn't that part of the whole Ragnarok myth?"

"What were we supposed to do? If Daria hadn't intervened, we'd be dead now."

"Would we?" she asked. "It seems to me that every step we take to *avoid* this stupid, prophesied fate is like trying to find the way out of Dr. Destiny's Funhouse Hall of Mirrors. In the end, there's really only one way we can go. The only choices we make aren't really choices at all and we're just deluding ourselves into thinking they are."

Roth's half smile was lacking humor. "Coming from the chooser herself, that's . . . unencouraging."

She glanced back over her shoulder to where Rafe was keeping pace with Fennrys, who still had one arm wrapped around his torso but was walking fully upright now and not as clenched with pain. She remembered again what the ancient god had said about prophecies always coming true—just not ever in the way anyone ever expected.

"I'm only theorizing." She sighed. "Doesn't mean I'm going to lay down and die anytime soon."

"Probably couldn't if you wanted to."

Roth elbowed her half jokingly, a shadowy semblance of the big brother she'd always loved so and looked up to. He was trying, she knew, for her. She nodded, swallowing the knot of sadness in her throat and tried, too. For him.

"Exactly!" she said brightly. "So really? Don't worry, be happy."

"Right."

"Hakuna matata."

"I don't even know what that means."

"*Lion King*," she said airily. "When this is over, we'll go catch the musical on Broadway. You'll see."

He winced. "And Ragnarok is suddenly sounding like an okay choice."

Mason smiled up at him for a moment, then looked away before the weight of his grief returned to burden his gaze. The trees of Central Park were in view and Mason somehow found herself breathing a sigh of relief. Shafts of silvered moonlight pierced the low-hanging cloud ceiling over the park, filtering down and lending the urban oasis an almost tranquil appeal. Halfway up the block from Fifty-Eighth, Mason thought she could actually feel a rise in the temperature, and she could smell green and growing things.

The Miasma hadn't had any kind of effect on the animals in the city—that much was evident from the number of dogs they'd seen, either wandering freely or tethered to their owner's wrists by leashes—and so Mason wasn't entirely surprised to see more than one of the Central Park horse carriages weaving, driverless, through the snarled traffic in front of the park's southern stone wall. Most of the horses looked spooked and unapproachable, eyes rolling white with fear as they smelled death and discord in the air.

But there was one carriage, yoked to a silvery-gray dappled beast with a long dark mane and tail, that was still parked neatly on the side of the road. The horse stood patiently, oblivious to the chaos around it. The carriage itself was a dark, lustrous black with silver accents, sapphire-blue velvet upholstery, and no driver to be seen.

"Fenn . . . Rafe!" Mason called quietly. When they

stopped and waited for her to catch up, she said. "Everyone is exhausted. I think we should horse cab it the rest of the way to Gos."

Fennrys shrugged, eyeing the carriage warily and probably remembering the last time he'd taken a ride in one, and how well that had turned out. But even Cal, who'd been carrying Heather the whole way without complaint, looked as though he could use a break. And, with the way they'd had to dodge and weave their way through obstacles, there was no way that they would make it to Gosforth on the Upper West Side in anywhere less than two hours. By that time, the Miasma enchantment would have faded and the city would be overrun with military and police.

"Let's do it," Rafe said.

"You guys should maybe hang back for a second, okay?" Mason said. "You probably . . . um . . ."

"Smell like wolves?" Fennrys raised an eyebrow.

"I don't know," she said. "I mean—*I* don't think so, but . . ."

She walked slowly over and held out a hand to the horse that nuzzled her palm and gazed at her with a calm, liquid-black stare. The beast whickered softly and it almost sounded to Mason as if it called her by name. She felt an answering swell of emotion in her heart and knew, somehow, this creature *belonged* with her. She turned and glanced over her shoulder to where Fenn and the others stood waiting, eyeing her warily.

"Come on," she said, and pulled herself up into the driver's seat. She settled herself on the bench and reached for the reins where they were wrapped loosely around a polished silver rail. "We'll cut through the park. There'll be a lot less traffic and we might just make it up to Gosforth before the fog wall falls completely and the National Guard comes thundering across the George Washington and down Riverside Drive."

Fennrys looked at the horse and buggy skeptically. "You ever drive one of these things before?" he asked.

"How hard can it be?" Mason grinned.

"I dunno," he said. "But the last one I hitched a ride in got blasted out of the skies over Valhalla and I woke up in a dungeon cell in Helheim."

"That's not going to happen this time," Mason said. She felt the grin on her face turn slightly feral as she gripped the reins. "Now climb in."

"That's my girl," Fennrys murmured as he pulled himself up.

She bit the inside of her cheek and, before she could stop herself, said, "You keep saying that."

His gaze flared with intensity. "Do I?"

"Do you mean it?"

"Mase . . ."

The sound of her name, the *way* he said it, made her feel like the breath in her lungs was full of sparks from a crackling fire.

His ice-blue eyes were dark with twisting emotion. "Of *course* I—"

"Stop," she said abruptly and held up a hand. "Forget I asked that. It wasn't a fair question and I don't need an answer. Not now. Just . . . get in."

Fennrys did so, throwing himself into the far corner of the

front velvet bench seat, turning so that Mason couldn't see the expression on his face, which, she suspected, had turned stormy. She mentally kicked herself as Toby climbed up and, in a moment of astute observation, decided that he should probably sit between the two of them to provide a bit of a buffer. It eased the tension crackling in the air, and Mason was grateful for that.

Behind them, the others climbed in and settled themselves with Heather, still unconscious, curled against Cal's chest. Maddox was the last one in and Mason saw that his keen gaze swept constantly over the park in front of them. He held his silver chain weapon, coiled and ready, loosely in his hand.

Mason remembered that he and Fennrys were intimately familiar with Central Park. They'd spent their lives guarding the gateway that was woven into the fabric of it, keeping the mortal realm safe from Otherworldly predations. They knew every fold in the earth and every knot in every tree that could conceal menace, and she was glad Maddox had stuck with them. If there had been any way to avoid traversing the park to get to Gosforth, she would have happily circumnavigated it. Frankly, ever since that evening when she and Fennrys had gone to the park together and had met Rafe for the first time, Mason had really never wanted to go there again. She used to love the place. Until she knew its secrets.

It seemed to her that the same kind of thing was happening not just with the places in her life, but with the people. She thought about Rory and her father. And she wondered what in hell she could possibly say to them the next time they met. She probably shouldn't have wondered any such thing.

Because, suddenly, at the very thought of her father, it was as if he was inside her head. She could almost see him. Hear his voice.

Mason . . . Honey . . .

"Dad?" she blurted the word out loud and Toby's head snapped around as he turned to look at her.

"Where?" he asked. "Mase? *Where* is Gunnar?"

"I . . . he's in my *mind* . . ." She shook her head sharply and slapped the reins, concentrating on the horse's gait as the animal broke into a trot. The sound of hoofbeats, steady and swift and reassuring, taking her away from there was balm on her rattled nerves. "It's . . . it feels like he's trying to find me."

"Roth?" Toby swiveled around to address her brother. "Anything we should know about dear ol' dad?"

"He drank from the Well of Mimir," Roth said, his voice tense.

"Damn." Rafe's face creased in a pained expression. "The Well of Sight? Great. He's got Odin sight. Were you gonna mention that little detail at any point?"

"Yeah," Roth said. "I thought I might get around to it when I wasn't being tortured or watching my girlfriend leap to her death."

Rafe glared at him silently and Toby let the matter drop.

"Mason," he said quietly. "Just . . . do us all a favor and try really hard *not* to think of Gunnar, okay? It'll make it harder for him to find us and maybe—"

He didn't get to finish his sentence.

The gray-skinned monster dropped from the tree above their heads and landed on the back of the carriage horse, digging into the animal's withers with sharp-taloned fingers and baring long yellow teeth. The horse screamed in pain and fear and the carriage careened wildly as it reared and took off at a bucking gallop.

"Draugr!" Mason shouted unnecessarily as the thing fixed its glowing, milky-white eyes upon her.

Fennrys was already leaping over the front rail of the carriage and onto the horse's rump. Before the storm zombie could react, Fenn ran his blade straight through the thing's rib cage and thrust the draugr off the horse onto the gravel path. The carriage wheels running over its desiccated frame made the sickening sound of bundled kindling snapping.

Maddox was shouting warnings that Mason couldn't make out over the chaos of trying to control the galloping horse. When she finally managed to haul the animal under control, she saw what he'd been yelling about. Through the mists that carpeted the park, illuminated by the sodium-orange glow of lamplight, Mason saw that the whole of Central Park was alive with lurching, snarling gray figures. They dropped from the trees and clawed through bushes and hauled themselves out of the lake . . .

And they were all converging on the carriage.

"Friends of yours?" Maddox yelled at Fennrys, who still crouched on the back of the horse, hanging onto the harness with one hand, his dagger clutched in the other, now stained black with monster blood.

"Oh, yeah . . ." Fenn grinned viciously. "I've missed these guys."

"I haven't," Toby grunted.

In all of the chaos, Mason hadn't noticed before, but she could swear that the fencing coach's beard had turned gray in just the last few hours. The hair at his temples, too. And there were lines at the corners of his eyes that she'd never seen before. But his aim was still dead-on as he stood up in the front seat and lunged over the side, driving his blade through the eye of a draugr trying to scrabble into the carriage.

They were surrounded.

In the backseat, Rafe manifested his coppery blade and hacked away at another snarling apparition, and Cal called up a wave out of the nearby park lake to sweep another pair of draugr back and drag them under the water. Maddox snared a draugr with his chain and hauled it close enough for Fennrys to punch it dead. But they just kept coming.

"We can't stay here," Daria said calmly, if somewhat impatiently, back to her frosty old pre-blood-curse-invoking self and clearly without time to waste on such apocalyptic Norse nonsense. "There are too many of them."

As if to emphasize that fact, another creature made a grab for her. Daria ducked, throwing herself protectively—surprisingly—over Heather's still-unconscious form. Roth leaned past her to deliver a blow to the draugr that looked like it shattered the thing's entire cranium—its face caved in and it fell to the ground, twitching.

"Fennrys!" Mason called, as he dispatched another draugr leaping for the horse's head with his blade. "Get *back* in the coach, dammit!"

"You heard her!" Maddox called, stepping down off the running board. He swung the silver chain in a slow circle over his head and it made a wicked, whistling sound that forced the draugr to momentarily back off. "Time for you lot to make a hasty exit. I'll hold the fort—"

"Like hell you will." Fennrys jumped down to stand beside him, shoulder to shoulder. "I'm not leaving you behind. Not again."

"Why not?" Maddox snorted. "I managed just fine without you last time."

"You got lucky."

"And you got away. Do that again." Maddox turned to him, his expression intense. "Listen. I told you that we've been strengthening the Gate here in the park since the last time, right?"

"Madd, I—"

"Shut up. I can access the magick the Fae used to do that. It's Green magick and you know that stuff is—"

"Incredibly volatile?" Fennrys sputtered in disbelief. "You're kidding me!"

"Nope . . ." Maddox shook his head. "Emergency use only and it'll probably pulverize a good chunk of the park. But it'll take most of *these* things with it in the process."

"Let me help you," Fenn pleaded, his expression anguished.

Mason's heart hurt for him. She'd never heard Fennrys plead for anything. Central Park was something he'd fought and bled to protect—that, and the otherworldly portal within it—and now he had to leave it up to his comrade to do that for him.

Because of me.

Fenn snarled in frustration. "Maddox—"

"You *can't*." Maddox's tone turned sharp. "And you'd be a damned fool to try. Just like I'd be a damned fool to let you. The other Janus Guards have got the Gate covered on the other side. We're outmatched here, boyo, and they"—he pointed to the carriage occupants—"need you to get them out and clear of the park and away from these things. Let me do what I can to help, yeah?"

"Maddox . . ."

"It's what friends do."

Fennrys went still, regarding the other young man. "I don't think I ever called you that to your face before," he said.

Maddox went still too. "Yeah," he said, "probably not. But you've clearly had a character growth spurt. I credit the love of a good woman. Go now. Keep her safe." He turned and winked at Mason. "And *you*, lass? You keep *him* safe."

"I will."

"Good. Now *go*."

Fennrys swore virulently and grabbed hold of the carriage, hauling himself up over the side. As he did so, Maddox flicked his wrist and the chain in his hand settled on the ground in a circle three feet wide with the Janus Guard standing at the center. He laid the end in his hand over the other end, completing the circle, and grinned over his shoulder at them.

"Show time," he said and slapped both hands, palms down hard onto the ground with a sound like a thunderclap. The earth beneath him seemed to ripple away in waves. The trees nearest the carriage groaned and began to shudder, leaves shivering as the branches quivered and twisted unnaturally. A huge old oak tree—it reminded Mason of the one that used to grace the Gosforth quad—suddenly reached out, as if its branches were fingers, and wrapped around a couple of shambling draugr, squeezing shut like a fist and hurling them into the center of the lake. Not without cost to the tree itself, though. Bark peeled back in wide strips and sap flowed from cracks in the venerable old tree like lifeblood.

The whole of the park shuddered animatedly. Tree roots punched up out of the mossy ground and thorny vines whip-sawed through the air, tearing the draugr to pieces. Maddox cried out with the effort of harnessing the dangerous forces flowing through the fabric of the park.

"Madd!" Fennrys shouted.

"Get him out of here, Mason!" Maddox yelled.

Tears of frustration hot on her cheeks, Mason cracked the reins and urged the horse to a gallop. The carriage lurched wildly forward, throwing Fennrys off balance, and in the few moments it took to right himself, they were too far away for him to be of any use to the other Janus Guard. Fenn pounded his fist on the brass rail and cursed until the woken trees echoed with the sounds of his fury.

Mason could feel the park's pain radiating all around her as she slapped the reins and shouted encouragement to the carriage horse. But she could feel a kind of righteous anger, too. The very earth was fighting—for *them*. She wouldn't let that fight go to waste. Some of the draugr carried torches burning with eldritch fire and a tree next to the carriage burst into flame as they thundered past. Mason screamed in rage. . . .

And felt the Valkyrie within her respond.

In her mind she heard the beating of raven's wings and

urged the horse to go faster. The creature responded to her commands with a burst of unnatural speed and suddenly it seemed as if they were flying over the ground. A swell of triumph bloomed in her chest as the ground mist shimmered with a fluorescence of rainbow hues and the contours of the park all around them turned hazy. Mason's Valkyrie power guided them into the spaces between the worlds as a thick, shimmering mist descended and the city faded away to pearly gray.

XII

Safe for the time being as they traveled the twilight ways, Mason glanced over at Fennrys, who was staring at her, frost and ice crystals glittering in his gaze. She knew that he had traveled in a Valkyrie carriage once before and that what she was doing now must be feeling familiar to him in a way that probably wasn't particularly reassuring.

She understood that. She could feel the lure of Valhalla so strongly, urging her to bring heroes to the hall of the Aesir, and the carriage horse—sensing her conflict—became balky and unsure. Lacking a firm hand on the reins, the animal bucked in the harness traces and Mason tightened her grip.

We're not going to Valhalla, she told herself—and the horse—adamantly. *I'm going to drive this carriage through this park and I'm going to take it all the way to the front doors of Gosforth Academy.* All she needed to do was resist the drumbeat in her ears urging her to go farther than that.

Much farther . . .

No. No Valhalla. Concentrate.

Easier said than done, when she was staring into the eyes of the hero himself.

The gaze they shared stretched out between them and Fenn must have seen the Valkyrie hunger growing in her eyes. He broke the stare and turned his face away, lessening the temptation, and she was grateful. But she still felt shaky. Looking away from Fennrys, she saw that she wasn't the only one who was feeling worse for wear.

"Toby?" Mason said, a twist of concern suddenly knotting in her chest. "What happened to your coffee mug?"

The battered old aluminum travel mug was so much a part of his demeanor that Toby looked odd without it. Even in one-on-one coaching sessions back at Gosforth, he'd rarely ever let the thing out of his sight, often fencing with sword in one hand and mug in the other. Toby stared down into his empty palms as if he was wondering the very same thing.

"I guess I lost it." He shrugged, his shoulders slumping loosely.

"It wasn't coffee," Mason said quietly.

Toby shook his head. "Nope."

"You're not human," she said. "Are you?"

To her surprise, he laughed. "Of course I am. I'm just a really freaking old one."

She blinked at him, startled, and he shrugged again.

"How well do you pay attention in Professor Leggatt's Shakespeare class?" he asked.

Mason raised an eyebrow at the seeming randomness of

the question, but Toby waited for her to answer. Ahead of them, the sleek black horse trod the Between path with sure feet now, pulling them along effortlessly through the murk.

"I actually liked that class," she said eventually. "I have a paper due on *Cymbeline* next week. I think it's next week. You know, assuming the world doesn't end."

"You guys study *Macbeth* yet?" Toby asked.

Mason nodded. "Yeah."

"Do you remember the very first scene, in the aftermath of a battle, before you actually meet Macbeth?" he asked. "Do you remember how the other thanes refer to him as 'Bellona's bridegroom'?"

"Uh . . . vaguely. Sure." Mason frowned, thinking back to the scene. She had liked that play. She'd liked Macbeth and secretly thought he'd actually gotten kind of a raw deal. "It was like a kind of honorary title, wasn't it? Like calling him 'Super Badass.'"

"Something like that, yeah." Toby laughed a little at the comparison. "They're equating him to the husband—or lover—of War. In this case, 'War' being a goddess named Bellona. Well . . . that's what the Romans called her. Later on. She was, in fact, Carthaginian. Before Carthage existed, really . . ."

"And?"

Toby pointed to his chest. "Just call me Macbeth."

"What?" Mason blinked. "You were . . . *what*? The husband of a war goddess?"

"*The* war goddess. The original. And we never formalized the union. But yeah."

Mason silently soaked in that information and tried to reconcile it with the man she'd known for a year, who'd been her mentor and her coach. And her friend. In fact, it wasn't so hard. It actually made a strange kind of sense.

"What happened?" she asked.

Toby laced his fingers together and stared ahead of them into the mists. "Falling in love when you're a goddess is . . . complicated. At least, it was with Bell. She was immortal, for one thing, and I guess she didn't want to lose me because I wasn't. So . . . she made me immortal too. Sometimes I think I was a coward for letting her."

"A coward? Are you *serious*?" Toby was one of the bravest men she knew.

"I didn't want to die, Mase. I was afraid to." He shrugged, but there was a gravelly hitch in his voice as he said, "Now? I would give anything . . . *anything* to make an end of it."

Mason flinched from the raw pain in that admission, but she appreciated Toby's honesty. His openness in the face of all the lies she'd been told by others. She could sense Fennrys silently listening to the exchange as he sat beside Toby, who clearly didn't mind him knowing.

"Professor Leggatt taught us that, in *Julius Caesar*, Shakespeare says: 'Cowards die many times before their death; The valiant never taste of death but once,'" Mason said. "Does that mean that I'm . . ."

She trailed off and Toby raised an eyebrow at her.

"Does that mean you're what?"

Fennrys shook his head, smiling grimly. "She means are we cowards?"

Mason ducked her head. "Are we? Think about it. We keep dying, right?"

But Toby just laughed. "I don't think that's exactly what ol' Bill meant, Mason. I think he meant that if you're *afraid* to die, you feel like you are dying every time things get hairy. There's death and then there's *death*. And when you finally get to the latter—when we all do—I think you'll definitely taste the difference." He exchanged a glance with Fennrys then turned back to her. "You're the bravest girl I've ever met, Mason Starling. Not least of all because sometimes you have the courage to be terrified."

"Thanks, Coach."

He snorted. "Especially of me."

"You got that right."

"So you really can't die?" Fennrys asked Toby.

"Nope."

"That's . . . huh."

For a Viking whose greatest desire was to die gloriously and live on in Valhalla, that must have been a difficult circumstance to contemplate, Mason thought. Then again, Fenn had experienced something of a perspective shift on that whole thing lately. She tightened her grip on the reins again when the carriage horse tossed his head.

"It's not exactly all it's cracked up to be." Toby's expression soured. "You know those cautionary tales about scatterbrained goddesses granting eternal *life* but not eternal *youth*?"

Fennrys nodded.

"Those myths had to have their roots somewhere."

"But . . . you don't look any older than my dad," Mason said.

"Good genes. And an elixir." Toby mimed his missing mug.

"So what happened to your lady?" Fennrys asked.

Toby shrugged. "The art of war marched on without her. War, for a being like Bellona, was an honorable, intimate interaction. Time was, if you were going to kill, you used to have to be close enough to feel your foe's dying breath on your cheek. Or see the whites of his eyes, at least."

Mason thought of Rory and his gun and guessed where Toby was going.

"The moment the very first gunshot rang out in the world," he said, "Bell *felt* it. And she started to die inside." He shook his head sadly, his expression full of memories of his long-ago lost love. "I had to hand it to her. She hung on until the Napoleonic wars. Saw me through a lot of battles, tended my wounds, cheered me from the trenches. But it was just so . . . ugly. So impersonal. War had lost its joy for the Lady of Battles."

"Joy, huh?" Mason murmured. And yet, the Valkyrie in her understood.

Fierce, savage joy . . .

Toby looked at her and his gaze sharpened. He saw that she knew *exactly* what he was talking about and there was both pride and sadness in that realization. For all the time she had known him, Toby had urged Mason on to greater lengths of martial prowess with saber and épée and foil. Exhorted her to reach deep for that drive to fight hard. Prodded Mason with every new bout to find her killer instinct. He'd clearly never expected to her succeed to the degree that she had. His brow furrowed deeply and he put a hand on her knee, squeezing gently.

"Where's Bellona now?" Mason asked, turning her face away from him.

"Gone." Toby sighed deeply. "One day, she just couldn't take it anymore," he said. "The ugliness. She walked out into the middle of a firefight and shed the mantle of her divinity. Never saw her so beautiful as in the moment when she gave up her immortality." He blinked rapidly for a few seconds before continuing. "*I've* never figured out the trick of doing that, but then I'm not a god. Just a really old, really tired grunt."

Mason bit her lip to keep from crying for Toby. Never in a million years would she have imagined that had been his life.

"She caught a bullet," he continued, the hurt in his voice a dull, ancient ache. "Just one. But it was enough. I never even saw who it was that shot her and *that* was when I realized that she was right. War up close and personal is bad. At a distance, it's monstrous. Humans in battle have become nothing more than killing machines. Things like honor, glory . . . they just don't mean anything anymore."

"You sound like my father," Mason said.

"Oh." Toby grunted. "Yeah. I suppose sometimes I do."

"Did you still fight?" Fennrys asked. "After that? I mean . . . I'm pretty sure what you told me about having 'buddies who were Navy SEALS' was a load of crap. *You* were a SEAL, weren't you?"

Toby laughed. "Yeah. I was. In a specialist capacity. A man gets bored and there's really only one thing I'm any good at. War. But I haven't fired a gun since I lost Bell."

"Pretty handy with a blade, I noticed," Fennrys said drily.

"Yeah." Toby shrugged modestly. "After she died, I went back to basics. And I won't kill a man unless I can look him in the eyes."

They rode in silence for a while as Mason threaded her way through the twisting mists of the Beyond. When she sensed that they were nearing the place where she could safely guide the carriage back into the mortal realm, she turned to Toby and asked him one more question.

"I was thinking about something Rafe said to me back at the Plaza," she said quietly, nodding back to where the Egyptian god sat, his coppery blade resting across his knees. "And about the whole valiant thing. He said in a battle, if I were to choose an Odin son, I would do it by choosing the most valiant."

"That's the way it works, yeah." Toby shrugged.

"What if I were to choose wrong?"

"Well," he said. "Now I guess that would be a hell of a thing. Wouldn't it?"

XIII

W hen Mason could sense that they had left the park and the draugr behind, she reached out with her mind and gently urged the carriage horse to tread its way back fully into the mortal realm. She guided it away from the shadowy path of the Between, out into the chaos of the city at the corner of Central Park West and Cathedral Parkway. In the distance behind them, some of the trees in the park were aflame, their ghastly orange glow painting the sky in an apocalyptic hue.

Mason had to concentrate fiercely on guiding the carriage around zombielike Miasma victims, some of whom staggered and lurched toward them, thinking they had come to help. But they couldn't afford to stop.

Especially not if Rory—

"We've got company, little sister," Roth called out from the backseat, interrupting her grim thought with the even more grim reality. Mason glanced over her shoulder to see a motorcycle roaring up the road behind them, weaving in and out of all the stalled and smashed cars, narrowly avoiding the waking sleepers.

"That little weasel stole my favorite bike," Roth observed. "I really am going to kill him this time."

Roth owned several bikes. At least one of them—his favorite, apparently—he kept in the garage at their father's penthouse. Mason knew that Rory used to bug him when they were kids to go dirt-bike riding on the paths around the estate. Roth indulged him for a while until Rory started doing stupid stunts and wrecked three motocross bikes over the course of a single weekend. Mason didn't know that he'd kept up his riding skills. Or maybe—judging from the reck-lessness with which he was steering the thing—he hadn't. But he was gaining on the carriage, and the horse was too played out to go much farther.

When a fire hydrant suddenly blew, directly in the path of the racing bike—and then another, right after Rory had managed to swerve past that one—Mason knew Cal was giv-ing her a chance to win the race. The white-water geysers that shot from the fireplugs should have caused Rory to slow down. It was so cold that the water was freezing into sheets on the road. But when Mason hazarded a glance back, she saw that he'd barely decreased his speed.

They might have escaped the draugr all for nothing.

"This can't be happening!" Mason snarled in frustration. "This has to be some kind of nightmare! It's not supposed to be like this. . . ."

"It's supposed to be exactly like this," Roth said grimly.

"Didn't you ever listen to the stories growing up, Mase?"

"No! I did not!" she said, snapping the reins. "I *hated* those damn stories. *This* night? This is how all those stories wound up sounding to me and I hated that. *Come on!* You can do it!" she urged the galloping carriage horse.

The animal's shiny, silvery coat was lathered and dark with sweat under the harness traces and its sides were heaving with exhaustion. But as Mason shouted encouragement, the horse's muscles bunched and released and the carriage surged forward as it poured on a burst of speed, taking the corner of 110th and Broadway on two of the carriage's tall wheels and almost spilling its occupants out into the street. Mason glanced over her shoulder to see Cal hanging on for dear life with one hand and reaching out—fingers stretched wide—with the other, as Rafe made a startled grab for Heather's limp body tumbling loosely through the carriage.

"Heather!" Mason shouted.

"Don't worry about her, Mase!" Rafe shouted over the roar of water from the burst hydrants. "I've got her—just get us the hell out of here!"

She wrenched her head back around, just in time to see a handful of linebacker-sized forms running toward them from between two Columbia U buildings. It took Mason a moment to realize that they *were* linebackers. At least some of them were.

"Rory," Roth snarled. "Damn that little—"

He ducked to the side as one of them threw what looked like an ancient Viking war ax with the accuracy of a champion quarterback throwing a winning long bomb. The tumbling ax missed Roth's head but sliced through his biker jacket and bit deeply into the top of his shoulder, leaving a deep gouge. Roth screamed and fell to the floor of the carriage, blood gushing from the wound.

"Roth!" Mason shrieked, almost dropping the reins.

"*Drive*, Mase!" Roth snarled, clutching his shoulder and sucking air through his teeth, his face twisted with pain. "Just . . . get us to Gos."

"Holy shit!" Cal exclaimed, dropping to his knees on the carriage floor beside Roth to help him.

"No!" Daria said. "Take care of what's behind us. I'll take care of him."

Mason hissed in frustration at not being able to stop the carriage and summon all of the Valkyrie power within her. But *that* was the very thing, she knew, that Rory and her father were trying to provoke. That was what would put Fennrys and Roth and all of her friends in vastly more jeopardy than they were already in.

Silently, she reached out with as much of her Valkyrie self as she dared and poured out encouragement to the brave, beleaguered carriage horse. It charged forward, heading straight for the line of football players. Rory had obviously been selling runegold magick enhancements to them and they were mad with it. Berserkers. Grimacing and howling like ghouls, they closed ranks and started to run, facing the onrushing carriage as a solid advancing wall of muscle. Their eyes glowed gold and they moved like animals. A pack of hyenas . . .

That would have to face a Wolf.

Before Mason could stop him, Fennrys was leaping over

the side of the carriage, his shape blurring like golden smoke as he shifted midair into the Wolf.

"Fennrys!" Mason howled, frantic, as he raced down the street.

"I'll get him," Rafe said, duplicating Fenn's leap and transforming with an added measure of grace and elegance.

The two wolves raced toward the wall of runebound muscle, their speed making them blurs as they took turns harrying the college football players like a well-coordinated attack team. Rafe was an old hand at being a wolf but Mason marveled at how Fenn's animal instincts drove his attacks, syncing his darting feints and savage lunges with the jackal god's as they drove the football boys back, splitting them down the middle so that Mason could drive the carriage past. The Fennrys Wolf was hanging on by his teeth to the bloodied sleeve of the quarterback who swung wildly with his other hand, which gripped another of the vicious Viking axes. He was unable to throw because Fennrys had him so off balance.

"Idiot . . . ," Roth panted, hauling himself up onto the bench seat behind Mason and holding his shoulder, blood seeping from between his fingers. "Should have aimed for the horse with his first throw . . ."

"What?" Mason hauled on the reins, narrowly avoiding an overturned Audi.

"He's right," Toby grunted. "That would have taken us all down and they could have finished us. Thank the gods they're just not that bright."

"Hurry, Mase . . . ," Roth urged, struggling for breath. "Rory. Gaining . . . on us . . ."

"Roth, will you *please* lie down or something?" Mason snapped at him over her shoulder, trying to concentrate on driving and not on all the blood covering her brother.

The carriage bucked and weaved, throwing Daria—who was struggling to tear a long strip from the hem of her white Elusinian priestess robe to use as a makeshift bandage—from one side to the other. She banged her head on the seat but shook it off and crawled back to Roth. Mason clenched her teeth, not quite willing to believe that Cal's mother was actually being helpful. Not yet. Daria Aristarchos was still persona non grata, a woman who'd been responsible for so much hurt and heartache.

There will be a reckoning, Mason thought. *A settling of debts.*

That would come later.

When the familiar stone turrets and walls of Gosforth Academy finally came into view, Mason guided the carriage right up to the shallow front steps. She whispered a frantic thanks to the animal as they all piled out and ran, and the horse whickered a weary reply.

They burst through the doors—Mason and Toby first, to secure the foyer and make sure the place was, indeed, still safe. Next came Daria with Roth, his arm draped heavily across her shoulder. Then Cal with Heather, cradled carefully in his arms. Rafe and Fennrys were last, shifting back to their human forms just before they entered.

The doors swung shut behind them as Rafe called an all-clear and ordered them locked up tight. Toby hurried to the electronic control panel off to one side and activated the mag locks by entering a coded sequence on a number pad. Mason remembered another time when they'd been locked into a Gosforth building that way. It had done nothing to stop the nightmares from finding a way in. She hugged her elbows and watched as Daria helped Roth over to a leather couch and Fennrys paced back and forth, his fists clenched and his chest heaving.

The sudden silence in the hall as the massive arched doors slammed shut was deafening. With the constant hiss of rain, the rolling thunder, and the snap of lightning strikes muffled to nothing, Mason could hear her heart pounding in her ears. She could hear everyone else's, too, including Fennrys's. It was like a drumbeat calling to her from somewhere far away, strong, insistent, hypnotizing . . .

Mason took a step toward him before she realized what she was doing but was brought up short by another pulse beat that suddenly registered at the edge of her awareness. This one was rabbit-fast and freaked out, and Mason turned to alert the others when, suddenly, Carrie Morgan came bursting through the double doors leading to the classroom wing.

The last time Mason had seen her, Carrie had made a concerted effort to publicly humiliate her. Thanks to Heather, the attempt had backfired gloriously and helped solidify a growing bond of friendship between Heather and Mason.

Carrie's head was down and she was clutching her cell phone in one fist, glowering at it fiercely and cursing its stupid crappy lack of signal. She clearly hadn't been expecting to see anyone else in the Gosforth lobby—certainly not the storm bedraggled collection of Mason and her unlikely group of companions—but when her head snapped up and her gaze landed on Heather, lying limp and pale in Cal's arms, she screamed.

Cal barely spared her a glance as he stalked past. He just continued on through the hall and out again toward the dorm wing without stopping, carrying Heather with him.

"Holy crap! Palmerston!" Carrie exclaimed. "Is she dead?"

"She's not dead, Carrie," Toby said.

"What did you weirdos *do* to her?" she demanded, ignoring the fencing coach and turning a glare that was probably meant to be withering on Mason, but that just came across as flustered and belligerent. "What the hell is going on?"

"Carrie?" Mason said quietly. "For once in your life shut up and be helpful."

Carrie's jaw opened and shut a couple of times as her expression wavered between mutinous and flooded with relief at the sight of other people walking around, seemingly unaffected by the chaos in the rest of the city.

"Do you think you can do that?"

"I . . . Yes." She glared stonily at Mason. "Of course I can."

"Good." Mason nodded. "How many students are left on the grounds?"

Carrie crossed her arms over her chest and said, "I don't know."

"That's not helpful." Mason turned to walk away.

"I *mean* I don't know exactly," Carrie blurted. She seemed utterly terrified at the prospect that she might be left alone. "Like, I didn't do a head count or anything. But it's not that many. Like, five of us maybe. A bunch of parents started pulling their kids out when the earthquake tremors started. Of course, *my* idiot parents chose this week to go on vacation and they haven't even so much as called to see if I'm alive." She shook the phone in her hand. "*Thanks*, Mom and Dad . . ."

"Are any of the faculty still on campus?"

Carrie tilted her head, disdain heavy in her tone as she said, "Are you kidding? Like our teachers actually care if we all die or something."

Toby glanced heavenward, no doubt silently begging for patience, before explaining to Mason and the others in a low murmur: "The headmaster and most of the teaching staff were scheduled to be at a curriculum planning session off-campus when this went down yesterday. I think they'd already canceled all the classes for the day. When the Miasma hit, they were probably just as vulnerable as everyone else in the city."

"A couple of teaching assistants were hanging around, but I think they must have taken off when things started to get weird with the weather." Carrie sniffed. "Losers. I'm going to tell my dad to get them all fired."

"Sure." Mason sighed. "You do that, Carrie. That's if any of them are still alive."

That was enough to shut her up for a moment.

"The faculty might try to head back here once the Miasma fully lifts," Daria suggested.

"Would you?" Fennrys asked. He turned to the school's fencing master—and current ranking administrator. "You guys get danger pay?"

Toby grunted in grim amusement and shook his head. "They're not coming back. I say we raise shields, load torpedoes, and hunker down. Daria? If you'd be so kind as to get the mag locks? The *other* mag locks?"

Cal's mother lifted a shoulder in an elegant shrug and strode over to a brass plaque set into the wall, engraved with various symbols. Mason had never given it much of a second glance. She always thought it was decorative—just part of the old building's gothic adornment. Daria placed her palm flat on the square and her hand seemed to sink into the metallic surface of the panel, which turned opalescent, and a shiver of light danced across her knuckles.

Cal raised an eyebrow at his mother. "Here all this time I always thought 'mag locks' just meant they were 'magnetic.' Not, you know, 'magick,'" he said.

"We've got both," Toby said. "The security in this place— when it's fully up and running—rivals the Pentagon."

"Does the Pentagon have magick?" Mason asked.

Toby just raised an eyebrow at her and remained silent.

"Oh . . ."

Quiet descended again for a moment as Mason and the others were left to contemplate that. And what and how the Powers That Be would respond to the otherworldly threat of the Manhattan situation if it looked like it might spill beyond the borders of the city and out into the wider world. Mason suddenly understood why Daria had invoked the Miasma curse in order to isolate the city and try to deal with Gunnar Starling in a contained arena. Mason wondered for the first time if the Elusinian priestess might have had the right idea, after all. She looked over at the leather couch, where Roth sat, pale and bleeding, and saw that he might have been thinking the same thing. His gaze was fastened on Daria, and while the hurt in his eyes hadn't lessened to any degree whatsoever, the hatred just might have.

Nothing, it seemed, was ever simple.

Not even hate, Mason thought.

Suddenly, the phone hanging on the wall beside the security desk rang.

Loudly. So loud it was like the tolling of a warning bell.

It kept on ringing until Carrie finally huffed, "Isn't anyone going to *get* that?" When no one moved, she huffed louder and stalked over to the desk, snatching up the handset. "Gosforth Academy; this better be Emergency Services telling us you'll be here with hot food and internet—oh. Hang on . . ." She rolled her eyes epically. "It's for you, Starling." She handed over the phone.

Mason stared apprehensively down at the handset Carrie had shoved into her palm and then slowly raised it to her ear. "Hello?"

"Hello, honey," said the voice on the other end of the phone. "It's your father."

Mason's blood ran cold at the sound of Gunnar Starling's voice.

"What do you want?" she asked, trying not to choke on her own words.

"I miss you, honey," her father said.

His voice was warm and soothing. Just like it always had been when she was little and had cried out in her sleep, racked by nightmares. She could almost feel her father's strong arms wrapped around her, rocking her as he chased away the demons that lurked in the dark corners of her room . . . and her mind. The one person who had always been there for her. She wanted to throw the phone down and run outside and find him and throw herself into his embrace. She wanted to beg his forgiveness.

"I wanted to talk to you," her father continued. "To tell you how proud I am of you. And right now, I want you to do something for me, honey. I want you to put the phone down and I want you to go outside. Rory is waiting for you."

And *that,* thankfully, threw cold water in Mason's face.

"Rory can go suck a magick acorn, Dad," she snapped. "And so can you."

The silence on the other end of the line wasn't exactly what she would describe as "shocked" although Mason had never, in her entire existence, spoken to her father like that—but it was heavy and deep and . . . *cold.*

"Here's the deal, Dad," she said. "I'm not going outside. I'm not going to end the world. I spent almost a month researching the paper I have due next week and I'm not going to let that go to waste. I have a ton of work to do on my saber technique if I'm going to get a chance for a do-over at the Nationals. And I *am* going to get that chance." She glanced at Toby, who gave her a thumbs-up. "For the first time in my high school career I have friends—real ones—and I don't want them to die in some stupid apocalypse. I have things to do, Dad. I have a *date.*" She glanced at Fennrys, who grinned a bit wickedly. "And as screwed up and selfish and out of whack as the world is, I happen to think it's worth trying to save. Not obliterate."

"You're just like your mother," Gunnar said in a soft, heavy voice.

"People keep telling me that," she said, a twinge in her heart. "If it's true, I have to think she'd be just as sad as I am that you're doing all this. Dad . . . can't you just *stop*?"

"Mason," his voice turned hard. "Listen to me. The people you are with are poisoning your mind. You have a destiny and it's not what you think. It's not evil. *I'm* not evil. I'm your father. Do you think I would have raised you to do something terrible? Is that what you think?"

Mason was silent for a long moment. And then she said, "You did raise me. And you raised Roth. But . . . you raised Rory, too, Dad."

"Honey—"

She hung up the handset, then grabbed the entire phone console, pulled it off the wall, along with a large chunk of drywall, and hurled it into the corner of the oak-paneled lobby where it smashed to pieces. As they clattered to the ground, the red rage that had momentarily wrapped around Mason's brain vanished. She turned back to the others to find Carrie staring at her, openmouthed.

"They're *totally* gonna make you pay for that!" she said.

"They can send the bill to my dad." Mason smiled acidly. "In Valhalla."

Carrie just flipped her hair over her shoulder and stalked off huffily, back to her corner of the lobby, where she could stare angrily at her useless phone some more.

"Is there an ancient cult dedicated to the god of pains in the ass?" Mason muttered drily. "Because I figure that's gotta be *her* deal."

"Actually," Toby said from over her shoulder, "Carrie

Morgan's family is dedicated on her mother's side to Epona."

Mason turned and raised an eyebrow at him.

"Celtic horse goddess." He shrugged. "Carrie has no idea, but I happen to know it's the truth. It's the reason she's won all those equestrian trophies."

"You're kidding," Mason said.

"Funny thing," Toby mused, "Epona is also the goddess of donkeys and mules, which might explain the temperament." He grinned at Mason.

"Wow," she said. "And that *totally* makes sense."

It did. And, in a weird way, it almost made Mason sympathetic toward Carrie because it meant there was a possibility that she had never really intended to be such a bitch. Maybe the circumstances at play at Gosforth Academy afflicted the student body in ways most of them weren't even aware of. It would go a long way toward explaining Mason's love of sword fighting. Maybe, she thought, it even went so far as to explain her brother Rory's behavior. She frowned, thinking about that. About him.

When did he become such a monster? she wondered. *And why?*

Was it something already inside of him? Some kind of destiny or fate or predetermined role that he was playing in spite of himself? And, if that was the case, could Mason ever find it within *herself* to forgive him for the terrible things he'd done?

What about the things I've done? And might still do . . .

She shook her head sharply to rid herself of the shiver of heat that ran up her spine and the redness that had begun, once again, to tinge the edges of her vision. The urge to just let loose and go haywire with a weapon at the slightest provocation.

Stop! she thought. *You have to* stop *feeling this way.*

Feeling like she would, at any moment, give in and unleash the Valkyrie that stirred so restlessly within her. It was a feeling that was so close to the panic attacks she would experience in enclosed spaces—except for one thing. Instead of fear, all she felt was rage. If the first instance evoked a "flight" response in her, the second most definitely evoked "fight." She was spoiling for it. Mason took a deep breath and turned to Toby.

"I think we should gather all of the stragglers left in the Academy," she said. "It'll be safer that way. Do you think maybe Carrie could help you track everyone down and bring them to the dining hall?"

Toby pretty obviously understood that Mason wasn't exactly responding well to irritants at that moment. "Sure, Mase," he said and beckoned to Carrie, who rolled her eyes. "Come on, Morgan. Let's go round up strays." He pointed to the hall doors. "I'll be right behind you." He went to check the security system one more time and drew the heavy curtains over all of the front windows before following her.

Mason turned her attention to Roth. His head was tipped back and his eyes were closed. Daria had produced a first-aid kit from behind the front desk and had managed to ease the leather jacket off Roth's shoulder. She poured antiseptic on the wound and Roth's only reaction was a slight fluttering of his eyelids. But his breathing was still slow and regular. It was most likely just a flesh wound—a bad one, but it would heal well enough, given time. Mason hoped he'd get that time.

She wanted to go to him and take care of him herself, but

something was stopping her. It was weird. But the sight of Daria, who had so cruelly used Roth—not once but twice now, as an instrument to perpetrate her own evils—so carefully cleaning his wounds was confusing and strange. And as much as she might understand that that was, in fact, what had happened all those years ago, Mason wasn't sure that she had forgiven her brother for killing her.

She wasn't sure she ever would.

XIV

Mason watched Cal's mother tend Roth's wounds and feeling very young and very helpless. Until she felt Fennrys standing close behind her. He radiated a heat that she could feel, without even touching him. She turned to look up into his face.

"Mase," he said quietly, "come with me?"

He nodded toward the glass-paned inner doors that led to the Academy's enclosed courtyard. She followed him out into the courtyard, where the raging storm seemed a little less rage-filled, mostly because the quad was so sheltered. Still, the lashing rain in her face made her close her eyes as Fennrys led her by the hand toward the wing of the Academy that held the gymnasium. The front facade and roof were screened in by plywood, and there was a stark empty space and a massive hole in the ground surrounded by heaped earth where the huge old oak tree used to stand.

For a moment, Mason could almost picture the ancient tree

still standing there, unfolding its massive branches to the sky. Her father had ordered the Gosforth administration to have the fallen oak sawed into firewood and transported back to the Starling estate in Westchester County. Mason fleetingly imagined that she could smell the smoke from the fires her father had built with it, and she thought of Yggdrasil, the mythical Norse world tree.

How fitting. Just like he wants the real world to burn.

For a moment, even with the rain falling, icy and stinging on her face, all Mason could do was stand in the middle of the quad and turn in a slow circle.

"You okay, Mase?" Fennrys asked quietly.

"No," she answered. "Not really . . ."

He reached out and squeezed her hand, his own palm slick with sweat, or maybe it was rain. She couldn't tell.

"This is . . . this *was* my home." She blinked back wetness that was no longer just the rain. Suddenly, it was all too much. "It's my school. I'm supposed to graduate next year. With a ceremony and everything, like a *normal* high school student. I don't care what Roth says. It's *not* supposed to be like this. *I'm* not supposed to be like this."

"I know."

"The other night, before I accidentally went to Asgard, I was lying in bed and I actually thought—I can't believe I'm even telling you this—I actually thought that maybe . . . maybe you might still be around when that happened." A bubble of bitter laughter caught in her throat. "Prom, I mean. I had this fantasy that . . . maybe you'd take me to the dance. Me. I've never thought anything like that about anyone. The only thing I ever cared about before you was fencing. And here you come crashing into my life, the one person who can make me a better fighter and suddenly it's *not* the only thing I'm thinking about. I'm thinking about going places and doing things and being with you and . . . and then all of this."

She waved her hand in the direction of the sky and was answered with a triple-tongued fork of lightning that ripped through the darkness, a deafening boom of thunder following close. Mason shook her head in disgust and anger. And sadness.

"Now all I want to do is survive the night," she said. "I'm not going to get a prom. And this place will never be my home again. It certainly won't be much of a school."

"Hey." Fenn took her by the shoulders and turned her to face him. "You're getting way ahead of yourself. And me."

"I'm sorry—"

"I mean . . ." He pushed a wet strand of hair off her face and tucked it behind her ear. "I haven't even had a chance to ask you to prom yet and you're already telling me you're not going."

Mason blinked in confusion, brought up short. "Fenn—"

"Will you?"

"I . . . what?"

"Let me take you to prom, Mason Starling." Fennrys reached for her hand and lifted it to his lips. His eyes glittered with icy fire as he dipped his head to kiss the backs of her fingers. He stared up at her and his mouth bent into the hint of a smile as he said, "I'll wear a tux. I'll get a limo and roll down all the windows before I pick you up. And I'll leave the weaponry at home."

Does that include the claws and teeth? Mason wondered fleetingly, dazed by the unexpected question and the way it had stolen her breath away. And then she realized that it didn't matter. If the two of them managed to live long enough—and if the world, or even New York City survived—then it just didn't matter. Fennrys. The Wolf. He was a package deal and she loved him.

"I'll get you a corsage," he continued, straightening up and stepping closer to her, his words filling the void of her stunned silence. "Do you like orchids?"

She gazed up into his face in wonderment, struck speechless in that moment and it occurred to Mason then that, for all his worldliness, all his weariness, Fenn was just a young man. One who'd never had a prom—or whatever the ancient Viking equivalent might have been—or really, as far as Mason had gleaned from what she knew of his life, even been on a date. Her heart thumped achingly in her chest. She wanted that. For herself, and for him.

"I love orchids," she said in a whisper.

He leaned down to kiss her and her lips curved into a smile against his.

"But maybe you could bring *one* weapon," she murmured. "Just in case . . ."

He laughed through the kiss and they stayed like that until, under her hands, Mason felt the muscles of his back and shoulders begin to shudder and Fennrys pushed her away from him. His blue gaze had turned stormy again and his face was pale.

"Fenn?"

He shook his head, taking her by the hand, and wordlessly walked her over to the construction entrance into the gym building. There was a padlock on the temporary door but Fenn struck it off with a blow from the hilt of his dagger. The gaping hole in the roof of the building was covered with heavy blue plastic tarps that filtered what little light there was from outside in aquatic shades that made it feel almost as if they were underwater.

Cal would look right at home here, Mason thought. At least, the "new" Cal would.

Her boot heel caught on an uneven ridge as she walked slowly into the middle of the dim vaulting space. What had been a brand-new wooden floor, freshly installed just before the incident, was warped and ruined. Lightning flashed through the tall windows of the gym's long wall, reminding her of the moment she'd seen her very first storm zombie—the draugr's hideous, grinning visage captured in the same kind of flashbulb illumination, framed by one of those very windows. It was a strange sensation being back in the spot where it had all started. Same place, different Mason. If the same thing were to happen again, that very night, she knew that she wouldn't hesitate to fight. She wouldn't hesitate to kill.

If she'd been like that before, maybe Cal wouldn't have gotten hurt.

She shook her head.

Cal wasn't there now and she wasn't about to waste time thinking about him. Not after what he'd done to Fennrys, who *was* there, standing right beside her—even after what *she'd* done to him. She looked up at him and, in the wash of blue haze, saw that there was a sheen of sweat on his brow even though the air in the gym held a damp, clammy chill. His eyes looked feverish.

"What is it?" she asked. "What's wrong?"

"I need your help," he said.

"Is that why you brought me here?"

He nodded stiffly. "I . . . I'm having a hard time keeping it—the wolf—under wraps. I think I have to . . . change. Just for a few minutes. To ease the pressure, sort of like . . ."

"Like a safety valve?" she asked.

"Yeah." He nodded. "Like a safety valve. But I need you to keep an eye on me if you're okay with that. You know, make sure I don't go on a rampage and eat a student or something."

Mason nodded and tried to sound casual as she said, "I can do that."

"Thank you."

For turning you into something that might eat a student? she thought. *You're welcome.*

He led her over to the place by the little raised stage at the end of the gym where there was a metal ring set recessed into the wood floor. He twisted the ring and lifted the trap door that led down to the storage cellar where they had all hidden when the draugr had attacked that first time. Mason looked down at the steep staircase that led into inky-black darkness and paused. She hadn't really experienced a claustrophobic episode since she'd drawn the Odin spear and she wondered if that was because Valkyrie didn't get claustrophobic. Or any kind of phobic. Valkyrie were fearless. She just wasn't sure she wanted to push that theory.

Fennrys raised an eyebrow at her as she hesitated. "Right. I sort of forgot about that . . . are you going to be okay with this?"

"Hanging out in a storage cellar? Yesterday, I would have said no freaking way. Today, I'll do whatever you need me to. Just . . . go." She gestured to the staircase. "I'll be right behind you."

Fennrys closed his mouth and pressed his lips together. He nodded tersely and descended into the cellar with quick, agile steps down the ladder. Mason followed on his heels. When her boots touched the floor of the cramped chamber, she looked around in the gloom to see that Fenn was already on the far side of the rows of wire-mesh storage racks. She reached up to where she remembered Toby getting a flashlight from and found the thing, flicking on its pale beam. Fenn was prying aside some kind of a grate that looked almost like the barred door of a medieval prison cell. She hadn't noticed it the one and only time she'd been down there, and she shot him a questioning look when he glanced at her over his shoulder.

"I found this when you and the others were unconscious, the last time we were here."

"You mean when you knocked us all out with a spell."

"Yeah. Then."

"And stole Toby's boots."

"I gave them back." He gestured her closer, pointing to the curved lintel above the opening. It looked like the mouth of a cave, but the stone archway was smooth, carved stone, inscribed with symbols and signs. "Look here."

He passed his hand over symbols that looked similar to the

ones on his medallion. And on the Odin spear. Norse designs. They went farther down that tunnel. In one of the deeper alcoves they passed, they saw that someone had made something of a cozy little nest on a rock shelf.

There was a camping lantern and a colorful crocheted throw that Mason recognized as usually draped over the couch in one of the common rooms. There was a small travel bag in one corner and on an overturned storage crate, there was an aluminum water bottle, a stack of energy bars, and a couple of paperback novels. There was also a framed picture of her brother Roth and Gwen Littlefield.

In the center of the dirt floor, there was a long silver knife, lying inside a circle drawn in what looked to Mason like rock salt, broken by the swipe of fingertips. Beside the knife, there were dark reddish stains in the dirt.

"The haruspex," Fennrys said, the breath rasping in and out of his lungs as he tried to keep a handle on his surging wolfish temperament. He waved a hand at the ground. "That's a casting circle. Magick practitioners use them. She must have been doing a divining."

"The last one she'll ever do," Mason murmured and picked up the picture of her brother and the purple-haired, pixie-pretty girl he had his arms wrapped around protectively. Roth in the photo was almost unrecognizable to her. He looked . . . happy. Relaxed. In love.

Now, she thought, *he'll never look like this again.*

After a moment, Fennrys gently pried the photograph from her hands and placed it carefully back on the upturned crate. Mason felt a sob hitch in her throat and turned away, but suddenly, Fenn's arms were around her. She felt his breath in her hair and her shoulder blades pressed against the wall of his chest.

"I swear to you, Mason Starling," he whispered, "we *will* make this right. Gwen's death will not be meaningless. I promise you that."

"I didn't even know Roth had a girlfriend."

Fennrys ran a hand over her head, smoothing her hair.

"He just looks so broken," she said. "I mean, now that she's gone. I can't . . ." She twisted around in his embrace and stared up into his eyes. The planes of his face were tight and the muscles on the sides of his neck stood out like cords. His ice-blue eyes sparked cold fire. "Fenn, I *can't* go through that with you. I can't lose you the way Roth lost Gwen."

"You won't." His voice was almost a growl. It echoed off the rough walls and melded with the vibrations of another tremor. A drift of dust spiraled down from the cavern ceiling and Fennrys puts his hands on the sides of Mason's face. "I will tear the world apart to keep us together," he said.

"I'm afraid that's what they want," she whispered.

"They're not going to get what they *want*, Mase." His expression turned fearsome. "They're going to get what they *deserve*." And then he pulled her close against his chest again.

Mason stood there, her shoulders quivering with emotion and let him hold her. She could feel him pressing his face against the crown of her head as his hands kneaded the muscles of her back.

"God," he whispered, "you smell . . ."

"Sweaty?" Mason choked out a muffled laugh. "Horrible?

In need of a half-hour shower?"

"Delicious." Fenn's voice was a husky rasp. "Um. Edible."

Mason pushed away from his chest and looked up into his face with wary amusement. "Oh . . . kay?" she said. "Fenn, are you all right?"

He nodded sharply and stepped back, pushing her all the way to arm's length. His nostrils were flared and his pupils were so dilated his eyes were almost black. "Yeah," he said. "I have to—"

"Safety valve," Mason said, holding up her hands. "I get it. Let's put a leash on that puppy."

Fenn raised an eyebrow at her. "Not funny."

She shrugged. "Kind of funny."

"Right." He reached down to the knife sheath strapped to his leg and, pulling the long-bladed dagger free, handed it over to her again. "Here. Take this."

Mason wrapped her fingers around the hilt of the weapon with a sigh. Was it a bad sign, she wondered, that the sensation of being armed and dangerous was becoming so familiar to her that it was almost blasé?

That's life as a Valkyrie, kiddo. Get used to it.

"I'm not going to stab you, Fennrys," she said.

"Not unless you absolutely have to, I hope," he said with a feral grin.

"Seriously—"

"Seriously?" he interrupted her, his expression turning stern. "Don't think about it if it happens. Just do what you have to do. You're the only one strong enough to stop me if I lose control, Mase."

"You mean me, the Valkyrie, is the only one," she muttered.

"Well, yeah. That's why I brought you along."

"What about Rafe? Or Toby?"

He shook his head. "You're stronger than Toby. Even he knows that. And Rafe . . . is afraid of me."

"He said that?"

"No. Not out loud, but I can smell it on him." His nostrils flared slightly, as if Rafe stood there in the chamber with them. "Fear really does have a particular scent. Even on a god. Who knew?"

"But he *is* a god. Why is he scared of you?" Mason frowned.

Fenn shot her a look from under his brows. "I don't know, Mase. Why do you think?"

She didn't have an answer to that. Or, at least, she didn't want to.

Fennrys slipped the medallion off over his head and handed it to Mason. She put it in the pocket of her jeans and stepped back. She was scared down to her boots and horribly excited all at the same time.

"Are you . . . can you do what *he* does?" She made a snout-shaped gesture in front of her face. "When Rafe changes? The whole man-wolf thing?"

Fenn grinned slightly and shook his head. "I don't think so. I don't have that kind of control. I think it's either me . . . or the wolf. I don't think there's an in-between. Not yet, at least."

Fenn took a deep breath. The air in the cavern grew hot and, where it touched his skin, seemed to shimmer like a heat wave. In the blink of an eye, the man was gone. And the fearsome golden wolf had taken his place. Mason held her breath and swallowed the lump of fear that knotted in her throat. She hadn't really had much of an opportunity to really look at him back in the Weather Room. He was beautiful and awe-inspiring.

And terrifying.

In the torch light, the thick fur that covered his sleek, muscular frame shone like molten gold. The eyes that stared out at her from above the finely sculpted muzzle were the same pale blue, but the deep black at the center of those irises was fathomless.

Mason stood frozen, mesmerized by his stare.

There was a raw intelligence in the depths of his gaze, and a familiarity, but she also knew better than to think that Fennrys the man was in control of Fennrys the wolf. She held herself utterly still as he lifted his nose and sniffed at the air. A low, sonorous growling shuddered through the cavern and suddenly, the great beast leaped, snarling and snapping his jaws.

Mason gasped and, in a moment of panic, threw herself flat to the ground, covering her head, instead of transforming herself into a Valkyrie. She expected to feel teeth on her neck, but the Fennrys Wolf hadn't been attacking her. Rather, he'd vaulted her prone form, to position himself between Mason . . . and the unexpected majestic presence that was suddenly sharing the cavern *with* them. Mason pushed herself up onto one elbow and shoved the hair out of her eyes. There was an archway of deeper darkness framing him—another catacomb tunnel that Mason hadn't even noticed. It looked as if it led steeply down, and she thought she could hear far-distant moans, like a mournful wind or a chorus of tortured voices, drifting upward toward them.

The Wolf was snarling and barking, hackles raised, and as she watched he seemed to grow in stature. Even more than Rafe, when the god was in his Anubis wolf-guise, Fennrys conveyed such raw, savage power. It was frightening and awe-inspiring at the same time. The man now standing in front of him saw it. And it brought a deeply satisfied smile to his face.

"There you are," Loki murmured. "Poor pup . . ."

Mason felt an ice-shock moment of horror at those words.

"Oh no," she whispered. "*No* . . . Loki . . ."

The god stepped forward, shedding the shadows that cloaked him in the darkness where he seemed so comfortable and the light in his crystal-blue eyes shone so bright. Tugging the embroidered sleeve of his magnificent tunic straight with one bejeweled hand, the elegant god strode toward where Fennrys crouched on the cold stone floor.

His beard was neatly trimmed and his hair flowed back from his forehead in a shining, dark gold wave. His clothing was rich and spotless, accented with gold and silver and precious stones. Loki looked remarkably well. Especially considering the last time Mason had seen him, he'd had half of his handsome face destroyed—melted down to the bones of his skull—by the venom of a serpent set to torment him for all eternity.

Loki knelt before the great wolf and stared into the beast's blue eyes, and there was no way in the world that Mason could deny the truth any longer. In spite of everything Fennrys had just told her, Mason had still held out hope that it was all an elaborate setup and that Fennrys *wasn't* Fenris.

She had believed that deep in the core of her heart.

How could he *be* the thing he'd been *named* after? It didn't make sense.

It doesn't have to. Nothing about any of this does.

Norse legends looped and knotted around one another in the same way that Norse art did. It was impossible to tell where one design ended and the next began. With sudden clarity, Mason realized that Fennrys hadn't been named after the legendary apocalypse harbinger of Norse mythology. In the twisted way of those tales, which had or hadn't yet come to pass and who the hell even knew, Fennrys *was* that harbinger. He *was* the Fenris Wolf.

Because I made him so.

"Well . . . I might've had a hand in it, too," said Loki, the God of Lies, turning toward her with a wide smile, seemingly having read her thoughts.

Mason felt her mouth go dry with fear as Loki knelt down in front of the great wolf, who whined piteously and crouched, his tail curling under as he backed away from the trickster god of the Aesir.

"Poor pup . . . my poor boy," the god said in soothing tones. "There you are, now. There . . ."

"Poor pup" was how Loki had described his missing monstrous offspring—the Fenris Wolf, the mythic beast that Mason had always thought Fenn had been *named* after—when he'd told her about him in Helheim.

Mason thought she might actually be ill. Or faint again. All the blood was rushing from her head and she could feel herself starting to sway. This . . . this was all her fault. All of it. She'd run her sword through the eye of the serpent tormenting Loki. The pain of the venom had been the only thing keeping the dangerous, chaos-loving god from directing his energies toward freeing himself. And she'd been so blinded by her feelings for Fennrys that she hadn't even stopped to consider what transforming him into a werewolf—a *wolf*, for the love of god, she *knew* that was what would happen if Rafe turned him—would do to him. Or to the world. The world that was prophesied to end with the unleashing of the Fenris Wolf, the harbinger of Ragnarok . . .

"The Great Devourer."

Mason's heart was shocked back to beating with those words from Loki's mouth. It beat with a heavy, dull throb that made her chest ache. She had heard that title before. And she had made a promise that, when the time came, and she faced the Devourer, she would do her best to make an end of him. Two promises. Two grave mistakes. She wondered if she'd live long enough to make a third.

Loki reached out one elegant hand, long-fingered and glittering with rings, toward the wolf, and the beast shrank from him.

"Ah," Loki murmured, "apologies, my son . . ."

Mason watched as he twisted the thick bands of gleaming metal and precious stones off his fingers and handed them over to her.

"Silver," he said. "Anathema to werewolves."

"I thought that was a myth," Mason murmured. Then she realized how ridiculous that must sound, since she was standing in a cave under her high school with two of the biggest myths there were.

Loki just smiled and dropped the rings into her hand with a wink, saying, "Not to the *wolf*, it isn't."

Then he turned back to Fennrys and began running his hands over the great golden animal's head, staring him in the face and murmuring words in a low voice and a harshly musical language that Mason couldn't understand. But the wolf cocked his head and seemed almost as if he could. Mason let them commune in private for a few moments.

"Ah, my son . . . ," Loki murmured, his voice almost reverential. Triumphant. Full of grim satisfaction. "You are magnificent." He grinned back at Mason, who stood frozen. "I'll have to send a thank-you note to the Fair Folk for rearing him up right," he said, the lilt of mocking laughter touching his words for a moment.

"How . . ." Mason's voice stuck in her throat. She swallowed hard and tried again. "How did you get free?" she asked.

"How did *you*?" he countered. "A trip to Hel's realm doesn't usually come with a two-way ticket."

"I think I was set up," Mason said. "I was allowed to escape."

"Heimdall. Yes . . . It's what he does best." Loki's grin never faltered, even as he spoke of the god who was destined to bring about his death. Maybe because *he* was destined to bring about Heimdall's. "The fact that the pompous old horn

blower didn't even have to coerce you into stabbing the serpent that tormented me was either a stroke of genius or pure
luck on his part. But the end result was the same. I was able to
regroup and gather my power. And, as you say, escape."

Mason felt the bottom drop out of her stomach.

Loki winked one blue eye at her and, when the golden wolf
whined, turned his attention back to him. "I've been wanting
to meet you for a good long time, Fennrys," he said. "But
this is not the way. Let's see the man you've grown into now,
eh?" He glanced at Mason. "You have his medallion. The one
you were wearing when you so delightfully visited me in my
Asgardian . . . accommodations." His eyes wandered over her,
unfocused, for a moment. "It's in your . . . left front pocket,
I think."

Her hand twitched toward it before she could stop herself,
and he grinned.

"I can feel the magick. May I have it?"

When Mason hesitated, Loki's expression twitched with a
slight, subtle annoyance. Beneath his hand, the Fennrys Wolf
whined.

"Mason. Please." Loki held out his other hand. "I only
want to help him. The power in that medallion can be used
by Fennrys to help control the beast. I know you've used it
yourself to help facilitate that, but it's not been completely
successful. I can help him cage the Wolf whenever he wants.
For as long as he wants. I think that's something we'd all like
to see happen, yes?"

She shifted on her feet, uncertain. Maybe Loki really could
help him.

"Please," the god said again.

Mason nodded, once, and fished in her pocket for the gray iron disc, inscribed with its twisted, tortuous designs. She felt the tingle of energy that raced across the surface of the metal as she handed over the talisman, placing it in Loki's smooth upturned palm.

"Thank you." The god inclined his head graciously. "Now. I'd like to be alone with my son for a few moments, if you don't mind."

XV

There was a god in the catacombs. He was alone with Fennrys. And, according to every version of Norse prophecy Mason had ever read or heard, he was responsible for Ragnarok.

And you thought it was a good idea to leave him there.

What I think is hardly material to the situation.

Loki had made it perfectly clear that he was in control of said situation and nothing a seventeen-year-old high school student—fencing champ or no fencing champ—said was going to have any sort of impact on that whatsoever. Also? If she was really going to be honest with herself, she still kind of trusted Loki.

He could have just taken the Janus medallion from her, but he'd said "please." Twice. And "thank you." That was more than she could say for any of the other major players on the whole insane chessboard. And she still wasn't convinced that he was evil. But she also didn't really want to head back up to the dining hall where the others waited, just so she could tell Toby and Rafe that she'd left Fenn alone for a little father-son time with Loki, his dad.

Mason stood outside the ruined gymnasium and felt utterly powerless.

Her gaze drifted toward the dormitory wing and she saw that, behind a drawn curtain, Cal's third-floor room had a light on. She knew he'd taken Heather there and her thoughts turned to how the other girl really *was* powerless. Alone among all of them, Heather was the one who had made it that far with no magick, no blood curse, no elixirs or transformative powers or parental demigods. And she'd been brave enough to give up the protective runegold to save her friends. Mason wondered if there was something she could do for her in return.

And then she had an idea.

She ran across the rain-drenched quad and in through the closest door to the dorms. There was a staircase right inside the door and Mason took the steps two at a time, then ran down the hall to the third-floor dorm room that belonged to her brother Rory as fast as her feet could carry her. The empty corridor echoed hollowly, but she could sense that there were still one or two scattered students in some of the rooms. It didn't matter. She didn't have time to stop and gather up lost lambs. Toby and Carrie could take care of that.

Of course, once she got to Rory's door, she realized that the first challenge she faced was actually just getting into the damn room. To be honest, Mason couldn't remember with any certainty the last time she'd even had her own room key.

And she was certain that Rory would never have left his door unlocked. She was right. The heavy antique door was shut tight, secured with both knob lock and deadbolt.

"Great . . ."

A surge of frustration filled her head for a moment with that increasingly familiar red rage. Mason backed off a few steps and then, before she'd even consciously thought about what she was doing, she took a run, and kicked the solid oak slab off its brass hinges. She heard herself yelp in astonishment and hopped around gingerly, expecting that her foot would be broken—or at the very least spectacularly sprained—but when she put her full weight on it, it felt surprisingly good. *She* felt surprisingly good. Mason grinned and flexed her hands into fists, reining in the urge to randomly punch holes in the plaster—just because she could—and instead, searched around for the thing she'd come to find.

The thing she knew Rory would have hidden somewhere.

His desk was a mess, littered with glossy mens' lifestyle magazines and expensive gadgetry and empty beer cans. His phone was sitting there and, without thinking, Mason picked it up and shoved it into her pocket. Like her keys, she had no idea where her own phone had gotten to over the last few days. Chances were that it was sitting on the bottom of the East River, a shiny useless trinket for a Nereid to play with. Rory's laptop was there too, half hidden under a draft of an unfinished English paper for the very same class she'd told Toby about in the carriage on the way to Gosforth. The assignment was technically due in less than a week. Mason picked up the sheaf of paper, fanning through the pages. At a glance, it seemed Rory was defending Iago as the misunderstood hero of *Othello*. She shook her head.

You would think that, wouldn't you, Rory?

She tossed the pages back on his desk and tried to remember, fleetingly, what her own thesis had been. At the time, it had seemed so important. Now . . . she couldn't even remember when she'd started writing it.

This? she thought. *This is how my life has changed.*

A storm. Monsters in a storm. A naked hot guy in a storm . . . that was how it had all started. And while it had seemed a little bizarre at the time, it paled in comparison to what had happened since. Mason Starling had been to hell and back. Literally.

Also? That night wasn't when all this started. It all started before I was even born.

She searched through Rory's desk drawers and found a huge wad of cash rolled up and circled with a rubber band, three bottles of brandy from Gunnar's private reserve (one of them empty), and a pair of leather driving gloves that still had the store security tag attached. Mason rolled her eyes and shoved them back where she'd found them. On the shelf above his desk there were books. Textbooks for class, a couple of paperbacks, a box set of *The Lord of the Rings* DVDs, and a book with no title, just an embossed leather spine decorated with the intertwined branches of a tree. Mason plucked that one off the shelf and opened the front cover. The book was a fake with a hollowed-out core and it contained two things. The first was a folded sheaf of photocopied pages. The second was a golden acorn.

Mason unfolded the pages and immediately recognized the handwriting as her father's. In the middle of the top page was what looked like a bit of poetry:

One tree. A rainbow. Bird wings among the branches.
Three seeds of the apple tree grown tall.
As Odin's spear is gripped in the hand of the Valkyrie,
they shall awaken Odin Sons.
When the Devourer returns, the hammer will fall down on the
earth, to be reborn.

She frowned at the odd stanza and, folding the papers back up, shoved them into her pocket. Then she plucked the runegold acorn out of its hiding place and snapped the cover shut. She went to replace it on the shelf, but something at the back, something reflective hidden behind the row of books, caught her eye. She pulled the rest of the books off the shelf. It was—surprisingly—a framed picture of the whole Starling clan. Mason and her father, and her two brothers mugging for the camera. Mason couldn't remember who'd snapped the picture, but she knew it had been at one of the parties her father had thrown for his insanely rich friends, taken on the waterside dock at the Starling family estate, the summer before, on the shores of Lake Kensico, with the water glinting like diamonds spilled on blue velvet behind them.

Mason's grinning face sported a smattering of freckles across her nose and cheeks, Gunnar's mane of silver hair was blown back in the breeze off the water, and Roth was actually smiling at the camera, although the dark sunglasses he wore hid his piercing gaze from the camera. Even Rory, tanned and handsome, had actually looked happy. As happy as he ever looked, at least.

And it was all a lie.

How could she have gone through life so blind?

There wouldn't be any more summer parties, she thought. And all of her dad's wealthy pals, if Gunnar had his way, would be dust and bone lying scattered in the long grass gone to seed when nature reclaimed the Earth from man. She thought of all the bodies—living still, and dead—that littered Manhattan's streets outside the confines of Gosforth. Spilled blood. A fine red mist lowered in front of her eyes and she spun and hurled the framed photo across the room. It shattered on the wall beside the open window, the sound of breaking glass louder even than the machine-gun rattle of ice pellets lashing the slate roof of the dorm.

It must have been good weather when Rory had last left his room, otherwise he would have shut the window. Not Mason. When she was little, after the hide-and-seek incident, Mason had demanded that her bedroom window always be left open. It was the first manifestation of her devastating claustrophobia, but Gunnar had accommodated her wishes. He'd never complained about rain-soaked curtains or warped wooden sills, nor had he ever chastised her for being foolish or frightened. And on nights at the estate up in Westchester, he would come and sit with her during thunderstorms and read her stories of gods and heroes. The stories had never mattered to Mason—and she'd certainly never suspected that she'd one day become a part of them—but having her father there to take care of her had.

She realized then that she still loved him.

But she would destroy him, if she had to.

With that thought, the red rage suddenly ebbed, washed away by a feeling of clarity that Mason had been lacking ever since she'd first drawn the Odin spear. Her hand dropped to the hilt of the sword at her side and she made sure it was pushed firmly down into its scabbard. She walked over to the window and picked up the shattered picture frame, shaking the shards of glass into a wastebasket. The picture inside was creased, and the glass had sliced through the paper, severing off the upper left corner with surgical precision. The empty space in the photograph where, if she'd still been alive, Mason could picture her mother's face. One big, happy family.

If only . . .

She laid the picture down on the windowsill, careful to avoid a puddle of rainwater that had pooled there, and then she reached up . . . and slammed the window closed. For a long moment she stood there, feeling the closeness of the room without the ever-present breath of wind that she was used to. She stared out into the darkness of the storm and thought about the missing element in the picture.

Mom . . .

Suddenly, a massive spear of lightning stabbed down from the sky and Mason closed her eyes against the blinding brightness.

With her eyes closed, she felt a hand on her cheek.

She'd felt that touch before—firm and graceful—but that

had been an imposter. And when Heimdall had worn Yelena Starling's shape, her hands had been ice-cold. The hand Mason felt now was warm. Soft. Strong . . .

"Mom?" she whispered.

"Mason . . ."

She honestly wasn't sure if the voice was just in her head. Then she opened her eyes . . . and she *still* wasn't sure. Because her mother—her real mother—was standing there, right in front of her. But the Gosforth dorm room was gone. Instead, it seemed almost as if Mason had fallen into the photograph. She found herself standing on the wide expanse of a sun-bleached deck, perched on the shore of Lake Kensico, with the lake and trees and the Starling manor house in the far distance.

And her mother, wrapped in cool shadows, standing right beside her.

Mason blinked and looked around. Everything had a kind of oversaturated quality to it. A patina of memory, laid like a filter over the scene, sparkling and gauzy and just a touch surreal. Only, this was no memory that Mason had ever had.

If only, she thought again, turning back to the woman beside her.

As their eyes met—sapphire and sapphire, identical—Mason recognized her mother as *truly* that. And she could barely believe that she'd been so thoroughly duped by Heimdall's impersonation of her. The features were identical, certainly, but *this* Yelena Starling looked out of those same deep blue eyes with a fierce, shining love and wit and wisdom. And an obvious sense of humor that had been completely lacking in her doppelgänger. *This* Yelena's mouth seemed as if it quivered perpetually on the edge of a big, broad grin or unbridled laughter.

In that moment though, she just smiled gently and said, "Hi, honey."

Mason fell into her arms.

"Mom!" she exclaimed, and knew that this time, she really was.

Father . . .

The word was strange and alien in his wolf mind.

But there was also a rightness to the sound as the man the Fennrys Wolf had heard Mason call Loki placed his hands—wide, strong, long-fingered, and warm—on either side of the wolf's head and began to speak in a low tone. Ancient words that Fennrys could feel wrapping around the human mind buried in his beastly form. When the transformation had first taken him, Fenn had been almost dead. Lying in a pool of blood, wondering what it would be like for him once he'd finally, for the last time, crossed over the threshold into death. There was no fear, no pain, and only one regret. That he would be leaving Mason Starling behind.

Mason, of course, had had other ideas.

And when Fennrys had regained consciousness, it had been as if waking inside a nightmare. For the first few minutes, he'd tried to convince himself that *that* was what was happening. That he was still asleep. Dreaming. Or delusional. Or already dead and gone and experiencing the afterlife in a markedly unexpected way. But then the scents and sensations had flooded him, and suddenly every nerve ending in his body—his four-legged, fur-covered body—had screamed at him to get up. Get away. And claw or chew through anything that stood in his way. He had felt the wolfen instincts redrawing pathways in his brain in ways that had made his wolf body feel more his own.

But now, with Loki's help, he could feel his buried humanity begin to resurface.

He could feel his way back out through the transformative enchantment that Anubis's wolf bite had bestowed on him as he lay dying. He watched, through his wolf's eyes, as his black-clawed front feet stretched out, the shape of them blurring, twisting, reforming as hands, fingers splayed wide on the cold stone floor.

In the blink of those eyes, he was human again. On his hands and knees, dressed in the same jeans and T-shirt and boots as before. The weight of his iron medallion hanging from his neck.

"Hello, pup."

Loki's voice, Fennrys realized, was the whispered one he'd heard when he'd been imprisoned in the dungeons of Hel. The one that had sounded like lies. Or maybe it had been more like promises. Strange, subtle ones.

Fenn regarded the god warily, and with a mess of tangled emotions. It was disconcerting to see so much of himself reflected in the face of the other man. Loki's mouth was thinner, more apt to twist into a sardonic grin, and the planes of his face were sharper, more angular, but they had the same cheekbones and the same nose. The eyes, though, was where the similarities ended. Fennrys knew that his own were the shade of the glacial north; his gaze guarded, remote. Loki's were like cauldrons into which the fates had poured the gleam of the Northern Lights and the mysteries of the twilight skies above the ice sheets and mountains and hidden secret valley fjords of his mythical home.

Suddenly, for perhaps the first time in his life, Fennrys wondered what his mother had looked like. He'd always assumed that he'd probably somewhat resembled his father. He'd just never expected his father to be a god. Certainly not *that* god. He wondered what his father saw in him in that moment. He'd been silent for long enough now that Fennrys was starting to think he must surely be some kind of disappointment. And then, in the next breath, he wondered if that wouldn't be the best possible thing for everyone. In the breath right after that, he wondered why it was upsetting to him.

And then his father smiled and shook his head.

"Mason told me when I first met you that you were perfect," Loki said, an amused grin curling the corner of his mouth beneath the thatch of his dark gold beard. "I think she might have been right."

"I . . . uh. Sorry?" Fennrys stammered, startled.

Loki laughed. "You're exactly what this conflict needs, pup."

"Ah," Fennrys said. Well, that made sense, he supposed. He was, after all, skilled in the arts of destruction and death. A perfect harbinger for the end of the world. "I guess you probably would think that."

"You misunderstand me." Loki shook his head, hearing Fenn's thoughts in the tone of his voice. Those extraordinary eyes of his glittered with fierce intelligence and something that looked a lot like . . . fun. Or, at the very least, mischief. He leaned forward, every line of his body quivering with vital, barely contained energy. "I don't mean that you're the great doom everyone seems to think you are. Although, of course, there's every possibility that you *are*. What I *mean* is, you are a wild card. Like Mason herself. Did you know that she is the reason I'm now free?"

"No. I didn't know that."

He chuckled. "She did some fine damage to the serpent that has tormented me through the ages—she's very good with a sword, by the way, did you know?—and the bloody thing slithered off and finally left me alone long enough for me to be able to turn my mind and talents to the task of freeing myself. I really have to thank her for that."

"And now?" Fennrys asked, intrigued in spite of himself, and the fact that he knew he should probably be terrified down to the soles of his boots at the moment. "Now that you're free? What will you do?"

"What do you think I should do?"

"Don't you have an apocalypse to stir up?"

Loki shrugged. "Seems to be moving along quite nicely without my help. Listen carefully, pup. I told Mason this and I'm going to tell you. The thing *is* . . . I don't know how it ends, Fennrys!" He grinned delightedly. "I honestly don't. I've never read the things they've written about me, although I can guess at many of them, I don't doubt. But I'm not the only shape changer in Valhalla and I'm not the only subtle mind. And when I hate? I do it honestly. There are others who, it saddens me to say, cannot claim the same."

"Heimdall," Fennrys said.

"Ah . . . have you met the great blowhard then?"

"He impersonated Mason's mother."

"I know. Hel is dear to me." Loki's voice took on a dangerous edge. "He will pay for that."

Fennrys shrugged. "Yeah, well, Mason might get to him first. She was pretty pissed when she found out he'd taken her for a ride."

"Good girl! So she discovered the falsehood then?"

Fennrys shook his head. "Not until we told her about it. And it didn't even matter in the end. Son of a bitch still managed to trick her into taking up the Odin spear."

Loki's eyes glittered. "But she has yet to choose, am I right?" he asked sharply. "There is no third Odin son yet."

"Not yet."

"Good. Then there's still time!" He bounded to his feet and headed for the cavern mouth.

"Time for what?"

"To find out what I've been missing!" He waved a hand in the direction of the tunnel Fennrys had come through to get to that chamber. "Have you *seen* what's up there? That city? It's fantastic! Wine and women and song . . . well, I'm sure it's a little more lively when it's not reeling under a blood curse but, Thor's beard! It's an endless feast for the senses. I'd like to sample some of it before it all comes crashing to an end."

"Wait. *What?* It's Ragnarok and you're going to play tourist in the Big Apple? I wouldn't have expected that from you." From Rafe, maybe, Fennrys thought. But then he realized with a start that Loki reminded him an awful lot of the Egyptian god of the dead.

Loki laughed at Fennrys's confusion. "That's because *I'm* unexpected!" he said with delight. "Unpredictable. Unstable. Chaotic. Random. Poised on the knife blade's edge . . . And so are *you*."

"I am not."

"Ha!" Loki slapped his palms together. "Look at your track record so far. You, my very dear boy, *are* choice. And she—that mad, lovely girl you love madly—is the chooser. It's poetic, really. Go forth. Make beautiful music together. Burn bright. Be brilliant. Defy!"

"How do I do that?"

"You know the stories—you've read them—so all you have to do now is figure out how to change the plot." The trickster god laughed. "Tales are told by the victors. Be victorious. Be happy! Write your own ending. Make it a *beginning* if you want."

A beginning, Fennrys thought. *Wait . . . there's something to that. How in the hell did this really all begin in the first place?*

"That's it . . . you'll see . . . The clues are all there." Loki's voice grew strange and echoey. "They always are. That's something your mother knew."

"My mother?" Fennrys drew back sharply, as if those two words had been a slap that had awakened him from a deep sleep. Or sent him tumbling into a dream . . .

My mother. If only . . .

XVI

The torch on the opposite wall suddenly flared, blindingly bright, and Fennrys put up a hand to shield his eyes. When he lowered it again, a figure stood before him, silhouetted in the glare of the sun's light. Startled, Fennrys turned to Loki, but the so-called trickster god of the Norse was gone.

So, for that matter, was the catacomb Fennrys had shared with him only a moment before. In its place, he found himself outside beneath a brilliant blue sky dotted with puffball white clouds. The air shimmered with a kind of dreamy haze and Fennrys wondered for a moment if that was what it was—a dream. But he'd never had a dream so vivid. He could smell the pine sap from the nearby trees and feel the feathery brush of long grasses waving around his knees. He stood near the edge of a precipice that dropped away, falling in a gentle slope toward a vale, cut through by a sparkling river that twisted like a giant blue snake below. Through the trees, Fennrys thought he could see some kind of boat bobbing on the surface of the water, but he wasn't really concerned with that at the moment.

What concerned him more was the tall, striking woman who stood before him, smiling. As his eyes adjusted to the brightness, he saw that she wore a long belted tunic woven of green wool and her arms and feet were bare. Her hair was long and plaited loosely down her back. And "tall" might have been an understatement. She was well over six feet. But she was slender and her face was pretty, if slightly weathered. There were fine webs of lines at the corners of her eyes and she had a deep tan. Even with that, the skin on the bridge of her nose was peeling and just a little pink. It looked as if she had spent the last year outside without any shelter from the elements. It didn't look, though, as if such circumstances would be any particular hardship to this woman.

She looked at him and smiled.

"You grew up strong," she murmured in a gentle voice.

While she spoke in a language Fennrys didn't know, somehow he understood what she was saying, and he had an immediate sense of déjà vu. He felt as though he might have once heard that same voice singing lullabies in the darkness in that same language. The woman cocked her head and a gleam of wry humor sparkled in her blue eyes.

"And handsome," she said. "Like your father."

"I'll tell him you said so," Fenn said, swallowing the knot that had tied itself in his throat.

"I used to do that." She chuckled. "Even though he already knew it. He's a touch vain, you know."

"And completely mad."

"Do you think so?" She cocked her head, seriously contemplating that. "I always thought he was the only one of them who wasn't."

"The only one of who?"

"The Aesir."

Fennrys shook his head, wearied by the further confirmation—assuming he wasn't actually dreaming or delusional in that moment—of his origins, and his impending disastrous destiny. "My father really is a god, then. Really."

"I'm afraid so."

"And so I really am the Fenris Wolf."

She nodded. "Really. It's why I sent you away. To live with the Faerie."

That brought Fenn up short. He frowned in confusion and took a step toward her, as if needing to hear her answer more clearly as he said, "Wait. I thought they *stole* me."

"I wish I could say that was truth."

The woman sighed, but her gaze never wavered from his face. Fennrys recognized the similarity of her features to his own, even though her eyes were an even paler shade of blue— so pale they were almost dove gray.

"I wish I could tell you that I fought to keep you. Fought to find you . . . never stopped looking for my stolen babe. But the *truth* of it is that I called the Fair Folk to you. And I gave you to them freely. Because it was the only way that I could think of to save your life. And the world—although I cared rather less about that than I did about you."

"I'm not sure I understand," Fennrys said, his voice tight.

"The truth of the matter is this: when I was young and not unpleasant to look upon, a young man—a traveling skald calling himself 'Lothur'—came to my village. As much as he liked my looks, I liked his."

"Let me guess. Loki."

His mother nodded. "I didn't know. Not until the morning he left me. He thought I was asleep when he bent down to kiss my cheek and, in a mournful whisper, called me 'she who offers sorrow' before walking out the door."

"'She who offers sorrow'?"

"'*Angrboda*' in the language of your ancestors."

Fennrys knew enough of the Norse myths to understand what she meant. "Which just so happened to be the name of the Fenris Wolf's mother in the myths," he said.

The woman smiled wryly. "Imagine my confusion. Until a few months later when my dresses grew too tight around my waist. Now, *my* mother was a Celtic princess, captured on a Viking raid, and I was raised on the stories of her myths and legends, as well as those of my father. I also had a dowry of her captured wealth. I used it to bribe a crew of sailors. I knew I would never see my lover again and I knew that if I brought you into a Viking world, eventually you would be killed. Whether you were the real Fenris Wolf or no. I bid the ship's captain sail west, hoping to find the Faerie lands my mother had talked of. Instead, we found *this* land. And the Faerie, having heard my cries as I gave birth to you onboard that ship"—she gestured to the boat on the river far below—"found us. I gave you to them before you ever set foot on the soil of this world, hoping to save both."

Fennrys didn't know what to say. He just looked at the woman—his mother—and his open mouth produced no sound. He'd spent his entire existence hating and resenting the Fair Folk for having stolen him away from his rightful destiny. And now he'd just been told that that belief—the core resentment of most of his life—had been a lie. Well, not a lie, really—Faerie couldn't actually lie—but a mistake, an assumption he'd made as a very young child that no one had ever bothered to correct because it had suited their purposes to let him accept it as truth. He really didn't know what to say to that.

His mother reached forward after a moment and, again with that amused look in her eye, gently nudged his jaw shut with her fingertips. She left her hand there for a long moment, just touching his face, and a look of longing crossed hers.

It was strange but, where Fenn expected there should be a smoldering coal of rage waiting to burst into flame in the center of his chest, he instead felt a kind of lightness. From the moment he'd come back to himself after Rafe had turned him into the Wolf, he'd felt as though he'd barely been able to contain his fury. But in that moment, the beast inside was quiet. Like it had been when Mason had pulled her magick trick and transported him to his Safe Harbor.

"I don't expect you to forgive me," his mother said. "But my name—my real name—if you would like to know, is Sigyn."

"I'm Fennrys," he replied, his mouth quirking up at the corner as he reached up to take her hand in his. "But I guess you already know that. Nice, subtle name choice there, Mom."

She laughed, and it was a lovely sound, echoing off the distant hills.

Fennrys felt a tightness in his throat. He'd meant it as a joke. But it was the first time he'd ever called anyone by that word. His heart felt bruised.

"It seemed there was little reason to hide the fact from the very people I was sending you off to live with," Sigyn said. "They already knew who—and what—you were. *That* was the whole point. To remove you from this world so that you would no longer pose a danger to it. Although I must say, I do like the Faerie spelling."

"Sounds the same."

"It does." She lifted one shoulder. "But I've found that what a thing sounds like is often not at all what it is, if you know what I mean."

"I'm not sure I do," Fennrys said. "But if it means there's a chance for me to become something other than what I'm supposed to be, then I'll take it."

"Oh, my son." She squeezed his hand. "You have become *exactly* what you were meant to be. That is the thing. You will do what you have to do. And you will be magnificent."

"I'm not so sure about that."

"I think Auberon, the Faerie king, would dispute that."

Fennrys grimaced, thinking back on his life growing up with the Fae. It had been like living in a paradise from which there had been no escape. The unrelenting, extravagant beauty of the Faerie Courts had driven him to seek out its darkest corners and most dangerous creatures. He trained himself to become a monster hunter.

Maybe, he thought, *it's because I was always secretly terrified I* was *the monster.*

In time, Fenn's exploits made an impression and he was appointed a member of the Winter King Auberon's Janus Guard. And then, eventually, around the turn of the century in the mortal realm, he was stationed along with the other Janus in New York City to guard the Faerie gate in Central Park during the one time of the year when it opened. In order to make sure nothing crossed over into the world of men to threaten its inhabitants. The way Fennrys was threatening it now.

Is that irony? he wondered to himself. *I can never tell.*

"The fact that they let you back into the mortal realm even as a guardian of their Gate means you earned their trust," Sigyn said.

"Or maybe I was just really good at killing things," he said bitterly, "and they decided to put that skill set to use in a way that kept the mortal realm safe, and gave the Otherworld ogres a break from me once a year."

"You are a guardian, Fennrys," Sigyn said. "You *and* Mason Starling."

The mention of Mason's name sent a stab of longing through Fennrys's heart so sharp it was almost physically painful. He missed her in a way he'd never missed anything else in his life. Almost from the moment he had met her, he'd felt as though they were meant to be together. And then the whole "Rush to Ragnarok" thing had begun and he'd realized that, in the way of horrifying prophecy, they were. And that was the worst thing in the world.

But now, to hear his mother talk of it, she had an entirely different take on the situation. He felt a tiny, moth-winged flutter of hope stirring inside and he just couldn't find the ruthlessness within himself to crush it.

His mother seemed to sense what he was thinking. Her gaze sharpened on his face and she said, "Everyone—even me—has been so eager to tell you what you will do, what you must do, and what you cannot help but do. Prophecies and portents and doomy truths are the first things to spill from the lips of those eager to write the future. But there are spaces between all of those words where you are free to write your own. It's time you were given the freedom to do that."

"What about the Norns?"

"They have been trying to bring the End of Days to fruition down through all the long years." Sigyn sighed. "I'm sure they thought they'd finally succeeded when I bore you as my son. So I sent you to the Faerie to thwart them, because I did not yet believe that you might one day be perfectly able to thwart them yourself."

"But what if I can't? What if everything plays out just the way they think it will?" Fennrys asked, turning to stare at the valley that stretched out below him. "So far, every move I make seems to play into their hands. Every time I try to make something right, it just takes a sharp left onto the highway of wrong. Even Mason. I tried so hard to keep her from taking up that damned spear. Now she's a Valkyrie."

Sigyn smiled. "She is, indeed."

Fennrys raised an eyebrow at her. "That's *bad*, Mom."

"Is it? She is powerful now, beyond measure. As are you."

"Isn't that what the Norns wanted?"

"Yes. Of course." Sigyn waved that away with one strong hand. "But there's a wild card in there that I'm quite sure those hags never would have thought to make allowances for. Because it is a thing they do not understand."

"And that is?"

"*Love*, Fennrys."

His heart clenched at the word. But he wasn't convinced. "I was hoping you were going to say there was a magick ring or sword or something hidden under a rock in a cave some-where that I could use. Maybe even an *actual* wild card."

His mother laughed again and Fenn was struck by how unconcerned she seemed about the impending end of the world. And how infectious that carefree attitude was. He felt better in that moment than he had in a long time.

"There have been magick rings and enchanted swords down throughout the ages," she said. "None of them is as powerful a weapon as the love you carry in your heart for that girl. Do you think the Norns ever stopped to consider the consequences of their machinations if the Fennrys Wolf and a daughter of Odin took the initiative, *not* to end the world, but to fall in love?"

"I thought there was no escaping destiny."

"I heard your Egyptian friend tell you otherwise."

"How did you hear that?" Fennrys asked warily, think-ing suddenly that this entire conversation could be occurring wholly in his brain. That maybe Loki had broken open Fennrys's mind with his terrible revelation, and so Fenn had manufactured this lovely, serene version of his mother to comfort him in his madness. It would explain why he felt so much more at peace than he had.

His mother just shook her head, though, and said, "It doesn't matter how *I* know. *You* know. And you only have to prove him right."

"'To hell with Destiny,'" Fennrys murmured. That was what Rafe had said to him and Mason. Maybe he really had been right. "Or maybe he was really just saying to *Hel* with destiny. Seems to be where this whole thing is headed."

"Well . . ." And here his mother's eyes flashed like glittering pale blue gems, sparkling and full of mirth. "If you're going to charge headlong into such a place, you should travel in style!"

"Wha—"

Fennrys didn't have the faintest idea what she was talking about. But he didn't have the chance to ask her, either, before Sigyn thrust out both hands and shoved him, gently, but with enough force to send him sprawling backward over the edge of the cliff where they stood. With barely a yelp of protest, he went tumbling on down the hillside, falling head over heels toward the river that wound like the track of a teardrop down the cheek of the world he was born to destroy.

There were tears on her cheeks. Mason could feel their slow slide.

For the first time since she couldn't remember when, she wept because she was laughing. And the reason was because her mother had started laughing first. Yelena's shoulders shook with the force of the joyous laughter that poured out of her as she held her daughter wrapped tightly in an embrace. It was as infectious as it was incongruous—so much happiness in the face of such grim, gray circumstances—and Mason couldn't help herself.

Finally, Yelena's mirth subsided enough for her to be able to release her. "I sent the Wolf to find you," she whispered, and raised a hand to Mason's cheek, wiping away the tears there. "To help you. *Now* you must find me . . . so that we can help each other."

"Okay," Mason said, not knowing exactly how she would do that. "I will."

"I know. With such a handsome helpmate, how could you not?" Yelena's eyes glinted with a hint of wicked fun and she gestured over her daughter's shoulder. "You are so strong, honey, all on your own. But you're even stronger together. *Stay* together. Don't let them tear you apart."

A breeze lifted her mother's dark hair and Mason swore she could smell the rich, sweet scent of apple blossoms carried on the air, even though the day felt more like summer than spring. Her mother smiled. And then, just as suddenly as she'd appeared, Yelena Starling was gone.

And Mason turned to see a shirtless, dripping-wet Fennrys climbing the ladder of the dock. The grin that split his face at the sight of her standing there brought a flush to her cheeks. That, and the fact that for an instant, she thought he might be naked again. She felt a mixture of relief and disappointment when he pulled himself all the way up the ladder and she saw that he was lacking only a shirt and shoes. His jeans, soaking wet and clinging to the muscled contours of his legs, were intact.

He left a trail of wet footprints across the bleached wooden deck boards as he strode toward her and, heedless of his sodden state, took Mason in his arms and lifted her off her feet into an embrace that she'd been longing for . . . forever.

"Wow," she murmured against his lips when he finally let her up for air. She pushed him to arm's length and felt a wicked grin spreading across her own lips. "See?" she said. "I told you Abercrombie model was a good look for you."

Fenn rolled his eyes heavenward.

"I swear," he groaned. "I *swear* to all the gods, I was wearing a shirt not two seconds ago. And a jacket. And . . ." He looked down at his bare feet. "Boots. With socks inside the boots. I had to take all that off when I fell down a hill and wound up underwater. Why does this keep happening to me?"

"Do you see me complaining?"

"You never lose *your* clothes," he grumbled, tugging at the scooped neckline of her tank top and pulling her closer to him. "We're standing on a dock beside a lake and you're not even wearing a bikini. It's grossly unfair."

Mason ran a finger down the center of his chest, noticing with detached wonderment that all of his scars seemed to have disappeared. "Again," she said, "no complaints here."

Fennrys kissed her a second time, and after another long, blissful moment, he sighed contentedly and glanced around. "Speaking of lakes and docks . . . where are we? Really?"

"I don't know." She lifted her arms and wrapped them around his neck. "Well, actually, I do know . . . but it's not important."

"How did we get here?" he asked.

"No idea," she murmured, staring up into his eyes. "Not important."

"What—"

"Fenn, shut up."

"Wh—"

"Shh." She put a finger to his lips. "I love you."

The wave of emotion that surged over his face made it look like he'd been electrocuted, and for a moment Mason was afraid that those were the last words he wanted to hear. But she'd said them, and she wasn't going to take them back.

"It doesn't matter where we are or how we got here. There are no monsters here," she murmured. "No peril. I don't care where 'here' is. I said to you back on Roosevelt Island that I would tell you how I felt when that happened. I don't know if that's ever going to happen again in the real world so I'm telling you now because I *need* for you to know. I love you, Fennrys Wolf."

The kiss he gave her then, even more so than the two that had already gone before, told her everything she needed to know. When he bent and wrapped one arm around her legs, lifting her off the ground and cradling her to his chest, she laughed and kicked her feet. He carried her up onto the gently sloping bank and set her down, collapsing beside her in the sweet-smelling grass. He propped himself up on one elbow and gazed down into her eyes.

"Tell me you love me again," he murmured, sweeping the long ebony hair off her shoulders.

She stared up at him. "I love you."

"Then you're right," he said. "It doesn't matter where we are. I don't care what this is. Dream, vision, spirit-walk, Safe Harbor, happy place . . ." He grinned.

"Very happy." Mason nodded, grinning back.

"And even if monsters and peril come thundering out from beneath those trees, right this very second, I don't care." He moved so close to her she could feel his eyelashes brushing her cheek. "Say it again," he whispered.

"I love you, Fennrys Wolf."

"I love you, Mason Starling."

She kissed the sharp contour of his cheekbone and whispered, "Good. That means that we can do anything together. So long as we *stay* together."

"We will."

"As far as I'm concerned, we never have to leave—wait." She sighed and closed her eyes, remembering suddenly, everything that had gone before. Remembering that what she had just said to Fennrys was almost exactly what her mother had said to her only moments earlier. Mason sat up and gazed back down toward the dock, and the empty space where her mother had stood. "Yes, we do."

"'Yes, we do' what?" Fennrys asked, reaching up a hand as if to pull her back down beside him.

"Have to leave this place."

"How can we do that if we're not even here? And I don't even know where here is," Fennrys said, but he sat up too, as if he already knew the moments in that place were ticking away.

"*Here*," Mason said, "is the place we need to get to. In the real world."

"How do you know?"

"Because I think someone is trying to tell us something with these shared visions. Here, and in your loft. They're leaving us clues. Or we're leaving them for ourselves."

"Clues." Fennrys quirked an eyebrow at her. "Okay . . . I remember you said something about a heart in the elevator—I'm assuming, hopefully, that you didn't mean one that had been removed from its owner."

"No. I drew it." She traced the same shape on his chest with a fingertip. "On the glass plate you smashed. Before you smashed it."

"You mean, like the kind of heart you carve into a tree?" His other eyebrow quirked up too. "With initials inside of it?"

"Um. Yeah." Mason bit her lip. "Like that."

"*Were* there initials inside it?"

"There were before you punched it, yeah."

Fennrys grinned, but instead of teasing her, he just went on to unravel the clue that Mason seemed to think they'd found. "Okay . . . so what's the significance?" he said. "I know why we were in the loft—Safe Harbor, right?—but what was the deal with the elevator? And . . . now that I think of it . . . why did it smell like *this* place?"

"You could smell that too?" Mason asked. "Pine trees and water and fresh air?"

"And apple blossoms."

"Right! Just like here!"

"Yeah . . ." He sat up then, working through the puzzle. "And I also think I was here—a different version of here—just a few minutes ago. Before I wound up in the lake, that is.

Only there *was* no lake, just a river down there. And nothing but trees where that mansion is." He waved a hand in that direction.

Mason glanced over her shoulder. "You mean my house?"

"You *live* there?

"When I'm not at Gosforth," she said sourly. "Yeah."

Fennrys whistled. "I've seen Faerie palaces that *that* place would make look shabby."

"It's okay." She hated the estate, with its conspicuous opulence, but she could understand why it was impressive. "As for where it is? It's in Westchester county. North of New York. On the shores of a lake—well, it's really more of a man-made reservoir—called Kensico."

"Man-made?"

Mason nodded. "They dammed a river to create it."

"Maybe that was the river in *my* dream." Fennrys frowned in thought.

"Maybe," she said.

"So what's the significance of this place?"

"Beats me." She shrugged, frustrated. The connection to what was happening to them in the real world wasn't appearing to her. The estate was miles and miles away from Manhattan. She glanced back at the house. "I've never really felt particularly at home here, even though the land the house is on has belonged to the Starlings since the days when we were still calling ourselves the Sturlungars."

"Wait. What?"

"That used to be the family name," she explained. "One of my ancestors anglicized it at some point, I guess."

"Right," Fennrys muttered. "I remember now . . ." When Mason looked at him quizzically, he just gestured her to continue.

"We've been living on this same plot of land since way before they built the dam in, like, the 1800s or something," Mason said. "In the early 1900s they displaced an entire town to create the reservoir, and I guess we were just lucky that the Starling estate was on high enough ground. All the flooding did for us was increase the land value. Instant lakefront property. Lucky, huh?"

"Maybe." Fennrys squeezed his eyes shut and pinched the bridge of his nose. "Although I kind of doubt it."

"What do you mean?"

"I mean I don't usually consider Faerie bargains 'lucky.'"

Mason cocked her head and looked at Fennrys, waiting for him to explain.

"Do you remember—and I only phrase it that way because it seems like it happened a million years ago, but—do you remember when I didn't know who I was?" he asked. "Where I came from?"

"Yeah." She grinned. "I actually do have a vague recollection of those days."

And those nights . . . *on the High Line. In your loft . . .*

"Well, I spent some time trying to find out back then and the only clue I came up with at the time sort of turned out to be a dead end." Fenn shrugged. "I probably should have mentioned it to you earlier. But I didn't and then . . . well, things started to happen pretty fast and I found out who I was and I kind of forgot about that one little piece of information."

"Which was?"

"Back in my loft, on the mechanical certificate in the elevator, I found the registered name of the property owner—Vinterkongen Holdings—only it didn't ring any kind of bells. But then I found out that the same party was involved in a land transaction, in the early 1800s with another party by the name of Sturlungar."

"What?" Mason blinked. That wasn't what she was expecting to hear. "Seriously?"

"Yup. Your ancestor bought a piece of land off my landlord."

"Mr. Vinterkongen," Mason said skeptically.

"Or," Fenn's voice turned a bit brittle, "as he's more commonly known, Auberon the Winter King. Of Faerie."

She blinked. "The guy you used to work for?"

"Yup."

"And you think it was the estate land that a . . . um . . . a Faerie king sold to my family?

"I think it makes sense." Fennrys shrugged. "Don't you?"

"Seems to." Mason frowned, trying to shake the puzzle box in her mind so that pieces fell together. "But why did a . . . Faerie own it in the first place? And what makes it so special?"

"No idea. Other than the fact that I think I might have been born around here."

Mason blinked at him, thoroughly confused, until he explained to her what his mother, Sigyn, had told him earlier in the dream-vision.

"I think we should go here," she said finally.

"We *are* here."

"I mean when we get back *there*. The real world."

"Right. Okay. Why?"

"I guess we'll find out when we get there."

"And how are we going to do that?" Fennrys frowned. "In the real world, we're currently stuck in your high school. And when the fog wall falls, there will be no leaving Manhattan. Not for a good long while."

He was right. There was no earthly way for them to move around freely.

But then a picture flashed into Mason's head—something she had seen carved into the door lintel above the entrance to the cavern Fennrys had gone down into—and she realized that they didn't need an *earthly* way.

She pictured the image, twisted and knotted, of a fantastical creature . . . and knew, with certainty, what they were going to do. She turned and kissed Fennrys for as long as she thought she could get away with and—before the vision faded and she found herself back in Rory's dorm room—she pulled away from Fennrys and said, "I have an idea."

"I do too," Fennrys said, and drew her back toward him. "My idea is that you should keep doing *that*."

She grinned and put a finger to his lips. "Saving the world first, kissing after that."

"The world had better appreciate my self-control," he said, and sighed languidly.

"If it ever finds out about it, I'm sure it will."

Even though here in this place, it felt like they had all the time in the universe, Mason was starting to feel the real world pulling insistently at her.

"You go find Toby and tell him to meet us back here," she said. "I mean, back in the catacombs. Where you are now. Don't tell anyone else. Not even Rafe. I'll meet you, but there's something I have to do before we go."

And with that very thought, a sudden slash of lightning, bright and pale, forked down out of the clear blue, and Mason found herself alone again in Rory's dorm room.

Mason gasped painfully at the sudden loss of Fennrys's presence and struggled against the surge of chaotic emotion that flooded back into her mind, displacing the peace she'd felt in the dream-vision. Outside the window, the afterimage of the lightning strike that seemed to have sent her to that place—or triggered the vision of it within her, or however it had happened—was just beginning to fade. She'd been "gone" for only a moment.

But how she wished she could have stayed there forever.

She looked back down at the photograph with its missing corner.

"I promise," she said. "I'll find you, Mom."

She folded the thing carefully and slipped it into the back pocket of her jeans.

XVII

When Heather finally awoke from the effects of the Miasma, it was to a splitting headache that was overshadowed by an even greater heartache. She found herself stretched out on the neatly made bed in Calum's dorm room back at Gosforth.

For a long moment, she let herself imagine that she was back in the days when she and Cal would study together lying side by side on the narrow bed. They'd called it "studying" but, of course, it had been mostly goofing around and making out. Back in the days before the world had come crashing down.

Reality sucks, Heather thought wanly. *Especially when it's so unreal.*

She groaned and rolled over, squinting in the dim light from the bedside lamp. Cal was sitting in the reading chair at the foot of his bed, staring at her. He held a glass of water in his hand and when he saw Heather open her eyes, he stood up and warily held it out to her. The look in his eyes said that he thought she might throw it in his face, but she just took it and said, "Thanks." It was warm and she wondered how long he'd been sitting there holding it.

She must have grimaced, because he said, "Sorry," and reached out to touch the side of the glass, which turned suddenly frosty in her hand. Heather took another sip. It gave her an instant brain freeze and she gave up, putting the glass on the bedside table and pressing the heel of her palm into her forehead.

"So . . . that Miasma thing?" she said groggily. "That *really* sucks."

"I know . . ." He paused and took a breath as if to say something.

"Cal—"

"I've been a complete ass. I know that."

"Uh, okay." Heather struggled to sit up. "I was actually just going to ask you for an aspirin. . . ."

He sighed and shook his head. "Sorry."

"No, actually, you're right. You have been a complete ass." She gazed at him for a few long moments before relenting. "Okay. Are you going to tell me what happened to you over the last couple of days? Or am I just going to have to make up stories to tell myself?"

"I tried to save Mason. On the bridge."

"I know," she said quietly. "I saw. You—"

"I failed. And I fell. And I almost died." He shrugged one broad shoulder. "And then I found out that's easier said than done for someone like me."

"How did you find that out, exactly?" Heather asked.

"My dad told me."

Heather blinked, startled. "Oh," she said, and fumbled for what to say next.

She and Cal used to talk about his absent father sometimes, back when they were dating. About what he might have been like and why he left. Heather guessed why he must have come back, of course. Word of an impending mythological apocalypse must have gotten around. She said as much to Cal, but he shook his head.

"Actually, that was before we really knew what was happening," Cal said. "A bunch of mermaids went and tracked him down after I smashed my head on that girder and fell into the East River. I guess he was worried about me. Or something."

"That's . . . well, I don't actually know *what* that is," Heather said. "Is it good? I mean, is he . . . nice?"

"He's a god," Cal said flatly.

"You mean . . ."

"A real one. Yeah. At least, he's part god." Cal shook his head in frustration at trying to explain the unexplainable. "Jury's out on whether he's nice or not. Seems okay, but of course my mom hates him."

"Why?" Heather asked. "I mean, I never really understood that."

"Neither did I. Until now," Cal said, and uttered a brief laugh. "Turns out, she hates him for the same reason she hates me. She thinks that the gods—*her* gods, at least—are there to be worshiped. Served. Not, y'know, 'partied' with." He shrugged awkwardly. "And that the results of any such 'partying' are . . . unnatural."

Heather's mouth worked soundlessly for a moment as she struggled to find something to say to that.

"I'm a freak, Heather. And according to my very own mother, I shouldn't even exist."

There. He'd said it. And from the look on Heather's face, she understood exactly what he'd told her. But Cal couldn't be sure what she *thought* about it. What he was sure of was that he could feel the sudden chasm that had opened up between them.

She thinks I'm a freak too.

And why not? His mother always had. Mason certainly did . . .

Only, he hadn't expected it to hurt so much, coming from Heather. He didn't think anything coming from her could ever hurt him again—not after the night she'd left him standing alone in Sakura Park across the street from Gosforth, as the cherry blossom petals drifted down like snow, so white against the night sky, and told him she was cutting him loose. He was wrong.

He shook his head to chase away the memory of that night. "Mom didn't know who—*what*—my dad was when they first got married," he continued. "But it turned out that was the deal. He's—*I'm*—descended from Triton. Y'know . . . the sea god with the three-pronged spear."

"So it's a family heirloom," she murmured. "Nice to know." From the look on her face, the implications of what Cal had told Heather was beginning to make her head spin and—apparently—throb. "Oh boy." She put a hand to her temple. "Seriously . . . aspirin?"

"Right, sorry." Cal got up and rifled through a desk drawer.

He pulled out a little white plastic bottle and shook a couple of gel caps into the palm of her hand. She picked up the frosted water glass with her other hand and tapped a fingernail against it.

"Is this ice-maker added feature something that comes with the whole *Super Friends* thing you've got going on now?" she asked, raising an eyebrow, clearly trying to remain sanguine and Heather-esque about the truth of what Cal had just told her.

"I guess so."

"And the remote, godlike, very un-Calum demeanor?"

"I don't know." He shrugged his shoulders, uncomfortable. "Is it a cop-out if I say maybe?"

"*I* don't know," she echoed him. "Are you serious?"

Cal tipped his head back and he sighed, staring hard at the ceiling. "Heather . . . until you told me something was wrong between us, I honestly had no idea. I actually thought we were good together."

She paused, obviously taken aback by the sudden topical tangent.

"We were," she said.

"I didn't know you were unhappy."

She laughed a little. "I've told you before. I wasn't. *You* were."

"And I told you that I didn't know I was unhappy." Cal

shook his head and gazed out the window. The view used to be screened by the branches of the Gosforth oak. Now it was unobstructed and the empty sky frightened him. It wasn't the only thing. "I've been thinking a lot about it," he said. "About you, and about . . . Mason. About how I really, truly feel. And it terrifies me."

The waves of Heather's blond hair fell over her shoulders and it struck him how absolutely beautiful she was. And how easy it *should* have been to love her.

"What does?" she asked quietly.

"All of it. Everything that's happened over the last few months. I know the way I'm acting—the way I'm feeling—is wrong. But I can't help it."

"Yeah, well." Her lips twisted in a bitter smile. "Love sucks sometimes."

"It's wrong and it's hopeless!" he exclaimed. "And it's not something I even *want*. And you wanna know the really crazy part? I actually feel like one of those ridiculous characters in one of those stupid old myths!" A bubble of anguished laughter strangled his throat. "I feel like Apollo chasing Daphne through a meadow or Orpheus scrambling down into Hades after Eurydice—like one of those guys who just loses his freaking mind over some girl and then pursues her until he's dead or she's dead or some other god takes pity on them and turns someone into a tree or a flower or they get ripped apart by crazy nymphs—something just to put an end to the stupidity."

Heather frowned. "Maybe you are."

Cal paused. "What?"

"I'm serious," she said. "Maybe you *are* one of those guys in one of those old tales. Maybe this—this whole thing with Mason?—maybe it really isn't *you*."

Cal watched as her frown grew deeper and she stared sightlessly down at the glass in her hands and he wondered if she was right. Maybe what he was feeling really weren't *his* feelings, after all.

Maybe . . .

And then he realized that it didn't matter. It wasn't something he could change, even if he wanted to. A wave of dull gray despair washed over him and he said, "It doesn't change anything."

She looked up at him, a sudden shine of tears on her lashes.

"I wish I could love you, Heather," he said as gently as he could. It sounded about as gentle as a gunshot to his ears. "I wish I could hate Mason."

"No, you don't."

"Okay. Maybe not hate. Maybe . . . *un*-love. I really do, but I think it would actually kill me to try," he said, shrugging helplessly. "And that—I *fully* realize—is the stupidest thing that's ever come out of my mouth."

"I'm not gonna deny that," Heather said, with a stab at her usual wryness.

"Why don't *you* hate her?" Cal asked suddenly.

"What?" She looked at him. "Why would I?"

"Because you love me," he said, dropping his gaze to his hands clasped between his knees. His fingers were twisted around each other like a nest of newborn snakes. "And I love her."

"I dunno. Do you hate Fennrys?" Heather asked.

The look Cal gave her was so bleak that it was comical. She laughed, and then felt instantly terrible that she was making fun of his pain but, at the same time, she almost couldn't help herself. Everything about the whole situation was so horribly wrong and yet, here she was, back sharing Cal's bed—technically—with him, teasing him, alone with him . . . When Heather had broken up with Cal, she'd thought she was doing what was best for both of them. In hindsight, she probably should have just shut up and never let him know that he was in love with Mason . . .

Wait.

What if it had been her all along? Heather felt a cold chill crawl across her scalp. Her father was notoriously under Daria Aristarchos's thumb on the Gosforth school board. What if . . . what if it had all been a setup? What if Cal really *wasn't* in love with Mason? Not really—not under his own power . . .

There was a knock on the door and Heather realized that she was going to have to come back to that one. Cal walked over and opened it. Mason was standing in the hall.

"Everyone is gathering in the dining hall to figure out what to do next," Mason said to Cal by way of greeting. "I'm, um, gathering strays." She fidgeted for a minute and then, glancing over Cal's shoulder and seeing that Heather was awake, said, "Can I talk to Heather for a minute? Alone?"

"You go on ahead, Cal," Heather said, standing up and smoothing the bedspread. "We'll be there in a second."

Before Cal slipped past Mason and out of the door, one

hand lifted involuntarily to touch her cheek. She turned away from it before his fingers had a chance to make contact. His shoulders stiffened, but he just kept going, his footsteps quick and angry, down the hall.

Mason turned back to Heather. "Am I ever glad you're awake."

"Yeah. I would be too," Heather said. "If 'awake' wasn't currently synonymous with 'migraine.'"

"You gonna be okay?" Mason asked quietly, nodding her head backward in the direction of Cal's retreating form.

Heather knew she wasn't referring to the lingering effects of the Miasma curse and said, "Sure." Then she sighed and leaned against the wall. "I mean, I guess I can actually say that I was the girl who dated the Greek god at her high school, right? That's gotta count for something later in life . . . assuming there is a later in life for us. Gotta say, I was a little surprised when I found out."

"Yeah. Me too."

"Really? Because I'm kind of under the impression that you're, like, a charter member of the same club, Starling." Heather stared at her with keen eyes. "I mean, I get—as much as it's possible *to* get something like this—that the whole Gos student body are all weirdly dedicated in service to some pantheon or other. Whether they know it or not."

"Mostly not, I think."

"Right." Heather nodded. "But it seems *you* got the full-on mythological embodiment deal. And no, I am not jealous. I'm just not sure how it happened."

"It was only recently." Mason sighed. "*Not* my idea, and

I'm not even sure exactly where 'Valkyrie' fits in on the whole semi-demi-full-blown-god pie chart."

"How? Was it all that stuff that went down with Rory on the train?"

"Yeah. And even then, nobody—not even Rory—expected that it would happen like that." Mason shook her head. "It was an accident. Well, actually, it wasn't. It was . . . more like a setup."

Mason gave her the point-form rundown of what had happened to her in Asgard. When she got to the part about casually running into Taggert Overlea on the field of battle in front of Odin's legendary feast hall and how Tag had actually led some of the Einherjar against the draugr, Heather boggled at her, mouth agape.

"Oh my god!" she exclaimed. "Local ape makes good! Okay, that actually makes me feel a little better." She closed her eyes and shook her head, the mess of her hair curtaining her face for a moment. "I mean, I almost lost it when your dad—" She broke off abruptly and bit her lip.

"When my dad what?" Mason asked.

Heather shoved her hair off her face with her forearm and her eyes opened, her weary gaze locking with Mason's own. She was silent for a moment before she said, "When he killed Tag."

"*What?*"

Heather told her then what had happened on the train—how Gunnar Starling had torn the life force out of Tag's body right in front of her—and Mason couldn't even muster up real surprise. Her father was a madman. And he was a murderer.

Her brother was sick and twisted and full of an unfathomable darkness. And her other brother had killed Mason when he was a child. Was it any wonder then that she herself was destined to end the world?

"You're not."

She glanced back at Heather, having drifted away for a moment inside her own grim thoughts. "Sorry?"

"I said 'You're not,'" Heather repeated.

"Not what?"

"Whatever it is you think you're going to do. Or be. You're not defined by your family. Or your destiny. Or any damned thing else. Anything else except you." Heather huffed in frustration. "It's all just so much bullshit, Starling. It's . . . it's *marketing*. It's what they want you to buy."

"Yesterday I would have believed that with all my heart, Heather. But yesterday I wasn't a walking prophecy." She shook her head. "Right now, everyone is holding out hope that Fenn is just a guy who happens to have an unfortunately prophetic name and, coincidentally—or, y'know, thanks to yours stupidly—happens to also now be a wolf."

Heather's brow furrowed. "And that's *not* the case?"

"He's down in a tunnel underneath the school right now having a little father-son chat . . . with Loki."

"Oh. Shit."

"This whole thing is my fault," Mason groaned. "Fennrys wasn't *Fenris* until I made him that way."

"So *un*make him."

"How?"

"Find a way."

Mason shot her a look. "I *know* a way. Let Roth kill Fennrys before Fennrys kills my father in an epic battle at the end of the world."

"Yeah . . . no." Heather shook her head. "Find another way."

"That's what I wanted to talk to you about. Away from Cal and the others." Mason dug around in the pocket of her jeans. "Listen. What you did back at the Plaza? That was a really brave thing. I didn't want you to have to run around without that kind of protection, so I rifled through Rory's room and found this." She pulled out a golden glowing acorn and held it up. "I figured he would have left one hidden in his room just in case. Roth will know what to carve on it to make it work. Toby probably does too, but Toby's coming with me. I need him."

"And where are you going?"

"I'm taking Fennrys and we're leaving. I have to keep him safe, but we also have to find . . . something. I'm not sure what yet, but it might be the key to stopping this. To maybe—like you said—finding another way. One where Fennrys doesn't wind up getting killed."

"And you're not telling the others?"

Mason shook her head. "Just you."

"Okay, then. I guess I'll just stick with the Man from Atlantis until this blows over." Her gaze drifted back down the empty hallway.

"Oh, Heather . . ." Mason sighed. "Why are you doing this to yourself? You know you could just walk away from him."

"You've forgotten what I told you about love already?"

Mason snorted, remembering. "You're *not* a drooling brain-dead."

"Close enough." Heather shrugged. "Only it's more than that. Look, Starling . . . I saw the way Queen D looked at her darling boy when Cal got all glowy eyed with the trident and the demigod thing and the stabbing of your boyfriend. I *know* that look. Cal's mom might think her son is some kind of freaky unnatural hybrid, but she's smart enough to know that he's a *powerful* freaky unnatural hybrid. And Daria's scruples—assuming she has any to begin with—don't really stick when there's power to be had."

"Wow," Mason murmured, thinking of her father.

"Yeah." Heather sighed. "I don't know if she hates Cal or loves him to death. But I do know she'll use him if she can. I don't know how, and I don't know if I can do anything to stop that from happening, but I know I have to try. You get that, right?"

"More than anybody." Mason raised her gaze to Heather's face. "Did you ever think high school would turn out to be this complicated?"

"I did . . . just not complicated like *this*." Heather laughed. "I thought, you know, I'd have to deal with peer pressure and underage drinking and sex and flunking classes because I spent too much time shopping or because I wasn't smart enough."

"Yeah. A few days ago *I* thought blowing the Nationals trials was the end of the world." Mason snorted. "Perspective, huh?"

"Yup. Sucks."

"I also thought you hated me not so long ago," Mason said, wanting to get that off her chest. In case there wasn't another opportunity.

Heather looked at her and smiled. "I know. I tried." The smile faded. "Be careful, Starling. Okay?"

"Yeah. You too, Palmerston."

She forced the smile back onto her face. "Hey—I've got a golden acorn! Plus, you know, I'm packing heat . . ."

"What?"

Heather's purse was sitting on the end of Cal's bed. She grabbed it and opened it so Mason could peer inside. There was something shiny nestled in there, beside Heather's phone and a makeup compact. Mason looked closer at the thing that resembled a pistol with . . . wings.

"Is that, like, a baby *crossbow*?"

"Yup."

Mason raised an eyebrow. "Where did you get a crossbow?"

"Uh . . . I think a god gave it to me."

Mason stared at Heather and waited. These kinds of conversations were becoming disconcertingly commonplace between the two girls. Heather told her briefly of her encounter with the young man who'd called himself Valen on the train back into Manhattan on the night Mason had gone somewhere over the rainbow, as it were.

"Wow. I mean, I guess it makes sense in a weird way." Mason shrugged when she was done with her tale. "I know most of them faded away, but some gods—like Rafe—never left this world."

"Yeah?" Heather looked at her sideways. "Maybe I'm just

getting cynical, but it seems funny to think that Cupid was one of those."

"Ha!" Mason laughed. "Yeah. How does that old song go? 'What the world needs now is love, sweet love . . .'"

"And there he was, all the time. Wearing sunglasses and a leather jacket, riding the subway late at night." She shook her head, remembering. "He was *so* hot."

"Would've been a little disappointing if he wasn't," Mason said. "What do you think he meant when he said he'd been trying to find you?"

"I don't know. I don't *want* to know." Heather put up a hand, forestalling further discussion of the matter. "And anyway, it'll have to wait until after the world ends now, I guess. Or, y'know, doesn't." She closed her purse back up and patted it, as if to make sure that the little weapon hadn't vanished.

"Cupid's arrows." Mason shook her head in wonderment. "I think you'd better be really careful with that."

"That's what Gwen said."

Mason shivered at the sound of her name. "I can't believe she—"

"Yeah." Heather held up her hand again. "Let's not talk about that either just right now. Okay?"

"Okay." Suddenly, Mason folded her into a fierce hug. "Thank you for being my friend, Heather."

"Yeah, yeah. Don't get all sentimental on me, Starling." Heather rolled her eyes, but there was a distinct lack of snark to her tone. She paused awkwardly, as if searching for something un-mushy to say in return. But then her expression altered and she said, "Hey, do you have a phone?"

"Uh . . ." Mason fished the one she'd taken off Rory's desk out of her back pocket and held it up. "Yeah. No idea where mine is, but I took Rory's from his room. I don't know why, though; it won't do me much good." She hit the home button and the four-digit password screen popped up. "It's locked."

"Huh," Heather said, frowning, as she plucked the thing from Mason's hand. "Let's see . . . he's not smart enough to be subtle . . ." She stuck her tongue out of the side of her mouth and tried a couple of combinations that she figured someone like Mason's brother, with his delusions of god-hood, might use.

"F.A.T.E. . . ." Nothing. "O.D.I.N. . . . T.H.O.R. . . ." Still nothing. "L.O.K.I.?"

"Try 'N.O.R.N.,'" Mason suggested.

"Nada." Heather shook her head. "How about R.U.N.E. . . . dammit!"

The phone screen politely informed them that this next attempt would be their last and then the phone would lock permanently.

Mason put a hand out and said, "Wait. We're going about this all wrong. It's *Rory*, for crying out loud. What's the most important thing in his world?"

Heather waited, peering over Mason's shoulder as she carefully tapped in the letters R . . . O . . . R . . . Y . . . and the home screen sprang to life.

"Wow." Heather blinked. "It really *is* all about him, isn't it?"

"As far as he's concerned, yeah." Mason snorted. "I should have known. That self-absorbed little weasel."

"Here." Heather took the phone back and programmed her number into it. "Now we can stay in touch. Just do me a favor: If it looks like we might lose and there's a chance he gets this back? Delete my digits. Late-night postapocalyptic drunk dialing from your creep-o brother, I do not need."

Mason laughed.

"Go. I'll go down and stall Cal and the others for as long as I can so you guys can make a clean getaway. Keep me in the loop, okay?"

"Okay."

"And try not to do anything insanely stupid."

"I'll try," Mason said. But she didn't bother promising, knowing that was one promise she was unlikely to keep.

XVIII

L oki was gone when Mason finally got back down
to the caverns. But Fennrys was sitting on the stone
bench that Gwen had made into a bed, his eyes closed,
and a smile curving the corners of his mouth. Mason
silently crossed the floor and bent down to kiss him.

He kissed her back, slowly, deliciously, and said, "I can
still smell sunshine and apple blossoms in your hair. Chalk up
another win for the Safe Harbor technique."

"Yup." Mason grinned down at him. "Except the shirtless
factor didn't translate."

"And I'm not soaking wet."

He opened his eyes and his gaze was placid. Tranquil.
Maybe just a *little* on the smoldering-with-desire side. And
Mason felt her heartbeat quicken in response. Suddenly it felt
very warm in the cavern.

"Did you find Toby?" she asked.

"I did." Fenn nodded. "Went topside after the dream-vision

faded and found him wrangling a stray student down to the dining hall. Said he'll meet us here when he can get away unnoticed. So . . . what's this idea of yours?" He pulled her forward so that she had to put one knee up beside him on the bench to brace herself or risk falling on top of him.

"We're going for a little ride," Mason said and then felt her cheeks grow even hotter at the expression that crossed Fennrys's face. "On a *train*."

His smile was languid. "Because that worked out so well last time," he said.

"*Inside* the train, *not* on the roof, and heading in the *other* direction." She tilted her head. "Although, weirdly, our destination is Valhalla."

"Seriously?"

"The one in Westchester," she explained. "Picturesque little hamlet of just over three thousand people, none of whom know that Ragnarok is about to barrel over the horizon, and who hopefully never will."

"Ye olde family homestead, huh?"

"It has to be."

It really does, she thought a bit desperately. *It's the only clue we have.*

"Well . . . it's a long shot and more likely than not, wishful thinking." Fenn lifted a shoulder. "But it's the only shot we've got. And before she pushed me down a hill, my mother said something about traveling in style; a private train fits that bill. Only thing is, didn't your daddy leave that particular toy of his on the other side of a busted-up Hell Gate?"

"Yup. He did." Mason nodded. "But . . . riddle me this: When is a train not a train?"

Fennrys rolled an eye at her. "Is this one of those Victorian brain teaser puzzles? 'Cause I've always sucked at those. Even when I *was* a Victorian."

Mason blinked at Fennrys for a moment. It was easy to forget sometimes that he was several centuries older than she was. Good thing he didn't act his age, she thought. She grinned at him and ran a fingertip down the length of his nose.

"The answer," she said, "is when I'm a freaking Valkyrie with awesome superpowers, and the engine of the train is an eight-legged horse. *That's* when."

"That makes even less sense than Lewis Carroll." Fennrys grunted. Still, he didn't seem to mind. He moved his head so that he could kiss her. Mason found herself having a hard time remembering what it was she was supposed to be doing down there in that cavern with him.

Right. Save the Wolf. Save the world. Let's do that. First.

She pushed herself back off the bench and took a deep breath.

"Focus."

"Right." He nodded, his blue gaze glittering dangerously. "Horse. Train."

"Yes," she said sternly.

"How?" he asked.

"I just remembered something I saw when I was on the train the first time," she explained, "when it was crossing over the Hell Gate. I thought I was having a delusional episode, but now I'm not so sure. Now I think that what I saw was part of the whole Valkyrie thing. Kind of like with the carriage in Central Park. I think I can do this."

Mason walked slowly over to the mouth of the tunnel and ran her hands over the intricate, knotted carvings that ran in a broad band around the opening. The designs were similar to the patterns on Fennrys's medallion and the carvings on the Odin spear, and she recognized them now, with a kind of bone-deep familiarity, for what they were. Ancient Norse knot work carved with charms and subtle symbols, imbued with a kind of magick all their own. There were curses and warnings and spells woven into the pictograms, and Mason, with her Valkyrie eyes, deciphered them at a glance. One of them—the image of a fabulous beast, its seeming overabundance of limbs tangled around one another—told her of the uses of this particular tunnel. She knew what it was, what it housed, and where it went.

It was a lair, and it was a train tunnel. And, once summoned, its occupant would carry her away from the chaos of the city. It would take her home. She stepped inside and her hand dropped to rest lightly on the hilt of the glamoured spear she wore like a sword.

"Are you sure that's such a good idea?" Fennrys's voice suddenly murmured in her ear, startling her.

She hadn't heard him come up behind her, but now she could feel the heat emanating from him like sunlight streaming through a window, falling on her shoulders and back. She wanted to melt into the sensation.

"I mean," he continued, "I thought you were supposed to

keep your Valkyrie tucked away."

"In battle, yeah," she said. "We're not fighting anyone, are we?"

"Just ourselves . . ."

She turned to look at him and saw that his eyes were fixed upon her, fierce and blazing with cold blue light.

"This . . . is . . ."

"Not a good time?" He grinned. Wolfishly.

Mason heard herself laugh, a low, throaty sound. "Probably not."

"I'll behave. Promise." He put both hands up and backed off another few steps. "Do your voodoo. Whatever that may be."

"Okay. Okay . . ." Mason's fingers twitched spasmodically and her hand dropped to the sword again. "Here goes nothing . . ."

She drew the weapon. Crimson light bloomed like a sunset in the tunnel and Mason felt the brush of raven wings on her face. The heavy swish of her chain-mail raiment settled to hang once more from her shoulders and she felt the solid weight of the helmet settle on her brow.

She raised the spear, and called, "Sleipner."

When she was a kid, Mason would listen to the stories her father would tell of Odin's fabulous steed—the coal-black, eight-legged warhorse named Sleipner—and she would try and wrap her head around the mental picture of a horse with twice the normal horsey complement of limbs. She never could quite picture it, though. In her mind, the creature always wound up looking awkward and ungainly. A bit goofy, really.

The reality of it—and Sleipner, she'd discovered, was very much real—defied her feeble imaginative attempts. When it appeared, the horse—which resembled a regular horse in roughly the same way that a wolf resembles a Chihuahua—was utterly magnificent. For one thing, the beast was massive. Much larger than even a Clydesdale. Mason could have stood on tiptoe and reached as high as she could and her fingertips still would have been miles away from touching the thing's shoulder. It was basically the size of a train locomotive—which was exactly the guise Mason had first seen Sleipner wear, when she'd first encountered him. When Rory had abducted her in her father's private train. Like the spear she carried, or the Valkyrie guise she wore, like her father's transformation into the All-Father god Odin, or her mother's assumption of the mantle of Hel, or Fennrys in all of his Fenris-ness, the mythical creature standing proudly before Mason, filling up most of the cavernous tunnel, was a manifestation of power. And it didn't look the least bit silly standing on eight legs.

Behind her, Mason heard Fennrys murmur, "Holy . . ."

She also heard the measured tread of combat boots coming closer in the tunnel.

"Toby's coming," she said quietly without taking her eyes from the magnificent creature. "You can tell him our ride is here."

"I can see that for myself, Mase," Toby said, in a tone that came as close to awe as anything she'd ever heard from him.

Sleipner turned his massive head and snorted—a cloud of smoke and embers issuing forth from his flared nostrils, like dragon breath—and Mason saw herself reflected in the black globe of the creature's huge eye.

"Easy, boy," she said. If Mason had just been Mason, she would have been terrified. But she was a Valkyrie and she had summoned the fabulous Odin steed. He would obey her command. "Easy . . ."

The monstrous horse dipped his head and allowed Mason to run her hand between his eyes and down his nose. The fine black velvet of his hide shone in the dim light.

"I need you to take me and my friends to Valhalla," Mason said. "The one in Westchester, I mean. Would you do that?"

He snorted again and pawed the tunnel floor once with a hoof half the size of a compact car, raising a massive cloud of red dust that filled the tunnel. When the dust cleared, the eight-legged horse was gone and an eight-wheeled locomotive idled on a set of silvery tracks, hooked up to the elegant carriage cars of Gunnar Starling's private train. First the carriage in Central Park, now this, Mason thought. Valkyries, it seemed, traveled in style.

I might not even ask for a car for my eighteenth birthday, she thought wryly. And then she thought, *If I actually manage to live that long. . . .*

Mason turned to see Toby and Fennrys standing in the archway of the tunnel, mouths agape. The spectacle of Sleipner's transformation had made a clear impression, as had her ability to summon the great beast. When she took a step toward them, they both took a half step back. On some level, that made Mason just a little bit sad, but she ignored the feeling and walked over to Toby and, waving at the monster-horse-turned-locomotive, said, "You know how to drive this thing, right?"

Toby, for his part, regained his composure swiftly. He eyed the train with dry distaste. "If you mean, can I drive a *train*, then yes. Gunnar could have told me that I was riding in the belly of a big old horse when he hired me to drive his damned train, you know." Beneath his mustache, his lip curled upward in a faint sneer. "It's disgusting. I would have demanded a raise."

"You know that's not really how it works, right?" Mason grinned at the look on the fencing master's face. "And the train is only Sleipner because it crossed the Bifrost and took on the *power* of Sleipner. At least, I think that's right. Right?"

"Sure, Mase." Toby patted her on the shoulder and stepped past her. "But mentally, I'm still getting cozy with horse innards."

"You're a brave soul, Tobe."

"Yeah, yeah. Saddle up." He grimaced. "So to speak."

With that, he swung himself up onto the first rung of the shiny black ladder that lead to the locomotive compartment. Mason thought she might have heard a muffled whinny, but decided—for her own mental stability—that it was just her imagination.

Inside, the opulent coach was exactly as she remembered it. It smelled of leather and the faint spice of her father's expensive cigars, and she felt a stab of longing. She missed him so much. She had, Mason realized, worshiped Gunnar Starling growing up. As much as Rory had, in his own twisted way. As much as Roth had.

And now? She knew the coming conflict wasn't one where

there would be no losers. One way or another, the Starling clan would be shattered. And, in spite of the fact that Mason was determined that she would be the one to come out the other side a victor, that fact still made her ineffably sad. Which was strange, because the thought of the looming battle *also* made her want to tear the heads off her brother and father and hang them from her saddle horn as she rode her Valkyrie steed through the smoke and fire hanging over the field of battle—

Okay. Whoa. Let's dial down the bloodthirst, shall we?

Across the train compartment, Fennrys was staring at her with a look so intense, she couldn't tell if he wanted to tackle her to the ground and tear out her throat . . . or tackle her to the ground and tear off her clothes. She wasn't sure, in that moment, which she would have preferred. He grinned at her and his eyes sparked cold fire. Mason's heart pounded in her chest so loudly she was sure that the others could hear it. She wondered if there was any water in the bar fridge. She might just have to pour a bottle over her head if she couldn't get ahold of herself—

"I *said* . . . ," Rafe's deep voice suddenly broke in on her chaotic, overheated thoughts, "what are you going to do when you get to your dad's estate, Mason?"

Mason glanced up, startled to see that the door to the train compartment was open and Rafe was leaning against the frame. His sudden presence, and the grim look on his face, had exactly the same effect on Mason's raging Fennrys-lusting as an ice-water dousing would have. The ancient Egyptian god of the dead pushed away from the entryway and the door slid shut behind him as he strolled across the rich Persian carpet, his dark gaze sweeping over the interior of the opulent train car.

"Traveling in style, kids?" he said wryly. "I approve."

Mason and Fennrys exchanged glances, exactly like the children Rafe had just called them—ones who'd been caught doing something forbidden and dangerous, way past hand-in-the-cookie-jar guilty.

"So," Rafe continued, casually running his hand over the rich burled oak surface of the bar. He turned and leaned on one elbow. "What's it feel like to be one of us?" he asked Fennrys.

Fenn shot Mason a look. "You mean one of the pack?" he asked.

Rafe grinned and shook his head, dreads swinging gently. "No, Fennrys Wolf. I mean, what does it feel like to be a *god*?"

"I'm not a god." Fenn glared flatly, clearly in no mood to be mocked. "I'm a monster."

Rafe winced. "Harsh."

"Weren't those your own words?"

"Yeah." The ancient deity sighed. "I suppose they were. And I suppose you're right. Half right, anyway. I'm old enough and I'm damned well smart enough to realize when I'm wrong. And I've been very wrong about you."

"I don't understand."

"In spite of everything, I don't think I ever *really* thought you had it in you." Rafe's dark eyes narrowed as he gazed at Fennrys. "The Wolf, I mean. I thought you could beat this rap—that there had to be some kind of misunderstanding and it really was just a name."

"What exactly are you saying, Rafe?" Mason asked quietly.

"I'm saying that, all along, I thought *I* was being the good guy, sticking up for the underdog. No pun intended." He shrugged. "I'm sorry for that."

"Sorry as in you regret doing that?" Fenn asked.

"Sorry as in I apologize. I should have had more respect for you." He walked over to a leather swivel chair and sat in it like it was a throne, but in the way that a king would if he didn't care that it was a throne. "I'm not your maker, Fennrys. I'm your brother." His glittering stare shifted. "Just like I'm yours, Mason. We are gods among mortals. And I don't care what Daria Aristarchos and her ilk think, *we* exist to serve *them*, not the other way around. And I'm proud to stand beside you in your fight to save their realm."

Mason felt her jaw drifting open in astonishment. She had not been expecting *that*.

"Also?" He grinned at her, showing the points of his sharp white teeth. "When all this is over, you still owe me, big time."

Right. *That* was more like what she'd expected. The circle of his gaze threatened to swallow her whole and Mason suddenly understood what it was to play by the rules of a deity.

"How long till we get to where we're going?" Rafe asked.

"We?" Fenn said, warily seeking clarification. It seemed to Mason that he was still waiting for the other shoe to drop. Ever the lone wolf, he wasn't used to being believed in. Especially not by more than one person at a time.

Rafe laughed. "You don't think I'm actually going to

let you two run off all on your lonesomes to try to save the world, right?"

"How do you know that's what we're doing?" Mason asked warily.

"Please, dear girl." Rafe bent an eyebrow at her. "Wasn't born yesterday."

That much was true.

"Didn't *die* yesterday," Fennrys said, his voice dropping into a low growl.

He sat forward on the leather banquette and it looked as if he might actually launch himself across the car and attack Rafe in another moment. Mason figured that would end badly, so she interposed herself between the two of them.

"You're not going to try to stop us, are you?" she asked the god.

"Depends. Are you running away?"

She shook her head. "Running toward."

"Toward what?"

"Help. Hope." She shrugged. "Hel."

"Your mom?"

"The real one this time."

Rafe waited silently for an explanation as Mason exchanged a glance with Fennrys, silently seeking his permission to let Rafe in on the whole dream-vision thing. After a moment, Fenn let his breath out in a sigh and sat back, gesturing for her to go on. She told Rafe most of what the two of them had experienced—editing out the kissing parts—and the ancient god listened intently.

"I think Heimdall has her trapped somewhere," Mason

said. "And there has to be a reason for that, I figure. Of all the Aesir, he was the one who wanted Ragnarok the most, right?"

"You have a point." Rafe tilted his elegant head to one side, pondering her logic. "Odin accepted it as inevitable, and necessary, but I'm not sure that given what he thought of as a choice, he'd have chosen to go that way. He wouldn't have faded away in the first place if that was the case. It takes a lot of crazy to hang on that long just to bring about the end of everything. Heimdall, Loki, they're the only original personifications of the Aesir left. And they are, according to prophecy, destined to end each other. Two sides of the same coin."

"Right. That's what we were thinking." Mason glanced at Fennrys, who nodded. "So if Heimdall thinks my mom—if he thinks Hel—is some kind of impediment to him being able to trigger Ragnarok, then us finding her is something that can only help us, right?"

"Maybe." Rafe clearly wasn't wholly convinced. But it was also just as clear that he desperately wanted to *be* convinced. Almost as desperately as Mason and Fennrys.

"She told me to find her, Rafe." Mason held his black gaze, unblinking with her own. "I really believe she can help us. *All* of us. I think together we can put a stop to this whole mess."

Rafe didn't say anything to refute that and, after a long moment, they had a kind of answer from him out of his silence. The train car shuddered as Toby got them under way. They were heading to Valhalla, and it was too late for Rafe to abandon the journey.

The train carried along for some time in silence, the rhythmic clacking of the wheels sounding very much like the pounding of eight horse's hooves. After a while, Fennrys grew restless and went through the sliding doors connecting to the engine compartment to ask Toby how long until they reached their destination. In the silence, Mason remembered the folded, photocopied pages in her pocket that she'd taken from Rory's room. She pulled them out and read them all. It didn't take long, but the experience left her feeling as if she'd existed out of time for the minutes it had taken. She looked up from the words on the last page and found Rafe staring at her.

"What is it, Mase?" Rafe asked, when she was silent for a long time. "What's bothering you?"

"Nothing . . . ," she murmured, caught up in her tangled thoughts, fanning the photocopied pages of her father's diary, staring unseeing at the words he'd written so long ago. "I was just . . . wondering."

"About what?"

"You."

His mouth twitched up at one corner. "What about me?"

Mason shrugged, uncertain how to broach the subject. Her interaction with the ancient death god had been awkward—to say the least—since she had compelled him to turn Fennrys. But she had questions, having just scanned through the lines of Gunnar Starling's musings from that long-ago night in Copenhagen when he'd been young, bored, and had wandered into a club and met his fate—Fates—three strange women introduced to him by the club's proprietor, a smooth, handsome, dreadlocked character who'd called himself "Rafe."

"The night you met my dad," Mason said. "The way he writes it, it sounds almost like you were expecting him. Like you were waiting for him to walk through the door, just so you could introduce him to the Norns."

"Verda, Skully, and Weirdo . . ." Rafe nodded, his gaze turning inward as he recalled his "pet" names for the three creatures of Norse legend who'd come to his bar that night, dressed like punk rock princesses, to lie in wait for Mason's father. "I remember that night like it was last week."

Verdandi, Skuld, and Urd . . . Mason remembered their real names from the stories. They had always terrified her as a child. Like three black spiders, hunched and waiting at the center of a web, waiting for hapless prey. Like her father.

Mason frowned. "It sounds to me like . . ."

"Like what, Mason?"

Her eyes locked with his. "Like you set him up."

"Ah." Rafe nodded his head slowly. "I can see how it would, yeah . . . But I didn't. I'm not a precog, Mason."

"I don't know what that is."

"A seer," he explained. "A teller of fortunes and futures. Like the Norns are. Like Gwen Littlefield was. Me? I'm just a very old god. And when you're as old as I am—and you belong to that particular club, which, year after decade after century boasts an ever-depleting membership roster—you find yourself hanging around with other gods. Or find them hanging around with you. The ladies, and I do use the term loosely where those three are concerned, had been coming around my place for years. A god of the dead tends to attract the type of individual that the Norns are always on the look-out for."

"You mean individuals like my father."

Rafe nodded again. "Of course, Gunnar wasn't the first. And if there's any way we can stop Ragnarok from happen-ing, I doubt very much he'll be the last. This? This is what the Norns do."

"And the night Fennrys and I found you in Central Park? That wasn't a coincidence, either, was it? You said you'd been waiting for him."

"I was." He glanced at the door leading to the engine compartment. "Your boy already had a reputation in the supernatural community, thanks to the rather dramatic nature of his departure from the mortal realm. Iris, the lovely lady with the fancy wings you met earlier, had sent me a mes-sage through Ghost—you remember Etienne, Fennrys's fallen Janus Guard comrade?—that he'd returned. That he was potential bad news for the city, maybe the whole world . . . and I was just trying to assess the situation. I like the mortal realm, remember?"

"You *swear* you didn't set him up?" Mason asked, her voice a whisper.

"Do you mean Fennrys, or your father? Because the answer to both is an unqualified *no*." Crossing the salon car floor, he sat down beside her, taking her hand in both of his and look-ing her in the eyes. His fingers were cool and strong and his dark gaze didn't so much as flicker as he said, "I swear it to you on Ammit's blood-encrusted scales. I'm a god, Mason.

Even if I'm an old discarded one. I don't need to lie."

"You don't need to do anything you don't want to," she said.

"That's true."

"Then why are you here? Helping us?"

"Because sometimes, dear girl . . . ," Rafe said as he pushed a strand of Mason's midnight hair back behind her ear and smiled gently, "even an old discarded god finds something to believe in."

XIX

Cal's green eyes reflected back at him as he pushed angrily through the glass doors into the dining hall. He couldn't help but notice that the scars on the side of his face shone stark against the remnants of his summer tan, more so with his face flushed with anger.

"Mason and Fennrys are gone," he said to the room at large. It was occupied by Roth, Daria, Heather, and a handful of students—huddled as far away from that bloodied, bedraggled crew as the room's dimensions allowed.

"What?" Daria said, her perfectly arched brows knitting in a frown.

"Toby is too," Cal said.

"Taken?" Roth asked. "Or on the run?"

"How the hell should I know?" Cal snapped, seething with apprehension—and an underlying current of irrational anger that he could barely believe he possessed. Never in his life had he felt this way but, where Mason was concerned, it seemed as if someone else was controlling the ebb and flow of his feelings, opening up a mental floodgate and pouring emotion into him to fill a hollow space he hadn't known he had. His hands curled into fists at his sides as he struggled to keep from lashing out with his power. "How in hell did they get out of Gosforth without us knowing?"

"They can't have gone far," Daria said. "The security system would have alerted us to any breach of the wards around the school."

"Do those wards extend down into the catacombs *under* the school?" Roth asked in a strained voice.

Cal's mother did a double take and her brow creased in an even deeper frown.

Roth shook his head. "They're gone."

"Where?" Heather asked in a carefully neutral voice that meant she knew something the others didn't. Cal recognized the tone. Heather wasn't the least bit surprised to hear that Mason and the Wolf had fled. And Cal also knew, again by that same tone, that whatever other information she had, she wasn't about to share. Heather Palmerston was loyal to a fault. To Mason, to Cal himself . . . it was an admirable trait that might just get them all killed.

Roth looked at Heather and, in response to her question, shrugged his good shoulder. "Not a clue."

"But the farther away from here, the better, right?" Heather asked.

"Maybe. The truth is, I don't know. I don't know anymore how this all goes down, Heather. Without Gwen, I'm flying just as blind as the rest of you."

Cal saw that Roth was still in a great deal of pain, both physically and emotionally. His handsome face was drawn and ashen, his eyes red-rimmed with shadows beneath them so dark they looked bruised. If Cal had had any emotional room left, he would have felt sorry for Mason's brother.

"I can't seem to find that Rafe guy, either," Cal said.

"I think I know where they've gone," Daria murmured. "At least . . . I think I know where they will ultimately wind up."

Roth laughed mirthlessly. "Of course you do. You know, Daria . . . you could have done something useful with Gwen's talent over the years. Instead of hoarding it, collecting secrets, plotting. Now it's wasted."

"This isn't her fault," Cal said. "She *was* trying to stop *your* father and—"

"Oh, grow up, Cal." Heather scoffed, sounding suddenly as if she was so deeply weary of it all. "Stop defending her just because she's your mother. She's just as responsible for all this as Roth's dad. As all of the Gosforth founding families are. Our parents? None of them are innocent in this. I guarantee you my own mom and dad are just as complicit in this mess, even if they aren't actively trying to wreak havoc. They've *known*. All of them have known—for years—that this . . . situation was brewing." She waved a hand at where Carrie Morgan and the other students huddled, all of whom clearly had no idea what she was talking about.

Roth looked at Heather with a glimmer of respect in his exhausted eyes.

"She's right," he said. "Secrets . . . lies . . . all of what we've—*I've*—been trying to do through subterfuge and backstabbing and games . . . supernatural politics . . . none of it has worked."

"Of course it has," Daria said. She shook her head sharply and raked the hair off her face. "For hundreds of years it has. Because of this Academy and the accords that bound its founders. We've all kept the peace. Until now. So you see, I actually understand your frustration."

"*Frustration?*" Heather visibly boggled at the sheer understatement.

"You know, I've always thought of you like you were my daughter," Daria continued, a thin smile stretching her lips. "Both you and Gwendolyn."

Cal felt his jaw drift open in utter disbelief. Maybe his mom really was actually, *utterly* delusional, he thought.

"You have got to be kidding me," Heather murmured.

"Believe what you want. It's true." Daria shrugged. "I always rather hoped that one or maybe even both of you would someday grow to realize your full potential and perhaps join me and my own daughter in the ranks of the Elusinian priestesses. I actually spoke to your father about such a thing not so long ago, Heather. We'd discussed fostering you, in fact, but he kept putting me off. Of course, it's not something that's possible for Gwen now—"

"Thanks to you," Roth said sharply.

"—but I still hold hope for you, Heather. You're smart and you're beautiful, but you're naive. You have power you're not willing to use. And you're far too willing to play the victim.

The tragic princess." Daria pegged Heather with a pointed stare. "I wouldn't normally say this, but you could learn a thing or two from the Starling girl. Perhaps, in time, you will. But that's only if there *is* time." Daria turned to Roth. "I need my peace pledge from the safe in the headmaster's office. And I need your help to get it. There is a mystical lock on the safe that can only be opened using the blood of two or more members of different founding families."

"You want more of his blood?" Heather snapped. "Haven't you taken enough already?"

Daria rolled her eyes at her. "I don't make the rules of magick. Inside that safe are the artifacts that each family turned over as mutual ransoms to Gosforth for safekeeping when the school was built. The things left by *my* predecessors can provide me with the means to raise an army to fight against your father's Einherjar if it comes to that. I need them, and then I need someone to get me to the Upper East Side, while the city streets are still somewhat passable. Rothgar, if your sister and the Wolf join forces with your father"—she held up a hand to forestall any protesting outbursts—"under their own free will or not, then we have to be prepared."

"My car's parked in a Columbia lot not far from here," Cal said without hesitation. "I can drive."

Roth glanced back and forth between Cal and his mother. Then he nodded tersely and gestured her toward the doors. From the expression on his face, it looked to Cal that he thought Roth might tear Daria's head off—perhaps literally— if he let himself say anything in wake of what she'd just said about Gwen. Cal wouldn't really have blamed him if he had.

* * *

Heather watched Mason's brother and Cal's mom walk off down the hallway, the ultimate expression of "frenemies" in that moment, she thought. When they were gone, her gaze drifted over the familiar contours of the gothically elegant architecture of the place she'd spent most of her life, and which she was only now beginning to see with eyes wide open. She couldn't handle it anymore. It felt like she was suffocating. The other students were looking at her like she was supposed to be able to tell them everything was going to be okay, and she just couldn't. Instead, she spun around and stalked toward the kitchen, pushing her way through the service doors and grabbing a glass from a shelf. She poured water from the tap and gulped it thirstily. When she turned back around, she saw that Cal had followed her.

"Insane," she murmured. "All of them. Our parents are *all* completely off the rails and this place is a freaking monkey-house asylum. . . ."

"They've been trying to keep us *safe*, Heather," Cal argued quietly. "And we've been stupid. We should have stayed here at Gosforth and we should have left well enough alone."

"What are you talking about?" Heather looked at him, completely bemused.

"I'm talking about the one thing that started this whole mess rolling." He shrugged. "If Mason hadn't gone off chasing Mister Man-of-Action Badass after that first night, none of us would be in this position now. She went hunting for trouble."

Heather tilted her head and regarded him with disbelief.

"It came looking for her first, Cal," she said. "For *all* of us. Or have you forgotten?"

"Of course I haven't!" Cal snarled and it almost seemed that, in doing so, he was actually trying to emphasize the scars on his face that had marked him from that first terrifying encounter. "But she should have stayed with us."

"You left too. You went home."

"Only because she did. And I shouldn't have."

No, Heather thought. *You really shouldn't have.*

"If we'd all just stayed together and at the Academy, we would have been fine, no matter what happened."

From somewhere out in the city, over on Broadway from the sounds of it, Heather could hear a car horn wailing non-stop. Probably some hapless cabbie was either unconscious or dead, slumped over the wheel of his car and leaning on the thing. It sounded like a pathetic cry for help, but as she listened, it stopped. Maybe the driver was awake.

She shook her head. "Maybe," she said. "But everyone else wouldn't be."

Cal laughed and it was a harsh, bitter sound. "So? Since when have you ever cared about 'everyone else'? When have any of us?"

Heather shook her head. "You really think you're so much better than everyone out there"—she pointed in the direction of the body-filled streets—"and so much smarter than everyone in here. Well, guess what? You're not some kind of superior being—"

"Yeah, Heather," Cal interrupted her savagely. "I *am*."

He flung his arms wide and the double faucets on the industrial kitchen sinks suddenly burst from their mounting brackets, dual geysers of water blasting forth. The twin spouts writhed through the air like quicksilver snakes, leaping into Cal's outstretched hands, where they met and twined around each other, flowing into the shape of the devastating three-pronged weapon he'd conjured before. It had happened so quickly that first time that Heather hadn't really been sure of what she'd seen. But now, in that moment, Heather got her first full look at what Cal had truly become.

And it was . . . magnificent.

Heather had always loved Cal's eyes. The clear, sparkling sea-green shade, the way they flashed when he smiled or laughed. And Cal used to do both of those things a lot. Not anymore. Now his eyes flashed with something else. Power. Tiny spears of lightning forked along the edges of the trident's triple blades and the air around Cal was heavy and wet and smelled sharply of sea-brine. His golden-brown hair blew back from his face and the planes and angles of his cheeks and forehead seemed as if they had been sculpted out of marble. His skin was smooth and flawless with the very notable exception of the scars on the side of his face—which somehow made him look even more striking in that moment. Beneath the thin material of the T-shirt he wore, his lean-muscled fencer's physique stood out in sharp relief. He looked like some kind of god.

He is. He really is . . .

She remembered the feeling she'd gotten on the subway

train when she'd met the strange young man who'd called himself Valen. The way the air had seemed charged in his presence. It was the same thing now with Cal. And, frankly, if Heather hadn't been so terrified of him in that moment, she would have been drooling out the side of her mouth. Cal radiated strength and danger, and it was incredibly sexy.

And so not him.

The thought snapped Heather out of her momentary shock. She shook her head sadly and took a step toward Cal. She put a hand on the trident and felt the smooth, cold surface of the solid water sliding beneath her fingertips and she gently pushed it to one side.

"Where *are* you?" she whispered.

With her other hand, she reached up and traced the scars on Cal's face. He flinched beneath her caress and she saw the real Cal flicker in his eyes.

"There you are . . . Calum."

He reared away from her, but she wrapped both of her hands around the back of his head and held him there, surprising herself with her own strength.

"Cal," she said, her voice quiet but steady. "Listen to me. We're going to need you. *You.* Not this . . . someone else you think you need to become. Mason is going to need your help to get through this."

She didn't say out loud that *she* would too.

Cal looked down at her—*really* looked at her, for the first time in ages, it seemed—and blinked rapidly. The fierce gleam in his eyes faded, washed away by a film of unshed tears. For a moment, they were so close that Heather thought he might kiss her. She ached for that, but she wouldn't be the one to make that move. Instead, he leaned his forehead on hers for a moment.

"Heather . . . ," he said, so quietly she almost didn't hear him. "Help me. I'm losing myself."

"No, you're not," she whispered back. "I know where to find you. I'll always know."

After a moment, he pulled away from her again. This time, she let him.

"She'll be back soon," he said, glancing in the direction his mother had gone. "I'll have to go with her."

"I know. And I'm coming with you."

"Heather—"

"You gonna argue with me, Aristarchos?"

"Will I win?"

"No."

"Then . . . no."

Cal's Maserati was a thing of sleek, sublime automotive beauty. Painted a dark shade of metallic blue, it sported the venerable company's logo on the front grill that, up until that very moment, Heather had never even noticed.

A three-pronged spear. A trident.

"Coincidence?" she murmured to Roth gesturing to the symbol as they circled around the back end of the car.

He glanced at Cal's mother, settling herself in the front passenger seat, and then raised an eyebrow at Heather.

"Yeah . . . ," she said. "Probably not so much."

As they drove through the city, they noticed increased movement. Activity. People were beginning to wake up. Clambering to their feet, wailing in panic or weeping silently. Some just sitting on the sidewalk, others shambling like zombies. Everyone wondering what in the world had happened.

Cal slowed down to steer around a yellow cab that was on its side in the middle of the intersection at Lexington and East Ninety-Eighth. Under normal circumstances—and Heather almost laughed out loud as she framed the thought . . . *Normal? Seriously?*—Cal probably would have cut across the park at Ninety-Sixth. But on the way to the car, he'd told Heather about what had happened on the way up to Gosforth, when she'd been unconscious. And, yeah. She heartily agreed that, if there was a chance that any draugr were left alive in Central Park, it was best to avoid that—like the plague—in their quest to get to the East River.

With that supremely irritating arrogance she had, Daria had told them where they had to go—Wards Island—but not exactly why. Heather wondered how much of her information was guesswork, and how much Gwen had told her of what would come to pass over the years. She felt a stab of anguish at the thought of the purple-haired girl's slight body plummeting into nothingness. When she'd first come to find Heather in her dorm room, Gwen had told her she'd *seen* the place Daria had taken Roth—what had turned out to be the top of Rockefeller Center—but that she didn't know it. All Gwen knew was that, in her vision, she'd felt as though she would "fall into the sky."

And she had.

Because Heather had told her what that place was, and taken her there.

I am not going to think like that. Gwen's death was not my fault.

No. It wasn't. It was Daria's.

"I'm assuming you've recently become reacquainted with your father," Daria was saying to Cal, her voice tight and icy, like a frost-coated piano wire.

"Why would you assume that?" Cal asked.

She laughed bitterly. "Because the last time you and I had dinner together, your salad fork wasn't made of water."

"He didn't show me how to do that, you know," Cal said defensively. "I figured it out on my own."

"Once he told you what you are. I knew it." Daria sighed, and it was a genuinely weary sound. "I knew one day he would come back to try and take you away from me—"

"He saved my life! And he didn't try to take me away from you." Cal's hands tightened on the steering wheel in frustration. "In fact, *he* was the one who told me go to back into the city to find you. Mom . . . I just don't get it. He doesn't seem like such a monster—"

"That's *exactly* what he is, darling. A very charming monster."

"What does that make me?"

"The monster's victim. As I was."

"You really hate him that much?"

"Cal, don't pretend you know anything about such things at your age," Daria hissed. "You don't know what hate is. It's less than a hair's-breadth away from love, and I don't expect you to truly know what *that* is either."

Heather wondered what Roth, sitting silent and hollow-eyed beside her in the backseat, must have felt about that sentiment. She glanced worriedly at him. With the emotional and psychic trauma he'd experienced, compounded by the physical trauma of the ax wound to his shoulder, Heather suspected it might have been better if they'd just left him at Gosforth. Not that she considered it even a remote possibility that Roth would have agreed to that. Still, he looked like he was close to the point of collapse.

"Well, monster or not, Mom," Cal was saying, "I suggest you slip into charming mode yourself. Because the only way we're going to get to where we have to go, is if Dad helps us out."

"What—"

"I called him before we left Gosforth," Cal said. "He'll be waiting for us at the East Ninetieth Street ferry docks with his yacht."

His mother's knuckles went bone white as her hands clenched in her lap around a silk drawstring bag that looked yellow and brittle with age. She spat a string of words under her breath that sounded as though they may have been in Greek. They also sounded pretty impolite. Heather decided in that moment she would be very nice to Douglas Muir when she met him. Anyone who'd stomached being married to that gorgon long enough for Cal to have been born was some kind of saint or bloody-minded masochist. Either way, he deserved a healthy dose of sympathy.

"Why aren't we just using the foot bridge at 102nd Street

to get to the island?" she asked. "What do we need a boat for?"

"Because the footbridge will almost certainly be under guard," Roth said quietly. "Or the authorities will have raised the drawbridge middle section. The police and military are probably going mental wondering what the hell's going on behind the fog wall. And even though they can't get *into* Manhattan, it's a pretty sure bet they don't want anything getting *out*."

"Exactly," Cal said. "Because of that, we're going to have to time our own escape from the city carefully. Dad told me he's using a few tricks he has up his sleeve to keep the yacht itself hidden from any Coast Guard or NYPD patrol boats prowling the East River. But we're still going to have to get onboard unseen. I don't quite have that worked out just yet."

Cal pulled over as close to the ferry docks as he could without actually driving into the mist barrier and cut the engine. The Maserati was stopped in the middle of the road, but so was every other car, and Cal really didn't seem to care. They got out and clambered over a low section of a traffic barrier, heading toward where the fog edge stood between them and the water. Heather could see the docks. And she could hear the waves lapping against what sounded like the hull of a boat, but she couldn't see it.

All they had to do now was wait for the right moment when the Miasma wall fell, and make a run for it to get onboard. It already looked as though it was thinning in places, and Heather could hear voices drifting toward them from boats on the water. The authorities seemed to notice the change too, judging from the way they called out to one another.

The risk of being seen—and stopped—was huge.

"Wait." Heather dug into her pocket and found the second runegold acorn Mason had given her. "Roth?" she said. "Can you use this somehow to help us?"

He frowned down at the little golden orb in her hand. "Where do you keep getting these from?" he asked, bemused.

"The acorn fairy," Heather said.

"Right." He plucked the thing from her hand and, after a moment's thought, grinned a bit. He carved a mark onto the gleaming surface with the point of his knife blade that looked a bit like an hourglass turned on its side. "This is the twilight rune. You can use it to cast an obscuring pall—kind of like a Faerie glamour—that should grant you a sort of temporary invisibility."

"Cool." Heather nodded. "What about the rest of you?"

"Well." He glanced at Cal's mother and his grin twisted into a grimace. "I guess we'll just have to cozy up to you, hold hands, and hope for the best."

Daria returned his gaze with a stony glare. Then she turned, her eyes half-closed and one hand stretched out in front of her. Heather figured she would be able to feel when the enchantment had dissipated enough to allow them to safely make a run for it. It was, after all, her stupid evil spell . . .

"Now."

Daria reached down and took Heather's wrist—the one above the hand that held the runegold acorn in a tight fist—with fingers that were as strong as iron bands and surged forward, dragging Heather along. She barely had time to reach out and grab Roth as Cal put out a hand, grasping for her invisible shoulder, and together they walked hastily, as silently as possible, through the ferry dock gates that swung eerily open, past random people who'd been caught in the Miasma barrier when the curse manifested, all of them writhing like goldfish out of water, wide-eyed and gasping with the horrors they experienced in the nightmare fog wall.

Heather swallowed the acidy taste of fear that rose in her throat at the sight of the afflicted New Yorkers and kept moving toward the end of the pier, where a shimmery distortion in the air and water wavered like a mirage.

"Watch your step," came a low, deep voice from somewhere right ahead of them, just out over the water. "No, Daria—the gangplank's half a foot to the left. Careful now . . ."

In a linked chain like invisible schoolchildren, they trod the invisible ramp up onto the invisible luxury yacht of a semi-god. The sleek contours of the gleaming white craft faded into view as Heather clambered onboard and found herself standing on the smooth surface of a polished teak deck. She pocketed the acorn, now that the veil obscuring the yacht itself—and its occupants—kept them from the sight of any river patrols.

In front of Heather, Daria took a halting step toward a handsome man—like an older version of Cal—who was sitting in a wheelchair waiting for them.

"Douglas . . . ?" Daria's voice caught in her throat.

For a moment, Heather thought Cal's mom might actually faint. She could see the blood rushing from Daria's face, her pupils dilating as she looked down at her ex-husband, who smiled back benignly. Heather suspected he was enjoying his wife's distress, and she glanced at Cal, knowing full well from the expression on his face that he'd purposefully neglected to mention the whole wheelchair thing to his mom.

Daria swallowed noisily, struggling for composure. "What—"

"Fishing accident."

Heather blinked at Douglas Muir, startled by that. "But . . . you're a god," she said. "Aren't you?"

"Semi-god, really. We're not quite as 'bulletproof' as the full-blooded Olympians." He winked at her. "We're susceptible to injury under extreme circumstances. Especially if the wound is something inflicted by another . . . supernatural agent, shall we say."

From the corner of her eye, Heather saw Cal's hand flick up toward the scars on his face as Douglas rolled the chair forward and reached out a hand.

"You must be Heather," he said. "Welcome aboard."

"Uh. Thanks." She took his offered hand. It was warm and strong.

"And Rothgar." The two shook hands. "You look like your old man. Happy to know you don't think like him."

"Thank you," Roth said dryly. "Me too."

"Who did that to you?" Daria asked, her gaze still fastened on Douglas's blanket-covered legs.

"Perses," he answered.

Daria made an angry noise. "Damn you, Douglas—"

"He's a *non*-semi-god," he explained to Heather, ignoring

his ex-wife's outburst. "A very old, very grumpy Titan who thought he could alleviate his centuries of boredom by terrorizing the inhabitants of the smaller islands in a Mediterranean archipelago. He won't be doing that anymore." Douglas shrugged his broad shoulders, as if he was describing a successful pest-control job. "Unfortunately, he got a couple of good shots in before the end. In the water, I'm the same as ever. On land, I just need a set of wheels. I thought it was a fair trade. I think the fishing village Perses had already eaten half of did too."

"This." Daria's face twisted into a disdainful sneer. "*This* kind of thing is why I left you."

Douglas pegged her with a sharp stare, a spark of anger glittering in his sea-green eyes. "You didn't leave me, Daria. You had me surgically extracted from your life. And Cal's." His hands tightened on the arm of his chair and Heather noticed that there were very fine membranes webbing the spaces between his fingers. They didn't go far—not more than halfway up to the first knuckle and she doubted she would have even noticed them if she hadn't known who—what—he was. "I had to find something worthwhile to do with my spare time while I was busy *not* raising my son."

"I kept him from you because I didn't want him to end up like you."

"What? Free?" Douglas snapped angrily. "You'd rather he spent his existence as a servant of gods rather than as a god himself."

"I'd rather he spent his existence as a human. Not as

some kind of freakish hybrid."

"Hey!" Cal rolled his eyes. "I'm right *here*?"

Daria waved off his protest, as usual. "It's not your fault, Calum."

"She's right. It's mine." There was hurt and hardness in Cal's dad's eyes as he looked at his ex-wife. "Silly me, I thought a little thing like love was more important than some stray, sparkly bits of DNA."

"You can make light of it all you want," Daria snapped. "It's that kind of thinking that has brought us to this point. Ask Yelena—oh, wait, no . . . you can't, because she's *dead*. All because Gunnar Starling wanted to dress up and play Odin. Mortals are not gods and they should stop acting like them." There were angry tears shining in her eyes.

"You know, you might have a point, Mrs. A," Heather interrupted, able to stand the bickering no more. "Maybe Cal would be better off without the freaky-cool fish fork and superstrength. Who knows? But you know what? It's not going to matter in a few hours and we'll never know one way or another if we don't use every advantage we have— including Cal—because there will be nobody left to have the argument."

"She's right," Roth said. "Next to Fennrys, and probably Mason—and, quite honestly, with what's happened to the two of them, I'm not even sure we can trust what side they'll end up on when this all hits the fan—Cal's the strongest one of all of us." He turned to Daria and Douglas. "Whether you meant for him to be that way or not, he is. We're going to need that strength. And while I know it's almost unheard of for such a thing to happen in a Gosforth founding house, maybe you should put aside all the family crap and work toward a common goal. For once. Maybe we all should. Maybe, if we do that, we can actually achieve something worthwhile and stop the world from ending."

XX

The train pulled into Valhalla station and nothing seemed out of the ordinary. There was a side rail that was reserved for Gunnar Starling's private use, and that's where Toby guided Sleipner to come to rest. Mason wondered fleetingly if, after they were gone, the fabulous transformed beast wouldn't just vanish into thin air. Or take to the skies. Or whatever it was that mythical, monstrous horses did in their off-duty hours.

Together, she, Fennrys, Toby, and Rafe crossed the small, mostly empty parking lot. Like the dedicated side rail, there was also a small carport near the quaint little station that was reserved for the black town car that was always there, parked and ready to shuttle Starling family members to and from the estate a few miles away. Normally, Toby would have had a set of car keys—news to Mason but not surprising, considering what she now knew of him—but he hadn't thought to bring them along.

"Not a problem," Rafe said, stepping past them.

"Right. You've got some kind of magick trick." Mason nodded.

She assumed that's how a god would normally circumvent locks and keys, and was a bit shocked when, instead, he shattered the driver's-side window with a sharp blow from his elbow, reached in to open the door, and snaked under the dashboard so he could hotwire the ignition in under a minute.

Toby took the wheel and drove with Rafe in the front passenger seat. Mason and Fennrys sat in the dark, plushly upholstered back, both of them silently staring out their respective windows, watching the dark shapes of trees slide past. Mason had never been a party girl in high school. She wasn't much of a drinker and she didn't smoke pot like some of the other kids did, so she really didn't have much of a frame of reference when it came to the idea of intoxication. But that was really the only way she could describe how she was feeling in that moment. The inside of her skull felt as though there were currents of electricity firing across its surface—tiny spears of lightning forking through her brain and flaring behind her eyes. Her pulse was deep and steady and swift—and louder than she had ever felt—like a hammer pounding on stone. Her skin was ice and fire. A good six inches separated Mason's knee from Fennrys's, but it felt like sparks arced between them.

She knew, just by the way she felt, that she was right about where they were headed. The Valkyrie soul in her knew, and that's why she felt almost drunk with bottled excitement.

They were on the right track. She just didn't know if they were doing the right *thing*. The Estate was where Mason would find her mother—she was sure of it—and she knew, beyond any doubt, that was something she *had* to do.

If only to say good-bye before the end.

Ragnarok. The end . . . and a fresh beginning.

Her father's dearest wish.

Mason wondered then, if her mother *hadn't* died, would her father still have rushed headlong toward the fulfillment of the prophecy? If Yelena hadn't sacrificed herself, for Mason's sake, maybe *she* would have been the thing in Gunnar's life that kept him wanting to live. But she had made her choice thinking it was the right one to make. Now Mason was doing the same thing.

And maybe it's all for nothing, but the choice is mine . . .

She closed her eyes, and felt Fennrys's hand wrap around hers.

When she looked over at him, she saw that his eyes were gleaming, silvery-blue in the darkness. The Wolf inside him was just as keyed up as the raven inside her. There wasn't any way for them to turn back now.

"We will finish this together," Fenn whispered, lifting their joined hands between them. "To whatever end . . . we'll get there *together*."

He wrapped his other hand around hers and she kissed his fingers.

When she turned back to look out the window, it was to see that they were driving through the gates of the Starling family estate. Looming up in front of them, at the end of the long winding drive was the manor house, like a castle that needed storming. Only, Mason knew that the house itself wasn't why she was there. There was nothing in that grand, empty echoing monument to loneliness that she needed. The manor's many darkened windows glared down at her like the hollowed eye sockets of moon-bleached skulls, stacked for offering to a battle god.

She would find nothing there.

That was her father's place.

His study, full of secrets and locked boxes and books, with its cavernous fireplace hearth like a yawning maw, the apple-wood fire unlit within . . . that was where she could go if she wanted to find *him*. All of the pieces of him. The rune-gold, the regrets, the words in his diary and the picture of her mother on the mantelpiece that Mason wasn't even sure he looked at anymore . . .

In her head, there was another picture, suddenly: the image of three women, wild-eyed with wanton looks, lounging draped over the leather furniture in the study, surrounded by all that oak paneling, and Mason knew, with certainty, that the Norns had visited her father in that house. The house that, even with all of the windows open, had *always* felt to Mason like a prison cell. And she wondered for the first time if it was truly the incident in the garden shed, with Rory and the game of hide and seek, that had been solely responsible for her claustrophobia. . . .

"Oh!" she gasped suddenly, and opened the car door, lurching out before Toby had even fully braked to a stop in front of the sweeping stone steps of the house.

"Mase!"

Fennrys dove out of the other side of the still-moving car. She could hear him running up behind her, his boots crunching on the stone walkway, and she turned when she felt his hand on her wrist, but she didn't stop.

"Hey . . . are you okay?" he asked.

"I know!" she said, almost breathless with excitement. "Oh, Fenn—I know where she is!"

"Find me," her mother had said.

At least, that's what Mason had told Fennrys about her version of the dream-vision. Initially, he'd been skeptical about the possibility, even if he'd kept it to himself. When they'd left Asgard, Fennrys had promised Mason that, when all the craziness was over, they would go back and look for Yelena— the *real* Yelena—and rescue her from wherever Heimdall had imprisoned her. But truthfully, he'd suspected that might be a hard promise to keep. Because, short of crossing back over Bifrost—which Mason's brother Roth had so very helpfully blown to kingdom come anyway—Fenn hadn't had the foggiest idea how they were going to do that. Not really.

When Mason had puzzled out the message in their shared visions—that they would find the answers they were looking for at her home back in Westchester—he was still skeptical. But with New York City falling to pieces all around them, nowhere to go, and nothing *he'd* managed to figure out to help fix the whole bloody mess, Fenn had been willing to go with her when she'd called Sleipner in the tunnel. Largely because, really, who wouldn't? The sudden appearance of the mythic equine juggernaut, standing there docile as a petting zoo pony and willing to do Mason's bidding, was, in itself, a pretty persuasive argument. And once onboard the train and moving, Fenn had felt the pull of destiny. He felt it now as he ran along behind Mason, leaving Toby and Rafe still clambering out of the car in front of the house.

This estate must be huge, he thought as they ran, wondering how on earth they would ever find Yelena there.

The manicured grounds around the back of the house—a series of terraced, putting-green-perfect lawns bordered by flower-laden rock gardens—gave way gradually to wilder, less structured landscapes. A waving sweep of wildflower meadow rolled away to a rocky streambed that twisted through the property and, beyond that, there was actual forest. Not just trees, but *forest*—dark and deep. Mason leaped like a deer down the garden path, flat-out running through the meadow.

Eventually, Fennrys stopped shouting after her, asking where the hell she was going, and saved his breath so he could just run and keep up. The farther away they got from the house, the more apparent it became that the outer grounds of the estate weren't something that Gunnar Starling cared for with the same sort of meticulous attention as the ordered spaces closest to the house. An ornamental rustic footbridge spanning the tumbling stream near the forest had partially collapsed, the middle arch having rotted and fallen into the water.

It's like Bifrost in miniature, Fenn thought as he leaped from one bank to the other in Mason's wake.

She didn't even pause, just hurdled the stream and kept on running straight into the dense trees soaring up ahead of her, and Fennrys knew that, whatever instinct was driving her, there was a rightness to her actions. He could feel it himself and excitement surged in his chest. Suddenly, he realized that they were following an overgrown path, and Mason's feet pounded along the moss and leaves as if she knew every twisting inch of it blindfolded. In her wake, Fennrys saw the branches of trees along the path suddenly grow heavy with pale purple blossoms, as if caught in a wash of accelerated spring fever. The air grew perfumed and heady, like the scented breeze in the dream-vision he'd shared with Mason. When the track hair-pinned around a stand of elm, Fennrys lost sight of her and, after a moment, he heard a small, startled cry.

"Mason!" he called and poured on a burst of speed.

He rounded the trees and virtually screeched to a halt as the path suddenly widened into a small clearing ringed by blooming apple trees laden with drifts of lavender flowers and open to the sky above. Mason had stopped short too, and Fennrys almost ran right into her. She stood at the edge of the clearing, which boasted a small, squat structure at its center. Like something out of a fairy tale, it looked like a witch's cottage, windows shuttered from the inside and massively overgrown with ivy now. The roof, Fennrys saw, was made of glass panels in iron frames, like an old greenhouse. The glass was dark with years of grime, and some of the panels had shattered, allowing the ivy to creep inside. It reminded him uncomfortably of some of the decaying buildings on North Brother Island. There were wine-barrel tubs full of dirt and dead weeds on either side of the door, which was painted green, only faded and peeling.

And there was a slide-bar lock on the door.

"Mase," Fennrys whispered. "Is this . . . ?"

"Where I died," Mason said. She nodded silently and took a step forward.

Inside, she knew, there would be a wooden bench.

Once upon a time, it had been painted bright blue, decorated with red roses.

Her mother had painted it that way. Mason didn't know how she knew that; she just did. When Rory had locked her in the shed on that day of the hide-and-seek game, Mason had fallen asleep on that bench. The paint had faded, the blue washed to gray, green leaves pale and dull, but the roses had remained bright. Mason had counted the petals over and over in her loneliness and fear over the next three days. Roses. Her mother's maiden name had been Rose.

And this had been her place.

Mason walked toward the door of the little potting cottage as if she were walking through a dream. She'd never gone back there after they'd found her. Never even thought to. Never dared cross again over the stream that ran before the forest. There was a newer lock on the door—a chain and padlock that Gunnar had obviously put there after the hide-and-seek game—but Mason wondered why her father had never had the old rotting little shack just torn down after that.

Because she's still here.

Her mom. This had been her place. Her orchard. Her garden shed. Her bench.

And she was still there. In more than just spirit.

Mason drew the knife that Fennrys had given her from her belt and struck off the padlock with a single blow of the hilt. The door swung soundlessly open and a dull red-gold flickering shaft of light spilled out through the gap. Which was strange, because the place was so clearly deserted.

"What the hell . . . ?" Fennrys murmured as he ducked inside after her.

No . . . Hel, Mason mentally corrected him. But she couldn't speak.

Inside the shed there was no glass-paneled roof, no wooden shelves or rusting garden tools. The bench was there in the middle of an otherwise empty dirt floor, surrounded by rough-hewn walls of stone. Rust-coated chains ending in manacles hung from iron rings pounded into those walls and the only light, the source of the wavering glow, was a single guttering torch set in a sconce. On one side, the wall wasn't a wall at all, but floor-to-ceiling bars. A prison cell. A cage.

And Fennrys knew it well. Mason knew that, too.

Because, before he could stop himself, his left hand was circling his right wrist in the place where the scars marked him as having been a prisoner here. And suddenly Mason could see him falling back into that place, the darkness and the stench of decay, wondering frantically if it had all been a delusion. Thinking that maybe he'd never left this place at all and was still there, chained to the wall, naked, alone . . .

"Fennrys?"

His head jerked back as her voice cut through his moment of panic.

"Fenn?"

She gently pried his fingers away from his own wrist and looked up at him, his eyes were so silver-blue bright they almost outshone the torch on the wall.

"Come on," she said.

Fennrys took her hand as she started to lead him toward the barred door.

A noise stopped them both in their tracks. They turned and looked back as slowly, tortuously, a shadow—like a clot of ink-black darkness—coalesced, draped across the bench. At first, it looked like a bundle of black rags, but as they watched, it resolved into a figure—a woman—who lifted her head and pushed back the deep, ragged cowl of the cloak she wore. Her face was carved thin and wasted, blue eyes sunken in her head. But she smiled gently when she looked on Mason's face.

"Mom!" Mason cried and lurched back toward the bench, folding herself around Yelena Starling's frail form and hugging her tight. "I found you! I told you I'd find you . . ."

"My baby," Yelena murmured into Mason's hair. "I never doubted that you would."

Fennrys knew, instinctively, what had happened.

When Roth, as a young child, had unwittingly caused the death of his little sister—and Yelena, by then a powerful death goddess in her own right, had intervened and sent her baby girl back into the world—a doorway into Helheim had been opened in that shed. And it had stayed open, if only a crack. Not big enough for anyone but Mason Starling herself to force a way through. But she had, and now they could bring her mother back out into the world. Heimdall had imprisoned Yelena in the very same cell that Fennrys himself had been locked away in when the Valkyrie Olrun had tried to take him across the Rainbow Bridge as a hero of Valhalla.

Only, there had been no blue bench in the cell when Fenn had been there.

None that he had been able to see. But Yelena had been his way out, just as he and Mason were now hers. He knelt down beside Mason and her mother and said, "Hello, Lady. It's nice to finally see you again."

Yelena looked down into Fennrys's face and smiled. She lifted her hand and placed it gently on his cheek. Her wrist was circled with one of the manacles from the wall. Fennrys recognized it. It was still stained with *his* blood.

"I knew I was right about you," she said. "I knew you would take care of my daughter." Her shoulders sagged in weariness and her hand went limp as her eyes fluttered closed.

"We take care of each other, ma'am," Fenn said in a gentle voice. His eyes locked with Mason's over her mother's dark head. "And we'll take care of you, too. Let's just get this fancy bracelet off and we'll be out of here in no time. . . ."

Yelena shook her head. "Heimdall has the only key. He stole it from me. The shackle is one of those things that the dwarves fashioned to keep 'monsters' like Loki and his offspring bound. Made of strange metals and impossible things . . . Without the key, it's hopeless. It would take Thor's hammer."

Fennrys grinned and looked up at Mason. "How about a 'mace' instead of a hammer?"

She blinked at him. "Did you just pun?"

"Horribly. Yes. I thought the situation could use a little levity. Y'know, chained mom and all, here." He waved a hand at the sword hilt at her side. "C'mon, Mase. What's made of more powerful magick than Odin's spear? Use it to break the chain."

Mason hesitated.

"It's just for a moment," he said. "If a battle looms, you can shift right back."

Easier said than done and he knew it, but Yelena had gone limp on the bench between them and seemed to be getting weaker with each passing second. Her eyes fluttered open briefly when her daughter drew the Odin spear sword and transformed into her Valkyrie self, bringing the head of the spear crashing down on the manacle with a furious cry. There was a flash of storm lightning and the sound of rolling thunder . . . and then darkness.

Mason muttered, "I'm getting really tired of the meteorological sound track that follows me around wherever I go. . . ."

She willed herself back out of her Valkyrie guise as Fennrys chuckled and threw the shattered manacle into the corner of the cell. He lifted Yelena up off the bench and cradled her to his chest as he stood. Mason led the way back out of the now-dark shed into the clearing, where the ground was frosted with twilight-hued petals that had fallen from the trees like confetti.

It felt like walking out of the prison cell all over again for Fennrys. Only this time he was wearing pants and had his memories intact. And Mason Starling was at his side. He could do this. This whole stop-the-Ragnarok-train-before-it's-too-late thing. *They* could.

As he carried Mason's mother in his arms out into the clearing in front of the shed, he felt her lift his medallion in her hand. "Loki . . . ," she murmured. "He has touched this with his magick. I can tell."

Fennrys looked down at Yelena. "Yeah," he said. "It sort of acts like one of those electroshock dog-control collars now. . . ." He saw her expression turn quizzical out of the corner of his eye and tried to explain. "He did it to help me keep control after Mason sort of, uh, accidentally turned me into the *actual* personification of the Fenris Wolf. Which is why Ragnarok is on its way, which is why we're trying to stop it, which is why we're here to find you and maybe get some help with that . . ."

He realized he was kind of babbling when Mason's mother began to squirm a bit in his arms and asked him politely to stop and put her down. He did as she asked. She stood and wavered a bit and both Mason and Fennrys put out hands to steady her.

"I'm fine." Yelena shrugged them away and pulled herself up to her full height. "My strength returns. I just needed a moment out of that shackle and away from that cell. But . . ."

She turned and pegged Fenn with the same fierce sapphire

stare that Mason always used when she was challenging him on something.

"I think you'd better tell me just what on earth you've been up to with my daughter since I set you free!"

XXI

Truthfully, before that moment, Mason and Fennrys had figured that Yelena—with her powers as Hel—already knew everything that had gone down between them and *that* was why she'd appeared to Mason in her dream-vision. But apparently that was not the case. In fact, Yelena told them, ever since she'd been captured and imprisoned by Heimdall, she'd been ignorant of everything that had happened in the mortal realm. And her awareness of all that had transpired there since the time of Mason's birth and her own death had always been inconsistent and incomplete. She'd known that her daughter would need the Fennrys Wolf, and so she'd sent him to her. But she hadn't, necessarily, known exactly why she would need him. Not that it mattered.

All that mattered to Mason was that her mother was there and she was alive.

"No . . . I'm not," Yelena explained hesitantly, disabusing

her of that joyful notion. "Mason, honey, that's something you'll have to understand. When all this is over, I'm not going to be able to stay here. My place is in Helheim now."

"We can talk about this later," Mason had said, not really willing to entertain the thought that, having just found her mother, she would have to let her go again once they averted the apocalypse.

That's if we avert the apocalypse . . .

In the end, she and Fennrys told Mason's mother everything that happened between the two of them, just as she had demanded. Well, everything relevant to the situation, leaving out the fact that the two of them were desperately in love. Neither of them was sure how Yelena would take the fact that the bodyguard she had sent to take care of her daughter was inclined to do more with her body—and the rest of her—than simply guard it.

As they talked, they walked slowly toward the boat dock, and that was where Toby and Rafe found them. Now . . . they were waiting. Mason really wasn't entirely sure what they were waiting *for*. But she was getting impatient. She'd thought about keeping her Valkyrie armor on—in case what they had to face next was something that warranted intimidating—but, really, it probably would have been overkill under the circumstances.

After all, the lake dock was placid and peaceful. And it was currently populated with no less than a centuries-old superwarrior, an ancient Egyptian werewolf god, a Norse—or, rather, *the* Norse—werewolf, and the goddess of Hel.

And, in the less than half an hour since they'd rescued her

from Heimdall's prison cell, Yelena seemed to have regained her full, fearsome composure as queen of an underworld kingdom. But every now and then, she would tuck a stray strand of Mason's hair back over her shoulder or give her arm a squeeze. Or Mason would catch her mother just staring at her. She could see herself reflected in those eyes that were so very like her own and the overwhelming love in that gaze told Mason that everything Yelena had done, she'd done without regret.

And she'd done it for her. The daughter she'd never even held in her arms.

It made Mason want to never leave that place. Even though she knew that wasn't a possibility. She sighed and turned to look out over the water. She was about to ask—again—what the holdup was when, out of the corner of her eye, she saw the flash of something stirring out in the middle of the lake. She took a step forward, squinting, and saw pale, pearly hair streaming out behind familiar shapes beneath the surface; nine lithe bodies with long, bright blue limbs and swirling, iridescent gowns that bubbled like sea foam. She reached over and gripped Fennrys by the arm, pointing to the darting, shadowed forms.

"Huh," he said. "The Wave Maidens. I was almost starting to wonder when they'd show up again. Should have known it would be here. Now."

"Why?" Mason asked.

"Because they're Heimdall's creatures," Yelena said, answering for him. "Some say the Bridgekeeper is the child of nine mothers. Others say that he is the father of nine daughters. The Maidens don't seem inclined to set the matter straight, calling themselves one or the other at a whim."

"Another Norse myth open to interpretation," Mason muttered. "You know, that's weirdly encouraging."

"Yeah," Fennrys grunted, glancing sideways at her. "Less so is the fact that Heimdall is the one dude who, in *any* version, really seems particularly hot on getting the whole Ragnarok ball rolling. I mean, other than the Norns and your dad, and maybe *my* dad—although I got the impression he'd rather hit the Meatpacking District and go club-hopping than hit the battlefield. Also, there's the worrying detail that, y'know, you made those ladies a promise a while back." He nodded his chin at the water, where one of the Maidens had surfaced, and was gazing at Mason with a smile on her face and an excited gleam in her bright eyes.

Yelena raised an eyebrow at her daughter, who reddened a bit under the scrutiny. "You didn't tell me that."

"I didn't know!" Mason sputtered a bit. "I mean, I forgot that part, and at the time, nobody had bothered to tell me what a bad idea that was."

"What was it you promised them again?" Fenn asked dryly.

Mason thought he was treating the whole matter a bit lightly, considering the fact that he knew perfectly well that she'd essentially bartered his life for that earlier rescue. How on earth was she to have known that Fennrys would turn out to be the actual mythical monster prophesied to devour Odin who, it turned out, was her very own father? All she'd wanted at that time was just not to drown. Not die. She would have promised the same thing, even if she'd known then what she knew now.

"Mason?" her mother prodded.

"I told them that when the time came and I knew the Devourer, that I would make an end of him."

"So there's that," Fennrys said and shrugged in a kind of resignation.

It infuriated Mason. "Stop that!" she said. "I'm not going to 'end' you."

Yelena raised a hand, a look of intense contemplation on her lovely face. "Is that *exactly* what you promised them?"

"Um . . . something like that," Mason said warily. "I might not have the exact sentence structure, but I'm pretty sure that's the gist of it, yeah."

"Mase?" Rafe said, stepping forward. Having recently extracted another promise from Mason, he was, perhaps more than anyone, qualified to offer up his thoughts on the matter. "I want you to really think about this one. Your father misinterpreted the punctuation in the prophecy of the Norns and it changed the whole meaning of the thing."

"How is that possible?" Mason asked. "I mean . . . this prophecy has been kicking around for so long, I can't imagine it was even written in English originally."

But Toby seemed to be onboard too, with whatever the others were thinking. "No . . . no. They're right, Mase." A thread of excited tension tightened his voice. "It's all in how it was communicated to him, but even *more* so, how Gunnar chose to decipher it. Interpretation is everything. *Think.*

What—exactly—did you hear the Maidens say to you in the Hudson River?"

Mason closed her eyes and thought hard.

Too hard.

It wasn't coming to her. Especially not now, with the constant drone of leashed-in Valkyrie blood lust humming in the back of her mind that she had to try so hard to shut out after every time she armored up.

"Relax," Fennrys murmured in her ear, his voice gently lulling like a hypnotist's, which was both helpful and distracting. "Just put yourself back there, cast your memory back to that moment. We were under the water. There were creatures below us and fire above, and I was with you. We thought we were going to drown . . . and then the Wave Maidens saved us and they spoke. They spoke to you . . ."

Mason pictured the beautiful water girls, with their long pale hair and their bright blue skin and glittering emerald eyes. She remembered their excitement as they chased away the dark, savage shapes of the Nixxie that had attacked them in the depth of the river. She could hear their voices, musical and liquid, like the water in her ears. They'd spoken directly into her mind. And they had said . . .

"You will know of the Devourer . . . ," she whispered, remembering.

There was an answering keen from the Maidens in the lake.

And then what?

"You will make an end of him—"

No. That wasn't it, exactly.

"You will make *of him* an *end*!" Mason said, her eyes

snapping open, heartbeat fluttering excitedly in her throat. "That's what it was. You will make of him . . . an end."

Fenn let his breath out in a controlled exhale.

"Okay," he said, his brow furrowing. "Okay . . . that's good."

"It is?"

"I think so. I think it means you don't have to kill me to satisfy your promise." He grinned. "Not unless you want to, that is."

Working through the semantics, the technicalities of her promise, Mason felt a surge of hope. As if the sun had suddenly come out from behind a dark cloud to warm her face.

"So it just means I have to . . ."

"Use me . . . to *bring about* the end." Fenn's jaw muscle spasmed as he ground his teeth together. "Right. That's *not* so good."

But Mason refused to let her hopeful sun disappear back behind that cloud.

"Wait!" she exclaimed, grabbing at Fennrys's shirt front. "I didn't promise them *what* end. Did I?"

Yelena glanced back and forth between the two of them. "Did you?"

Mason slowly shook her head.

"No," she said with certainty. She was sure now. Absolutely positive. "I promised *an* end. Not *the* end. Not their end . . ." Mason pulled Fennrys toward her, looking up at him, until her nose almost touched his chin. "And one way or another, Fennrys Wolf . . . we *will* end this."

His smile was a slow blooming thing of wild beauty. It

split his face as he lifted Mason off the ground. "Now, that is definitely my girl talking," he said, kissing her hungrily on the mouth.

Mason didn't even care that Toby and her mother and Rafe were standing there, pretending like she wasn't on the verge of totally making out with Fennrys. Her hopeful sun was still in the sky over her head and all was—at least, all *would* be— right with the world.

We will make it right.

The actual dark and storm-tossed sky above her head did nothing to dispel her sudden, fierce surge of optimism as she stepped reluctantly out of Fenn's embrace and turned to face the waters of the Kensico Reservoir.

Now, she thought. *How to fulfill my promise to the Maidens? How to use Fennrys to bring about an end?*

She cast her gaze out over the flat, pewter-gray glassy mirror of the lake, where the circle of goddesses waited and suddenly, she knew. She hadn't just come back to the estate to find her mother. She had also come back to find *his.* Before any of the others had a chance to question her, Mason drew the Odin spear, her Valkyrie mantle fell upon her once more, and she called out a name.

"Sigyn!" she cried. "Your son needs you!"

"Mase?" Fennrys exclaimed. "What the hell are you—"

His cry was drowned out as the surface of the lake began to seethe and boil, waves rippling out, silver rings crisscrossing as the Wave Maidens darted and dived, flitting with a single guiding impulse through the shadowy depths like a school of fish, flashing like lightning as they circled around and around, hair streaming, limbs knifing through the water. Mason could feel the waves of power gathering, flowing outward, as the Norse goddesses helped her call forth the impossible.

"What are they doing?" Toby asked in an almost whisper.

"Naglfar," Yelena whispered.

It was a word—a name—that Mason didn't instantly recognize. But even the sound of it stirred great fear, and even greater excitement in her.

"The Ship of the Dead," Rafe said, his deep voice hushed.

"The ship of my birth," Fennrys countered quietly.

The fleeting vision Mason had experienced of the cloaked figure sitting on a wooden bench in a sea-scented fog, holding a wrapped bundle, played over in her mind. Out in the lake, the Maidens keened an eerie song and slowly a dark leviathan stirred somewhere deep beneath the surface of the water. Beside Mason, Fennrys was holding his breath. Something she'd never known him to do before. And yet, she completely understood the reaction. The tension of the moment was almost unbearable. The clouds in the sky above seemed to pause, and there wasn't even a hint of breeze or birdsong.

The middle of Kensico Reservoir erupted in a mighty geyser, exploding upward in a diamond and rainbow shower of water. And a dragon-prowed ship of legend thrust high into the air. Like some kind of great ancient sea monster heaving itself up out of a watery slumber, *Naglfar*, the great, ghostly fabled Norse Ship of the Dead, climbed skyward and hung suspended for a moment before slamming back down onto the surface of the lake, sending a circular wall of water blooming out in a white froth. Then the low-sided, elegant long ship began to float gently, silently toward the shore where they stood waiting.

The bare skeletal finger of a single mast thrust up from the center of the ship, and the crossbeam, without a sail, was a stark black slash across the sky. A row of round shields, battered and battle-worn, hung from the ship's sides above the rows of oars that stuck out into the water, moving in unison, like the limbs of some prehistoric, many-legged creature. And pulling at those oars were the ghosts of the men who had rowed an extraordinary woman across an ocean so that she could give birth to a prophecy.

The Fenris Wolf. The Devourer. The Harbinger of Ragnarok.

The love of Mason Starling's young life.

Standing in the prow, her long, pale hair lifted by a ghost breeze, the tall, broad-shouldered woman in a green gown and cloak was not beautiful but, rather, handsome, with strong, angular features, and eyes that held the wealth of her will and strength and determination to shape her life according to her own desires and not the tenants of some apocalyptic foretelling.

Mason could see instantly why Loki had loved her.

She turned and glanced at Fennrys and was startled by the unaccustomed softness of his expression. He gazed out at his mother as the ship drew close, and Mason saw in him a rare moment of, if not pure happiness, peace, at least.

Fenn's past had always been a thorny issue for him—even when he hadn't been able to remember any of it—and to see him like that made Mason more determined than ever that they would forge their future according to *their* terms. She felt her own mother's arm lightly drop across her shoulders and, for a moment, she leaned against her, feeling the warmth that had been absent when Heimdall had impersonated Hel in her infernal realm.

The ship's keel scraped on the rocky beach and four of the gray, ghostly warrior sailors leaped over the sides, hauling frayed and weed-wrapped ropes with them as they pulled the shallow-draft warship up the strand. The tall woman nimbly hurdled the side wall of the boat and waded ashore, the hems of her tunic and cloak dragging with the weight of the water they soaked up past her knees as she walked with long strides toward Fennrys, who stood at Mason's side. She felt his hand tighten briefly in hers. Then he let go to step forward to greet his mother's ghost.

At Mason's other side, Hel also stepped forward.

Sigyn embraced her son—a brief, vigorous, heartfelt hug—and then turned to Mason's mother and bowed deeply from the waist. Mason got the impression that, had it been anyone but this woman, the occasion would have warranted a curtsy. But then the two women—or, really, the ghost and the goddess of death, if one was going to get technical—clasped hands like old friends.

"It has begun then?" Sigyn asked them.

No time for small talk or introductions, I guess, Mason thought. But she barely even heard herself over the inner clamoring of her Valkyrie spirit.

Rafe nodded. "We'd like it to end. But not The End, if you get my meaning."

"Whatever the outcome, whatever the end, you must meet the enemy on the final battlefield of Valgrind." Sigyn glanced back at the Wave Maidens. "They will demand it of you."

"I'm guessing we're nowhere near that at the moment." Toby grunted, glancing around. "We're nowhere near anything."

Sigyn smiled. "When I came here—when *we* came here— we crossed an ocean that we had been told was uncrossable. Endless until it fell off the edge of the world. But then we found this place. This land, untouched, unknown, and we sailed this ship up a river as far as we could until we reached this valley. When it used to be a valley and the river was navigable. We will make it so again. And we will ride that river to the end. To Valgrind."

The Wave Maidens began to keen with excitement and a shiver went up Mason's spine. The Odin spear almost seemed to quiver in response.

"I think I can help with that." Mason's mother stepped forward and, raising her arms, sent forth a thick cloud of ash-black shadow that flowed like liquid through the air toward *Naglfar*. Weaving and writhing, it crawled up the mast and clung to the crossbeam, unfurling like inky canvas. The Wave Maidens leaped and danced in the water and a ghost wind sprang up to fill the shadow sail.

Fennrys glanced at Mason. She nodded, and he stepped toward *Naglfar*, stopping before the gap in the line of shields hanging on the ship's side and, with a sweeping gesture, said, "All aboard who's going aboard."

★ ★ ★

"Am I the only one who sees the dam?" Rafe inquired casually.

The ship raced southward across the glass-smooth surface of the reservoir.

"The massive, solid, impassable dam?"

On either side of *Naglfar*'s dragon prow, the Maidens leaped and frolicked in the frothy wake, like dolphins cavorting. Thirty feet in front of them, the Kensico Dam loomed. Mason strode forward to the prow of the ship and hurled the Odin spear. A huge chunk of concrete exploded from the lip of the massive concrete wall.

"We're still not gonna clear that." Rafe shook his dreadlocked head as the spear returned to Mason's armored fist.

But then the Maidens sang, and the waters of the Reservoir surged forward in a huge wave, pouring through the gap in a gushing waterfall, taking *Naglfar* with it. They sailed over the gap in the dam wall—a crescent-shaped bite large enough to let the ship pass through without emptying the entire Reservoir and wiping out the valley to the south of them. Instead, borne on the wave that the Maidens had called up, the ghost ship rode the bucking froth down through the flood plain and into the winding path of the Bronx River, once a much larger waterway, now flooding with that single surge, like a tidal bore racing to the ocean and taking the long ship with it.

The path of the Bronx River snaked through the middle of a series of heavily industrialized and populated areas, almost entirely hidden in a rich green seam that no one knew was there, covered over at intervals by bridges and freeway overpasses. None of which proved an impediment to *Naglfar*. As they traveled abreast on a magickal wave on a river that had long since diminished to a stream, the smoke sail passed— insubstantial—through all obstacles, billowing and snapping in the phantom wind.

After she'd thrown the spear at the dam, Mason had sheathed the weapon, shaken by the surge of power that had flooded through her. Now she sat near the back of the ship on a bench empty of ghostly rowers, picking at a stray thread on the seam of her jeans, feeling shaky and uncertain, and just a little alone, in the ebb of her display of Valkyrie might. Fennrys was heads-down with Toby, discussing battle strategies—*not* that it was going to come to that—and Rafe had engaged Mason's mom in Underworld deity chat. Mason thought he might have developed a bit of an instant crush on her. Not surprising, they had a lot in common.

Mason sat there, lost in thought, when the bench beside her creaked and she looked over to see that she'd been joined by Sigyn. The striking blond woman smiled at her but didn't force conversation. After a while, when Mason felt like talking, she said, "You know my mom?"

Sigyn nodded.

"How did that happen?"

"I had been long dead, a shade wandering Helheim for a long time before your mother and I met," she said in a language that, while Mason's ears heard as foreign and unknown, her brain interpreted in lilting English. "When I found Loki there, bound and tortured by the serpent, I did my best to keep the poison from falling onto his face."

"You still loved him, after he left you like that?"

Sigyn simply nodded.

"He told me about you," Mason said.

Fennrys's mother smiled sadly. "After a long time, he begged me to leave him. He said that watching me suffer as he suffered was worse than the torment itself. Eventually I came to believe him. And so, as much as I loved him, I left him."

"Loki made my mother a goddess," Mason said. "Why?"

"Because *I* asked him to," Sigyn said. "I met your mother first when she was a new shade in the Beyond. The first Lady Hel had long since departed, like so many of the others, shedding the mantle of her power. Power that Loki, as the only god left in Helheim, gathered with his will and kept safe until such time as he could bestow it upon another. In much the same way that the Norns gathered Odin's power and the power of Thor after the gods themselves departed."

"It's all a little hard to wrap my head around," Mason said.

Sigyn nodded. "I imagine it is, yes. Yelena and I talked and she told me of the prophecy the Norns had given your father. She told me that she had denied her foretold fate and willed you to be born a daughter, and not a son. That's when I knew that Yelena had power of her own. And I took her to Loki, who granted her even more. Together, we vowed that we would one day set things right for our children if we could."

"Why didn't Loki give *you* the original Hel's power?"

"I had been a shade for too long by then." Sigyn shrugged.

"Yelena still had the echo of her humanity about her. And she had *willed* you to be born a girl. She had strength enough to withstand the bestowing. And she made a fine goddess."

Mason smiled at her mother where she sat, talking to Rafe. Pride for the woman who went through so much so that she could give Mason a chance to beat the prophesied odds. She vowed not to let her down. The only thing was, she didn't know how to make that happen.

"How are we going to win this?" Mason asked, and even she could hear the hint of desperation in her voice. "Everything we do seems to bring the inevitable closer. Now we've raised the Ship of Souls. Just another piece on the Ragnarok chessboard. Isn't this what my father wants?"

"He wants the game to go his way, yes. But in order to play by your own rules, you still have to put all the pieces on the board. How you move them is up to you." Sigyn reached out to lay a hand on Mason's shoulder. Then, without another word, she rose and moved to speak with the gray shape piloting the ship.

Mason watched her go and then turned her attention to the scenery passing swiftly by. She didn't know where they were going, and she didn't know what they would find when they got there. But it suddenly occurred to her that maybe she should find out. She reached into the pocket of her jeans and pulled out Rory's pilfered phone.

The boat was gathering speed as the river widened perceptibly in front of them, when Fennrys heard Mason utter a dismayed groan. He glanced over and, telling Toby he'd be right back, stepped over the rowers' benches to get to the back of the boat.

"What's the matter?" he asked.

Mason was holding a phone in her hand and with a look of weary resignation, she showed him the image on the glowing screen.

"What am I looking at?" he asked, staring down at the blue line snaking in a twisty squiggle across a field of variegated green and brown and gray. "Besides a map, I mean. I know it's a map."

"Do you see that?" She pointed to the place where the blue line thickened and spread out into a narrow wedge, flowing into a wider blue expanse that was dotted with a couple of green splotches and crisscrossed with a few straight lines.

"I'm going to assume that this is the river we're on"—Fennrys tapped the same place Mason had pointed to—"and this is where it ends?"

"Yup."

"And that is?"

"The East River."

Fennrys frowned and overlaid the image with what he knew of New York in his mind. Suddenly he understood Mason's reaction. "Ah," he said. "And *that* little dot, right there, would be North Brother Island. Yeah?"

"Yup."

"And *that* line . . . the one near the bottom of the screen . . . would be the Hell Gate Bridge?"

"Oh yeah." Mason nodded.

"So I fought the sea monster *there* . . . and Cal's Nereids attacked us *there*."

"Right." She smiled at him with mock enthusiasm. "Lucky us! We're heading straight back into the heart of New York City's very own supernatural Bermuda Triangle."

"Of course we are," Toby said, stepping over a bench to join them.

Fennrys saw that the fencing coach was moving stiffly, as if his joints pained him. Mason reached out a hand to help steady him as he teetered a bit and sat down heavily, and Toby batted it away irritably. Then he snorted and said, "Sorry, Mase. I'm fine. Just . . . I don't have my sea legs yet."

Fenn exchanged a fleeting glance with the old warrior and saw in his eyes that it wasn't just that. But Toby was stubborn and he was proud and he certainly wasn't about to admit that he was in anything less than fighting trim. Not on the cusp of what might well prove to be the biggest battle he'd ever had to fight in all his long life. Fennrys had respected Toby from the moment he'd met him, protecting his students in the Gosforth gym from an onslaught of monsters. But his admiration for him doubled in that moment.

Mason pretty clearly felt the same way. She left Toby's diminished state unremarked upon and turned back to the phone, tapping on the screen again. "I'm texting Heather," she said. "I just asked her where she is."

After a few moments, the phone buzzed and she turned the phone around to show them Heather's reply.

On Cal's DAD's boat. SO weird.
East River.
Me, Cal, Beeotch Face, and ur bro.
The hot non-psycho one.

"I guess they left the school after we did," Toby said. "They must have hooked back up with Douglas Muir somehow."

"I guess," Mason agreed, her eyes still scanning the text message. "There's more . . ."

Just off Wards Island I think??
Going there to sow dragons teeth. Yah.
Daria's idea. I'm all WTF??
Where r U??

"Dragon's teeth?" Mason asked.

"Well, at least Daria's not about to break her perfect track record of invoking insanely dangerous curses," Toby enthused with brittle cheerfulness. "Because that would be a bummer."

"Seriously. *Dragon's* teeth?" Mason asked. "Real ones?"

Because, at this point in her life, that would in no way be surprising.

While she waited for Toby to answer, she texted:

Close. Also on boat.
Heading same direction.
B there soon. Stay SAFE.

There was no immediate answer back, so she turned again to Toby.

He sighed wearily. "In the Greek myth of the origins of the warriors of Sparta, they were said to have sprung from the teeth of a great serpent—a dragon—sown in the earth like seeds."

"Daria's gathering an army," Fennrys said. "Or . . . *growing* one."

"It would seem so." Toby nodded.

"But why?" Mason asked. "There's no one for them to fight."

"Yet." Fennrys's brow was creased in a frown.

And there won't be, Mason reassured herself adamantly. *There will be no choosing. Therefore, no third Odin son. Therefore, no one to lead the Einherjar out of Asgard.*

She had to find her father and tell him that. In the strongest possible terms. She was the chooser of the slain and *this* was her choice.

I will. Not. Choose.

He couldn't make her.

Apocalypse averted. End of story.

Driven by the Otherworldly winds, *Naglfar* was approaching the place where the Bronx River widened and spilled out into the East River. At Yelena's command, the ghost sailors of *Naglfar* steered the ship to the west, rounding a point of land and skirting north of Rikers Island penitentiary. The ship sailed silently giving them a clear view to North Brother Island on the right, South Brother Island on the left, and the head of the Hell Gate Strait, dead ahead. In between the three points of land, Mason noticed that the water, black glass on the surface, looked almost as though it was boiling deep down, shot through with twisting currents and glowing, acid-green streaks of wild magick.

In the distance to the west, the sky over Manhattan was dark and angry, lit from below with a dull orangey-red glow from the many fires—Central Park included—that burned throughout the city. It was also full of helicopters, made tiny by the distance, like a cloud of gnats, hovering over the tops of skyscrapers. Even from this far, they could hear the thumping of rotor blades and the wail of sirens. With the dissipation of the fog wall, the military had flooded back into the city.

In sharp contrast to all that frenzied activity, the hump of land directly in front of them—the northernmost end of Wards/Randalls Island—had a silent, deserted feeling. Directly in front of *Naglfar*, a large expanse of ground had been turned into a multitude of baseball diamonds arranged like scattered four-leaf clovers: nothing but flat, unimpeded grass fields and sand that stretched out for acres. Perfect staging grounds for friendly sports contests . . . or unfriendly battle.

The eerie desolation was only heightened by the spirit-white shape of Douglas Muir's boat, moored at a jetty just south of the fields, sails furled and silent. And beyond that, the stark skeleton of the Hell Gate ruin. *Naglfar*, with its shallow-draft keel designed to sail up rivers and beach on shores, needed no place to moor. The ghost sailors just hauled on the oars until the dragon prow scraped up the pebbled strip of beach on the eastern point of Randalls and came to a stop, half out of the water.

For a moment, everything was silent.

Time stopped, balanced on the edge of a blade.

Mason held her breath and knew that, somewhere on that island, her father did the same.

XXII

"You should stay here," Cal had said to Heather as Roth leaped over the side of the yacht to secure the moorings. He didn't wait for Heather's answer but just followed Roth onto the concrete dock and held out his hand to help his mother ashore.

Heather didn't even have it in her to put up a fight. Not anymore.

She had a terrible feeling about the whole endeavor. Daria had promised that the Dragon Warriors were a last resort—simply a safeguard line of defense in case things went horribly south—and until such time, the bag full of teeth she was toting around would remain firmly sealed. Of course, Daria was also the only one of them who had any kind of foreknowledge of just what they might have to face.

Heather had asked Roth if Gwen had ever given *him* any kind of insight into how this night might play out, and he said she hadn't. She believed him, if only because of the fleeting shadow of dull hurt in his eyes when he'd told her—as if he'd felt somehow betrayed by Gwen for that—and she didn't press him. Roth was one big walking open wound and Heather could feel the cut threads of his love bond with the dead girl, like strings of barbed wire waving in an ugly wind.

Love, she thought. *Sucks.*

As Roth and Cal set off with Daria on their reconnaissance, Heather leaned on the railing and watched them go. She hadn't even realized that she'd reached into her purse and pulled out the miniature crossbow she'd been carrying until she looked down and saw that she held it in her hands. She toyed with the weird little weapon and was suddenly glad that Cal wasn't there to see the blush of shame creeping up her cheeks.

She could do it. With the leaden bolt tucked in her purse, she could twist his feelings for Mason Starling in the exact opposite direction. She could make him un-love Mason. But at what price?

"That one hurts like every hell there is," Valen had said on the train when he'd given her the crossbow.

It was funny but, there had been a moment, driving through the chaotic streets of Manhattan in Cal's Maserati, when Heather had thought—for a fleeting instant—that she'd seen the heartbreaker god, perched on an overturned street vendor cart, eating an ice-cream cone. She'd recognized the dark sunglasses and the carelessly super-sexy attitude. But when she did a double take, there was no one even near the wrecked cart and Heather chalked it up to imagination.

Only . . . she thought she might have seen others, too.

People that didn't look quite like *people*. Like the way you could spot tourists in the middle of a crowd, the beings Heather had glimpsed in the darkened, storm-drenched city under supernatural siege had given off different vibes than the plain vanilla mortals.

That's what the city is going to be like, she thought. *If it survives, it'll be full of gods and monsters, hidden in plain sight.*

Fantastical, equivocal, dangerous . . .

Better than the alternative.

At least there would still be a world.

Even if it's a world full of weirdos.

Weirdos like Cal. Her Greek god ex-boyfriend. She almost envied Roth—at least he'd *known* that Gwen had loved him as much as he'd loved her—and she almost hated Mason. Except that wasn't fair. Starling hadn't asked for Cal's insane, undying love. It wasn't like she'd set out to intentionally steal Cal's heart away, either. And Heather knew that Mason would never abuse that affection.

I mean, she just wouldn't, Heather thought. *Mason's not that kind of girl. But what if—*

Her train of thought was interrupted by Douglas Muir, politely clearing his throat from right behind her. Startled, Heather spun around and fumbled the crossbow, almost dropping it. Douglas's hand shot out and he grabbed the thing before it disappeared over the side of the boat. He opened his fingers and gazed down at the elegantly ornamented little weapon. Then his eyes flicked up at Heather.

"Now, what's a nice young girl like you doing playing with

a nasty old thing like this?" he asked. His tone was gentle, but there was a sharpness beneath the words.

"I thought it might come in handy." Heather shrugged nonchalantly and snatched the bow back, shoving it into the depths of her bag. She hoped Cal's father couldn't tell from her face just how she'd thought it might come in handy.

Especially the golden arrow . . .

"I mean, it's a weapon, right?" she said. "We might need every weapon we can get our hands on. Right?"

"Human weapons." Douglas shrugged. "Maybe. Things like that? They're not for us."

"What do you mean 'us'?" Heather raised an eyebrow at him. "No offense, Mr. Muir but . . . you're not an 'us.' Not exactly."

He sighed. "I know that. I do. I remember when I first discovered that."

"Must have been awesome," Heather said.

"Worst day of my life."

She frowned at him.

"Humanity is precious, Heather." Douglas leaned forward, hands gripping the arms of his chair and his green eyes sparking fiercely. "What do you think we're fighting for here? Frail, flawed, ridiculous humanity. And all the crap and pain and sorrow that goes with it." He sighed. "You might think you can solve your problems the way a god would with that little pop gun. And you might. But you have to think about what you might lose in the process. Because when you're playing games with gods? The toughest thing you'll ever have to do is hang on to your humanity." He rolled his chair back a bit and gazed past her, to where Daria and the boys were the size of chess pieces in the distance. "Especially in the face of war and love. Even more than the gods, those things can wreak havoc on your soul. Love more than war. Ask your friend who gave you that."

"I will," she said quietly. "If I ever get the chance to meet him again."

"I hope you do." Douglas smiled. "I hope you get the chance to tell him you didn't need his help."

His smile was so much like Cal's that it made her heart hurt. But something in his words felt like the taste of hope to Heather. She savored the sensation for a long moment. But then the sky split wide open above them, and gray-gold light poured down onto the island, bringing with it the sounds of battle cries on the wind.

And hope turned to ashes in Heather's mouth.

From where he stood beneath the Bronx Kill Bridge on the north end of Randalls Island, just over a quarter of a mile from where the Ship of the Dead had beached, Rory Starling lowered a pair of night-vision binoculars and tried not to grin like a madman. Top Gunn disapproved of excessive displays of emotion. Rory kept his face turned away from where his father stood in the deeper shadows beneath the arches of the bridge, silent as a tombstone and just as still. The only thing about Gunnar that gave any indication of life was the twisting serpentine gleam of light in his left eye.

He hadn't spoken since the Norns had shown up.

It must be driving him crazy, Rory thought, *to have to tolerate their presence here tonight.* . . .

Not that there was anything Gunnar could do about it. Those three bizzaros weren't going anywhere. Directly above Rory's head, he could hear them, and see them—three shadowy shapes scurrying back and forth on the rail bridge like spiders, keening and gyrating with barely contained, powder-keg anticipation. Wild haired, wilder-eyed, and dressed head-to-toe in ragged black clothing, their excitement sizzled and sputtered like the sparks from a firecracker pinwheel.

Even after all the times he'd read the excerpts in Top Gunn's diary, Rory still hadn't been exactly sure what to expect from the trio. Sartorially, it didn't appear that they'd changed much in appearance since those days. Rather, it seemed as though the Copenhagen punk rock scene had appealed so much to the sisters' collective sense of style that they'd just decided to roll with that particular look right up until Ragnarok descended.

Maybe it's because they've come so close this time, they don't want to jinx anything, Rory thought. *Whatever. I don't get their deal. Just so long as they stay out of* my *way* . . .

Gunnar had told Rory that the current Starlings weren't the first generation of Aesir devotees to try to bring this thing to fruition. But Rory swore on his new silver hand, and on the life of his once-dead sister, that they would be the last. They would do this thing.

I *will*, he thought, as suddenly the sky overhead split open and a strange, sepulchral light flooded down onto the island.

Bringing with it the sounds of approaching war.

That's my cue!

But then, a moment later, he felt a familiar jolt in the back of his mind—a kind of warm, tingling spark. Someone had brought runegold to the island. Rory didn't even have to see it anymore to know when the golden talismans were nearby. Not after so many years of learning the secrets of the little golden acorns. His father had taken back the ones Rory had stolen from Gunnar's study and he'd felt their absence keenly ever since—like an addict forced to quit cold turkey—and a sheen of sweat sprang up on his brow now. He glanced back at his father, who was wholly focused on the ghostly ship in the distance.

So here's where I go off-script, Rory thought, and suddenly took off running.

Ignoring his father's shouts in his ears, and using the elevated rail track to shadow his movement, Rory pounded south and east, his eyes scanning the playing fields, and he stripped the leather glove from his silver hand as he ran.

Standing at the prow of the beached Ship of the Dead, Rafe scanned the island with his keen, dark gaze. Eventually, he pointed to a small, angular structure—an elevated rail bridge, part of the track structure leading to the Hell Gate at the south end of the island—and said, "There."

Fennrys stepped up beside the ancient god, squinting in the direction he pointed, and saw three tiny figures dancing madly on top of the bridge girders. Carried on the barest hint of a breeze, he heard the three mad sisters begin to keen wildly, an eerie wailing ululating, voices tangling around one another like lengths of knotted skeins. Lightning flashed directly over the bridge, capturing their exaggerated poses like flares from a photographer's flash.

"Norns?" Fenn asked.

"Drama queens . . . ," Rafe muttered through clenched teeth.

Mason joined them. "Are they alone?" she asked.

Fennrys noticed there was a bright, hectic flush of excitement in her cheeks.

He turned from her to scan the terrain. Aside from the bridge, there wasn't much in that area other than the odd chain-link fence behind the baseball diamonds. In the far distance to the south, he could see Roth and Daria and Cal walking slowly across the field. They didn't seem as if they were on their way to meet anyone. No preplanned Gosforth family summits, then. Well, that was one good thing, he supposed.

Fenn pointed them out and then said, "I don't see anyone else . . ."

"Rafe," Mason was saying, "you knew the Norns. Maybe you can talk to them."

"I don't know what good that would do."

She put a hand on his arm. "Before anyone else gets here— before my *father* gets here—maybe we could put a stop to this."

"Mase—"

"Would it do any harm to try?"

"No. I guess not . . . ," he said. He glanced at Yelena and Sigyn.

Fennrys followed his gaze. The two women, ghost and goddess, had retired to the back of the boat, hoods pulled far up around their faces. The ghost warriors of *Naglfar* had faded to almost nothing and Toby was huddled on a bench. It seemed as if it was an effort for him just to remain sitting upright. There wasn't going to be much help for them from any of those quarters if it got to the confrontation stage, Fennrys thought.

"We might as well give parlay a shot before we have to fight," he said, and gave Rafe a reluctant nod.

The god shrugged and vaulted nimbly over the side of the ship. The effect was instantaneous, unforeseen, and horrifying. . . .

The moment the soles of the ancient god's modern, stylish leather shoes touched the ground, the darkness above Randalls Island tore open and the light of the sunless skies of Valhalla poured through, sullen and glaring all at once. Fennrys heard the thunder of charging feet—multitudes of them—coming from somewhere far behind the boat. He twisted and glanced over his shoulder to where North Brother Island was lit up like Times Square with coruscating, eldritch light. When he turned back, it was to the sight of a gray arm, ropey with desiccated muscle, suddenly punching up through the turf right in front of Rafe.

Mason screamed in warning, but it was too late.

Far too late, Fennrys thought. *It always has been . . .*

Another gray fist erupted from the ground. Draugr.

Rafe's expression was stricken as he slashed through the air with one hand, manifesting the slender coppery blade he used as a weapon. He spat a venomous curse and brought the sword down in a blurred circle, severing a draugr head from its neck. But Fennrys saw that the whole of the ground beneath Rafe's feet, from the scrubby shingle of beach to the mown green lawns of the baseball diamonds beyond, seemed to writhe and heave. It was as if the ground was alive.

No. Dead, Fennrys thought. *Dead Ground . . .*

"This here's Dead Ground."

Suddenly, he could hear the voice of the troll he'd met under the Hell Gate on his very first night back in New York City. He hadn't known what "Dead Ground" had meant at the time, but he sure as hell did now. In that moment, Fennrys recalled another conversation. The one he and Maddox had had with Rafe upon entering the New York Public Library, back when he'd gone on his quest into the Underworld realms in order to find Mason and bring her home. About how the ground where Bryant Park and the library now stood had once been the burial grounds for tens of thousands of bodies, mortal remains interred in a potter's field—unmarked graves for paupers and the unclaimed dead—and how those bodies had been dug up around the turn of the century and moved. Reburied.

Rafe hadn't known where.

Fennrys knew.

All those bodies, taken from a place where a path to the Beyond Realms existed—a path to Aaru, the lost Underworld kingdom of Anubis, Lord of the Dead—had been reinterred in the soil of Wards and Randalls Island. And by setting foot on that burial land, Rafe had just reopened that path.

And recalled to horrid un-life all of those many, many dead.

It struck Fennrys with the same kind of pristine, diabolical logic in the same moment as it hit the ancient god. Rafe whirled wildly around, the look on his face one of panic and terrible realization. His eyes burned with regret as he gazed into the distance. Fennrys followed that stricken gaze and saw that the three women who'd been gyrating madly in a war dance on the Bronx Kill Bridge had gone statue still.

"Mason . . . Fennrys . . . ," Rafe called back to them. "I'm sorry! I didn't set you up, Mase—I swear it! They set *me* up! Right from the start . . ."

"What's happening?" Mason cried, grabbing at Fennrys's arm and glancing around frantically.

The shaft of Asgardian light was spread out behind them and everywhere it touched the surface of the East River, the water turned to solid ground, racing back toward the shores of North Brother Island. When the land bridge reached those shores, Fennrys saw a flash of glimmering golden roofs, and he knew that the rift had torn wide open, all the way to the Beyond. All the way to Asgard. Far distant mountains ringed what seemed to be an endless plain, the leading edge of it creeping toward them as the rift grew, displacing the dark water of the East River with earth and grass that trembled with the sounds of feet.

They came like thunder, rolling across the Otherworldly plain.

The Einherjar.

The Hell Gate Strait was transformed into the foretold battle plain of Valgrind.

And Fennrys was faced with an impossible choice.

In front of the beached—now landlocked—ship, there were draugr everywhere, heaving themselves out of the ground in a widening circle all around the ancient Egyptian god. Fennrys knew that Rafe couldn't make it back to *Naglfar*. There were too many of the draugr between them.

"Go!" he shouted. "Get out of here, Rafe! There's nothing you can do now but run . . ."

The ancient god looked as if he might protest, then—when he saw it was hopeless—he snarled in frustration and, in the blink of an eye, transformed into his wolf self. There was a gap of about two feet in the ring of lurching gray monsters and he took it, leaping with his powerful hindquarters and clearing the reach of the draugrs and their grasping talons by inches. He ran south, along the shore, and Fennrys hoped he could make it to Douglas Muir's yacht and cast off before the river disappeared entirely and the only avenue of escape closed for the ancient god. His friend . . . the one person other than Mason who had actually believed in Fennrys right from the beginning.

The one person who'd given him a second chance . . .

And a third . . .

Fennrys looked back to where Mason's mother, and his, stood like statues.

They wouldn't interfere. They couldn't. They had made their choices a long time ago and now it was up to those who came after. He looked at Toby and saw an old man. There were tear tracks on his weathered cheeks. The eternal warrior who could no longer fight, only bear witness to the battle at the end of the world. It hurt just to look at him.

"Oh god," he heard Mason whisper. "Rafe's not going to make it . . ."

Fenn turned back to see the horde of gray-skinned monsters grasping at the black wolf's hind legs. Watched him falter and fall, and struggle gamely back up, only to be dragged again into the draugr melee. The cries and yelps from his throat were piteous and pain-soaked.

The Wolf in Fennrys whined in brotherhood.

He'd already left Maddox behind, now he was going to have to stand there and let Rafe go down under a horde of draugr. And it was killing him. But there was nothing he could do. He'd promised Mason. Fenn turned and looked at her and could see himself reflected in her eyes. He saw that his own were gleaming silver-blue.

But the magick Loki wove into his medallion held. He didn't change.

He wouldn't . . .

"It's okay," Mason said, and put a hand on his heart. "Remember you will *always* be Fennrys. Now it's time to go be the Wolf."

He hesitated. Rafe screamed.

"Go!"

Fennrys tore the iron medallion from around his neck and tossed it at Mason as he leaped for the side of the ship, vaulting over it and transforming midleap. Instantly, he felt his mind transform with his body. Every instinct, every impulse, clarified and refined. Emotions dropped away.

There was nothing for him but the fight. The kill.

He ran.

When the sky split open, Roth and Daria and Cal were standing in the infield of a placid-seeming baseball diamond. And then the ground started to heave. The three of them glanced around in confusion. Even with all of the tremors in Manhattan over the last few days, this felt different. Then they saw the distant golden-roofed halls of Valhalla, shining through the rift out over the river.

"No . . . ," Daria murmured. "We're too late."

"We can't be!" Cal protested. "Unless Mason's already chosen—"

"No." Roth turned a fierce glare on him. "Mason wouldn't do that."

Daria looked at him like he'd lost his mind.

"She has no reason to!" he exclaimed, thrusting out an arm toward the empty play fields. "There's no battle here. No one to choose *from*. And even if they're called to this place, the

Einherjar won't fight without a third Odin son to lead them."

"Then clearly we have nothing to fear," Daria said drily.

"Yeah . . . nothing." Cal pointed grimly in the direction of the ancient Viking ship with the shadow-black sail beached at the far end of the island. And at the multitude of gray shapes erupting like time-lapse-photography weeds out of the earth. "Except those guys."

"Draugr." Roth's gaze went stony.

Daria reached for the pouch hanging at her belt.

"Wait." He reached out a hand and clamped it around her wrist. "What are you doing?"

"Gunnar is very clever," Daria said. "Or, at least, those who are pulling his strings are. We may be able to keep your sister from fulfilling her prophesied role, but it won't matter. Because if we do not keep *those* things"—she pointed at the draugr—"contained on this island, then all is lost, whether Mason chooses or no. It won't be Ragnarok, but . . ."

"What will it be?" Cal asked.

"Worse." Daria reached up a hand and touched the scars on Cal's face—the one's given to him by just such a creature that night in the Gosforth gym—and said, "If you had been mortal, *this* would have ended you."

Cal pushed her hand away. "They told me Fennrys did something to heal me that night."

Daria nodded. "Without his magick, and without your own . . . particular physiology, you would have died. And *then* you would have become like them. Those creatures."

Cal frowned. "A storm zombie?"

"Call it what you want."

Cal looked at Roth, who shrugged, a look of confusion on his face.

"I didn't know," he said. "I didn't know that's what happened."

"Your father didn't tell you everything, it seems," Daria said.

"Hardly surprising," Roth snapped. "I didn't tell him I thought he was a lunatic. Or that I was really working for you."

"If I *don't* bring forth the Dragon Warriors now," Daria said, "then the draugr will just kill and multiply, and kill and multiply, until there's no one and nothing left." She glanced over her shoulder to the south, where they could just see the outlines of a cluster of large, institutional buildings, about a mile away. "And they'll probably start there—with the Wards Island psychiatric treatment facility, home to a number of criminally insane, dangerously violent offenders. Perhaps, after that, they'll move on to Rikers Island penitentiary." She pegged Roth with a flat, unblinking stare. "No? You find that an unacceptable situation? Perhaps you agree then that we'd best draw our line in the sand here, as it were."

Without waiting for his reply, she stalked past him over to the pitcher's mound, knelt, and gouged a furrow in the sandy earth with her fingers. Then she poured out the contents of the silken pouch into the furrow. Whispering words in a low urgent voice, Daria re-covered the gap and, gesturing for Cal and Roth to follow her, said, "I'd stand back if I were you."

Then the Dragon Warriors appeared.

A chasm split the middle of the mound, gaping wide

enough to let five men, shoulder to shoulder, fit through. The first of those five heaved themselves up through the opening, dressed in ancient bronze armor—horsehair-crested helmets, breastplates, studded leather skirts and sandals and greaves—each one bearing a sword, a spear, and a man-sized shield bearing the insignia of a coiled serpent. Their faces were identical. They were killing machines. And they were legion.

Fifty, a hundred, two hundred . . . they kept climbing out of that pit. Even after the first ranks had already engaged with the ragged leading edge of the draugr horde. Cal looked at his mother, expecting her face to be set in an expression of triumph. But all he saw there, in that moment when she wasn't aware that he was looking, was weariness and worry.

She doesn't think we can win. They won't be enough.

They need help . . .

The sight of so many warriors, armed and ready to kill or be killed, stirred something in Cal's blood. Something he never would have thought himself capable of feeling. Bloodlust. Battle fever. Maybe, he thought distantly, it was all part of the whole "god thing" but, whatever it was, Cal wasn't about to deny it. After all of the pain and frustration of the last few days, all of the chaos and uncertainty and searing anger . . . after days of being afraid, he finally *fully* let loose.

Maybe in doing so, he could prove something to himself.

And Mason.

Cal felt his eyes flash with lightning as he called the waters of the East River to do his bidding, and a funnel of whirling water suddenly climbed into the sky, arcing through the air toward him. It surrounded him in a spinning torrent, clothing his limbs in supple, hard-as-steel armor and stretching into the shape of a trident in his hand. And then he was running to join the ranks of his mother's Dragon Warriors.

Concealed, invisible behind the shimmery haze of her runegold glamour, Heather faltered to a stop as the ground in front of Cal's mom suddenly cracked open and a marching band procession of guys in skirts and funny hats poured forth. Insanely dangerous-looking guys in skirts and funny hats. Flinty eyed, muscle-corded, single-minded and purposeful, they almost hummed like high-tension wires with the need to inflict maximum damage against a foe—any foe.

And there just happens to be a blue-light special on foes, right here!

Those guys could fight to their unbeating hearts' content, she thought. They weren't even alive—not in any real sense Heather could conceive of—and she didn't care what happened to them. They were a video game army, everyone the same.

Everyone except one.

The one warrior fighting with familiar grace and elegance near the front of the ranks. The helmetless one with the golden-brown hair . . . and the trident.

"Oh no. Cal . . . ," Heather whispered and started running again.

This wasn't *his* fight. It couldn't be!

It was his mother's. And Mason's father's.

And Heather just knew that if Cal got involved it would end badly. It was intuition—a feeling of imaginary snakes writhing in her stomach—but that sensation quickly gave way to another one—a feeling of very *real* fingers wrapped around her throat. She staggered to a sudden stop and heard Rory Starling's voice whisper, "Hey there, Palmerston. I think you have something of mine."

He'd come up right behind her.

So fast—and then she remembered that Rory had always been athletic. He'd always just been too much of an arrogant jerk to participate in team sports. He must have been hiding beneath one of the only lonely trees in the park and she'd run right past him, so intent was she on getting to Cal.

"Where the hell did you think you were going?" Rory asked. "Were you gonna go save Cally boy? He looks like he's doing all right on his own for once. Probably won't last, though. Guy's got no spine. Or, y'know, he won't after I rip it out of him. If the draugr don't do it first."

His voice was an ugly, sneering thing. Heather could hear him, but she couldn't see him, and she realized that, because he was touching her, Rory was invisible too. He must have known she had the runegold. He was behind her, pushing her to walk forward, and her first instinct was to haul off and mule kick as hard as she could, hoping she hit something vital. But it was if he read her mind and the fingers around her throat tightened with more-than-human strength. Heather froze.

"Uh-uh," Rory said. "Not unless you've grown tired of having a trachea."

She remembered how broken Rory had been the last time she'd seen him. How his arm had looked shattered beyond repair. Apparently, he'd gotten all better since then. Physically, at least. He was clearly still a psychopath. And he'd just threatened to tear her throat out.

"Now, I'd rather not have us suddenly materialize in the middle of all those soldiers," he said. "That could get messy. So I'll keep my hands on you and *you* keep your hand on that runegold. Now *move*. Just keep walking—over there—toward that trestle bridge." He nudged her sharply. "I'm not sure how in the mood my dad is for company, but I always think hostages are money in the bank. And if he doesn't need you for that, he can always give you to the Norns to play with. They probably haven't had a nice healthy mind to snack on for aeons."

"Certainly not if they're hanging out with you," Heather snarked.

To her surprise, Rory laughed. "Y'know, Palmerston, I always thought you were more than just hot. I actually thought you were smart. When you wised up and dropped that loser Aristarchos, I thought there might even be a chance for us."

Heather found herself torn between the urge to guffaw or gag.

But then she found herself stepping beneath the shadow of the Bronx Kill Bridge and—when Rory suddenly grabbed the runegold from her hand and shoved her forward—falling on her knees to the ground . . . right at the feet of Gunnar Starling. One of the most terrifying men she'd ever known.

"Sorry I went AWOL there, Pops," Rory said. "Just thought she might come in handy."

Gunnar cast a baleful eye over his wayward son, who'd casually pocketed the runegold, and then he turned to look down at Heather. He stared at her in silence for a long time and all Heather could do was return the gaze, unable to look away, as memories flooded her mind of what the Starling patriarch had done the last time she'd seen him. Calmly murdering Tag Overlea with a golden acorn like the one Rory had just taken from her.

"Handy?" Gunnar asked in a deceptively conversational tone. "I rather doubt that now." He bent down in front of her and actually held out a hand to help her stand. Heather had no idea what to do or say, but when he spoke again, it felt as though she were turning to ice inside. "But that's not to say Miss Palmerston hasn't already helped us out immensely. And for that, my dear, I owe you a debt of thanks. Of course, I won't ever be able to repay it. Not after today. Now come, stand by me and let us watch the fruits of our combined labors grow ripe on this branch of the World Tree."

"Do you even listen to yourself when you talk?" Heather said, the shakiness in her tone undercutting the brash words. "This raging supervillain complex you're nurturing is a little over the top, don't you think? And for the record? I would never help someone like you."

"Not willingly, I'm sure." Gunnar ignored the supervillain jibe. "I was fortunate that your mother didn't feel the same way. She's an extraordinary woman. And really quite devoted to her patroness."

Heather felt an uncomfortable clenching in her stomach. "What patroness? What are you talking about?"

"The Roman goddess Venus." Gunnar's eyes were filled with an ugly satisfaction at whatever expression Heather wore in that moment. "Didn't you know?"

Of course she didn't know.

Of course I knew.

She'd known. She'd always known.

It was there in the strained, awkward relationship between her parents—the way they could seem so passionately in love with each other one moment, and like they hated each other's guts in the next. The gut-hating phases almost always happened after one of her mother's private solarium parties. The ones her father never attended.

The ones Heather had been forbidden from attending.

Parties—no, rituals—dedicated to Venus, Roman goddess of Love.

Heather moaned. "I think I'm going to be sick."

Of course, Venus had had a son. Cupid. A Valentine's Day cherub.

Valen . . .

Frankly, Heather preferred the James Dean wannabe guise.

Valen had said he'd been looking for her, but that he hadn't been able to find her. That must have been her mother's doing. For a fleeting instant, Heather thought that maybe her mother had been trying to protect her.

No. Not if what Gunnar Starling said was true.

"Your mother pledged you to her goddess when you were born."

To the goddess of love. So *that* was why she'd been able to sense the emotions in others ever since she was young. And it had left Heather feeling like a freak for her entire life.

Thanks, Mom.

"And, of course, your feelings for the Aristarchos boy have always been exceptionally strong." Gunnar smiled pleasantly, as if he were just one of Heather's teachers at Gos, complimenting her on a job well done on an assignment. "Strong enough that your mother was able to use them as a conduit— to turn *his* feelings toward my daughter."

"Why? Why would she *do* that?" Heather asked, barely able to choke out the words.

"Because I asked her to." Gunnar smiled a predatory smile. "I can be very persuasive. And to my way of thinking, it's never a bad idea to have a semi-divine being devoted to one's cause." His left eye glittered strangely as he glanced in Calum's direction. "Even if he doesn't know he is. Yet."

Heather felt a rush of heat to her face. They'd used her. Just to get to Cal. She had been *so* right when she'd told him their parents were all off the rails. All of them. Not just Gunnar Starling, although he was clearly the worst of a bad bunch.

He nodded at the field. "Watch now as Cal plays his part. . . ."

Pieces on the game board, Heather thought. *That's all we are.*

And now all she could do was watch how the game played out.

She glanced around to see where Rory was, but he was nowhere in sight. While Gunnar gloated, his son had used the runegold he'd taken from Heather and disappeared again. She wondered for a moment where he'd gone, but then she heard an inhuman howl of pain.

And she knew exactly where Rory was, and why.

★ ★ ★

Fearsome blurs of gold and black, thrashing among the sea of horrid gray, the two wolves fought gallantly for their lives against an overwhelming number of draugr. And there was nothing Mason could do to help. Not without manifesting the Valkyrie inside her.

The one thing, in this place, that she absolutely could not do.

She wanted to scream with frustration as she watched Rafe and Fennrys struggling to defend each other against a horrifying multitude, two against so many.

But then, suddenly . . . there were *more*.

A shout of encouragement escaped Mason's lips as bronze-helmeted warriors appeared—rank upon rank of them—from out of nowhere, wading into the sea of thrashing gray monsters, and it was like turning back the tide. They drove the draugr back, gave Fenn and Rafe breathing room and a chance to regroup and fight the way they were meant to—as a team. When an opening suddenly appeared in the sea of storm zombies, the black wolf surged forward toward the sleek white yacht, moored to the nearby concrete pier. Douglas Muir had seen Rafe and Fennrys coming and had already cast off the bow rope. As Rafe leaped—bounding over the side railing to collapse in a panting heap on the deck—Douglas cast off the stern mooring, because the Fennrys Wolf was right behind him.

Mason felt her hope soar.

They're going to make it! she thought.

And then the air right in front of the great golden Wolf . . . shimmered.

With only ten feet to the yacht, Fennrys's head suddenly snapped up as if he'd been hit by an invisible train and he flew backward through the air twenty feet, blood spouting from his muzzle in a bright crimson arc.

"Fennrys!" Mason screamed, confused and horrified.

When Rory suddenly faded into view, her confusion vanished.

But not her horror.

Dread flooded Mason's chest, drowning the hope that had so recently flourished there. Rory stalked after the Fennrys Wolf, lifting his gleaming silver hand high in the air to bring it down in a hammer blow on the Wolf's flank. Mason could almost feel his ribs breaking and she cried out as that gleaming silver fist descended again and again, pummeling the golden Wolf like thunder.

She saw the great beast struggle to rise and then fall again. And again . . .

She saw red staining the golden fur . . .

And then *all* she saw was red.

XXIV

The crimson mist that dropped over her like a cloak clarified everything. Simplified it.

She was what she was. Valkyrie. Her purpose was pure.

I will choose . . .

Who?

The one who will fight for me. Die for me . . .

Her far-seeing gaze scanned the combatants on the field as, behind her, the Einherjar waited. Poised on the cusp of achieving their promised destiny, standing at the brink of Ragnarok itself. Shields and swords, helmets and spearheads shining in the nonexistent sun, they stood in loose formation, not the undisciplined mob of berserkers she might have expected, wild with the joy of impending chaos, the fight, the kill . . .

That would come soon.

But not yet.

Bound to follow only the three Odin sons into battle, the

Einherjar were compelled to leash in their warrior rage until such time as there was a third son actually in existence. The one that Mason, as a Valkyrie, was supposed to choose. The very thing she had vowed not to do. And now, standing on a game board of gods that her own father had so painstakingly set up, it was the only thing in her mind. The sight of Fennrys, beaten, bloodied . . . so utterly broken, had shattered Mason's self-control.

She hadn't even realized she'd drawn the veiled spear from its sheath.

But she had.

And now, a raven circled over her helmeted head and silver chain mail clothed her limbs. And vengeance, bloodlust, battle madness were the only things she felt. Beyond the singular, overwhelming need to choose.

Choose . . .

Her Valkyrie gaze scanned the field.

Choose.

But who?

The Wolf . . .

No.

The Wolf had fought bravely, savagely, but the flame of his inner light sputtered like the burnt down wick of a candle, lit long into the night. He could not be the third Odin son.

Mason turned toward the Elusinian woman's warriors. Sprung from dragon's teeth, there must surely be one among them who would fight valiantly enough to be worthy of her spear's touch. Her eyes scanned the rows upon rows. All of the faces looked the same. Hard, cold eyes, like polished stones set in faces of chiseled marble, frozen in identical expressions beneath the severe brims of polished bronze helmets, the nose guards bisecting their features, dehumanizing them. War machines. They fought well, efficiently, but without passion.

She needed passion . . .

There!

Just behind the leading edge of the Dragon Warriors, she found it.

Cal.

Calum Aristarchos had passion. He was seared through to his skin by the burning coal of it at the center of his chest. Passion for *her*. For Mason Starling. The kind of passion that would make him do anything she required of him.

It was all so very clear to her now.

She needed him in the same way that he needed her. It was a perfect storm of desire and she was more than willing to dive into the heart of it. The roaring of wind and blood in her ears drove every other thought from her mind as she called a Valkyrie wind and, lifting the Odin spear high above her head, ascended into the skies above the field of Valgrind to claim her champion.

But first, he would have to fight. For her.

He would have to die for her.

"Calum Aristarchos!" she shouted, rising up off the deck of the ship to hover over the battlefield, her cloak spread wide like wings behind her. "Fight for me! Die for me!"

His face turned upward and his green eyes blazed.

"Win my love!" she cried. And her voice echoed across the field of Valgrind.

Somewhere deep inside him, a rust-frozen lock suddenly shattered and fell away.

And a door swung wide open.

All the years he'd spent as a medal-winning fencer, Cal had won because he'd been careful. Smart, strategic, never overcommitting or taking stupid chances. He'd worked his technique down to inches and studied his opponents minutely. His fighting had always been clean, crisp, passionless. And most of the time, he'd won.

That was before the Fennrys Wolf.

Before he'd started to lose everything.

But the Wolf, it seemed, wasn't the only one who could fight with berserker rage,

When Cal heard Mason cry out his name, his heart responded with a surge of emotion. He looked up to see her there, shining like an angel in the sky above him and he knew he'd never seen anything so beautiful nor so terrifying in all his life.

Die for her? It was his heart's desire.

Before he'd even made a conscious decision, Cal suddenly found himself out in the very front ranks of the Dragon Warriors, howling a battle cry and hewing draugr limbs from bodies. All the thwarted passion in his immortal soul found expression in the shining weapon in his hand . . . and the way it hacked through his enemies.

He would win Mason Starling's love, even if it killed him.

Which was, of course, the whole point.

"Oh no! No no *no*—*crap!*"

Heather watched, aghast, as the Valkyrie rose up from the decks of the phantom ship, into the skies over the battlefield. She heard the chooser of the slain cry out—in a voice like storm and fury—howling out words that Mason Starling would have been embarrassed to hear come from her own mouth.

If she'd still *been* Mason Starling, that is.

"Starling—*NO!*" Heather shouted, even though she knew that the other girl wouldn't hear her, intent as she was on warping Cal's already twisted feelings and tying them into a passion-fueled knot of killing rage.

She wanted to scream that it was all a lie. All of it.

Yes, she thought. *Cal loves Mason, but* that *is the biggest lie of all!*

So Heather decided that she was going to shoot Cal full of truth. Excruciating, throbbing-dull, needle-sharp truth. Away from Gunnar's line of sight, she eased her hand into the purse she still wore slung across her body, and felt around—carefully—for the crossbow . . . and the cold, heavy, dreadful leaden bolt.

"This one hurts like every hell there is . . . ," Valen had told her.

Of course it did. Hate always hurt like that.

Heather fumbled, one-handed, to load the leaden bolt into the crossbow slot, her fingers turning numb from the bolt's chill touch. She probably didn't have to worry about the need for stealth. Gunnar Starling's attention was fixed wholly on what was happening on the field of battle—on the epic, horrifying smackdown going on between Rory and the Wolf that used to be Fennrys—and on Cal and Mason.

From the corner of her eye, Heather saw Roth break from Daria's side and charge across the field heading straight for Cal, where he was busily hacking holes in the draugr horde in order to prove himself to Mason. Roth slammed into Cal from behind, thrusting him out of the main press of the fighting. He screamed at Cal, punching and pleading, trying to get him to stand down and stop fighting. With about the same success rate as trying to swat a hornet with a silk scarf. All he managed to do was draw Cal's fury down on himself, and the hunting knife he carried was no match for the silvery trident in Cal's hands. In short order, Roth was forced to retreat. He stumbled back toward the Bronx Kill Bridge and Cal followed, pressing his attacks. That was when Heather saw her chance. She pulled the crossbow out of her bag.

Over near the Bronx Kill Bridge, Roth ducked under the sweep of Cal's trident and threw a roundhouse punch. Cal staggered back a step, and swung his weapon backhanded in a vicious arc that left three parallel lines of blood seeping through the front of Roth's T-shirt. Roth fell to his knees and Cal advanced, raising the trident for a killing blow. Above them, Mason hovered in the air like a dark angel. Her face, beneath the brim of her raven-winged helmet, was the rigid, ecstatic mask of a battle goddess. Her blue eyes were incandescent.

She raised the Odin spear high over her shoulder . . .

Hidden in the shadows beneath the bridge, Heather raised the crossbow to her lips and—acting on instinct—she whispered Mason Starling's name to the dull gray bolt. She took aim, and pulled the trigger. It hit Cal square in the chest.

He screamed like a wounded animal.

In an instant, the madness dropped away from him—Heather *saw* it happen—and the look of anguish that washed over Cal's features as he looked up into the sky where Mason hovered . . . terrible and beautiful, ready to strike, to choose . . . it broke Heather's heart. In pretty much the same way she'd just broken his.

You set him free, she told herself.

But it didn't make her feel any better. She watched the trident fall from his hands, shattering into a million teardrops as it hit the ground. Cal's shoulders rolled convulsively forward and he sank to his knees, shuddering, in the mud of the churned field to bury his face in his hands. In the sky above, the Odin spear wavered in Mason's fist and the point of the blade drifted up. Her Valkyrie wrath morphed into an expression of confusion. Heather looked over to where Roth lay on the ground near Cal, staring up at his sister. His chest was heaving and bloodied. The tides of the battle had ebbed away from them.

Heather took a step forward . . .

And Gunnar Starling backhanded her across the jaw.

"You stupid girl!" he shouted. "What have you done?!"

He reared back, fist cocked. Heather scrambled to get out of his way and suddenly Roth was there, hauling Gunnar back, away from her. And then Cal was there too. He grabbed Heather by the wrist and dragged her away from the two Starling men as they grappled and swung at each other, cursing and frenzied with rage. When Cal got Heather out of harm's reach, he lifted the hand he held her by up in front of his face . . . and stared at the crossbow. Just stared at it, for a long silent moment. She could see it in his face. He knew what it was.

And he knew what she'd done to him.

"It was all a lie," he said, his voice scrapped thin and raw. "Wasn't it?"

Heather nodded, unable to speak the words that would tell him that *yes,* everything he'd felt for Mason Starling—all the wrenching heartache, all the moments of bliss when she smiled at him, all the things he'd wanted with her—had been a mirage.

His fingers convulsed on her skin as he held her by the wrist.

"It didn't *feel* like one . . . ," he whispered.

His other hand went to the place on his chest above his heart where the lead bolt had hit him. There would be a mark there, Heather knew. One that might not ever fade.

"Why?" Cal asked her.

"Why what?" Heather glanced at him from under her lashes, not quite able to make eye contact.

Cal shook his head, weary. "There's another bolt. Isn't there?"

She swallowed noisily and nodded.

"Why didn't you use it, too?"

Heather knew what he meant. Why hadn't she made Cal love *her* instead?

"I don't want the lie," she whispered. "No matter how beautiful it is."

With a shocking suddenness, the bright-burning passion was gone. The fight was suddenly gone, banished from the heart of the one she'd been about to choose. Uncertainty, sorrow, bitter regret . . . *these* were not the things that drew her spear. But suddenly, they were the only things in Calum's heart.

She would not choose him. She couldn't.

The red mist of battle lust cleared from her mind and her gaze roamed over the chaotic field beneath her. She saw Heather and Cal—her friends—heads bent toward each other, nodding over a weapon held in Heather's white-knuckled hand. And then Mason understood just exactly what had transpired. She descended slowly from the sky to stand before them and willed herself to become Mason again. . . .

And nothing happened.

The helmet, the armor, the spear . . . *none* of it disappeared. Mason remained a Valkyrie. But she was Mason, too. There was a moment of confusion, and then she understood. She was too far gone. Too much the Valkyrie to *not* choose. Not far away from where she stood, battles still raged. Draugr and Dragon Warriors battered ceaselessly at each other while the Einherjar still stood, waiting for her to choose. Roth and Gunnar swung battering fists at each other. And Rory and Fennrys were fighting to the death.

Fennrys's death.

With each blow he landed, Rory's silver hand seemed to shine brighter—even though red blood coated his knuckles.

Mason didn't understand it. As the Wolf, Fennrys should have been virtually unkillable. His strength was immeasurable, his ability to heal almost instantaneous. It was the reason Mason had begged Rafe to turn him in the first place.

Rory was just . . . Rory.

But he wears a hand made for a god. A silver *hand . . .*

Suddenly, Mason heard Loki's voice echoing in her head. She remembered his words in the catacombs under Gosforth: *"Silver,"* he'd said, taking the rings off his fingers so he could touch his son. *"Anathema to werewolves."*

Wolfsbane. Poison. A truth that had translated down through folk and fairy tales. Kill a werewolf with a silver bullet. Or a silver fist. And then Mason realized something else. In one hand, she held the Odin spear. But in the *other,* her fist was still knotted closed around the iron Janus Medallion that Fenn had tossed her on the ship. And it still pulsed with all of the magick that Loki had poured into it, to cage the Wolf inside his son.

Mason had used the medallion before—Fennrys had taught her how.

Make it happen in your mind, and make it happen in the world . . .

She poured all her will and all her heart into the iron disk and sent its magick out toward the Fennrys Wolf, pleading for Loki to help her help his son.

"Please," she whispered. "Help him find the *man* within the beast . . ."

Because Rory's silver hand was killing the Wolf.

But Mason knew it couldn't kill Fennrys.

Time spiraled out and away from her. She saw her brother

howl with cruel laughter and lift his arm high. Then the talisman in her fist blazed with eldritch light. She saw the Wolf's eyes flash in answer to her plea.

Rory unleashed another devastating blow, aimed at Fennrys's head . . .

And Fenn caught that fist in his hand.

Fennrys heard Mason's voice in his mind.

"Come back to me," she whispered.

Sweetheart, I can't. I'm so tired . . .

"Please, Fennrys. Together. We can do this."

Mason . . .

"I love you."

With those words, he reached deeper inside of himself than he ever had. He found his father's magick—Loki's magick—and he grasped it with his mind. And he felt it suddenly flood his heart and limbs, transforming them. Changing him.

And chaining the beast within him . . .

Forever.

He gritted his teeth and thrust out his hand, catching Rory's clenched silver fist in the iron cage of his fingers. In his human shape, the silver was nothing more to Fennrys than cold, hard metal. He lurched to his feet, the sensation of his broken ribs grinding against each other nothing more than background noise in his mind in that moment.

He smiled in Rory's astonished, furious face.

And then shoved him to his knees in the crimson-stained mud.

★ ★ ★

Mason's breath caught in her throat.

Fennrys was on his feet and Rory was on the ground. But she could feel, through the fading bond of Loki's magick, how weak Fenn was. How hurt. If Rory fought back, she wasn't at all certain Fenn would win. She glanced at Heather, and at the crossbow she still held in her hand.

"There's another bolt?" she asked.

Heather nodded and fished the golden arrow out of her purse. She loaded it into the crossbow with swift, precise motions, and handed it over to Mason.

"Just . . . speak a name." Heather nodded at the weapon.

Mason understood. All she had to do was tell the crossbow who to make her brother love. And her mad, vicious, damaged, humanity-loathing brother would finally know what it felt like to care. To feel. To *love*. It was the worst possible thing she could think of to do to him.

She raised the bow to her lips.

"The *world,* Rory," she whispered in a voice like judgment, "love the *whole damned world . . .*"

Then she aimed, and pulled the trigger.

The bolt struck Rory in the middle of his back, and Mason thought she'd never heard such a cry of anguish in her life. He fell to the ground, thrashing and kicking, his eyes white-rimmed, as a sudden, overwhelming deluge of emotion crashed over him like a tidal wave. His mind hadn't changed, she knew, only his heart, and he clawed at his rib cage as if he would tear that heart out rather than suffer a moment more of it beating. He screamed, rolling into a tight ball of agony, feeling every moment of every awful thing he'd ever done and knowing, for the first time, how truly rotten to the core he was.

He wouldn't be able to hurt anyone ever again.

It was over.

No . . . it isn't.

Mason looked down and saw that she still hadn't changed back. She couldn't. She had to choose. And so long as she didn't, the world—the one she'd just compelled her brother to love with all his sick, twisted heart—remained in peril. But once she chose, that same world would end. She almost sobbed with frustration . . . and then it struck her.

The most valiant combatant on that whole field had been the Fennrys Wolf.

And the one he'd fought so valiantly with . . . had been himself. Fennrys had fought the Wolf within—for her. He was the one who'd fought for her. He'd already died for her. . . . He deserved to be chosen. To be the warrior. And he would keep the Wolf at bay.

Which means . . .

Mason felt a thrill of excitement run through her as she hefted the spear in her hand, felt its weight of destiny, and threw.

"NO!" her father roared as the ancient weapon left her hand. "The Wolf must remain the Wolf!"

Which means no Ragnarok.

The Odin spear's iron blade glowed white as it flew through the air. It struck Fennrys in the very center of his chest, igniting like a flare, and then passed through him to stick in the ground, leaving only the mark of a glowing brand in the middle of his chest. Fenn stood there, a look of mild surprise on his face, as he pressed his hand to the mark.

"I guess I've died enough times already," he said in a ragged voice, "that this kind of thing doesn't even affect me anymore. . . ."

Mason felt a wave of relief flood through her as the chain mail and armor she wore faded from her like mist in a breeze. She turned toward her father and saw the golden twist of light in his left eye flicker and dim. "There can be no fulfillment of the prophecy if the Wolf and the Warrior are one and the same," she said quietly. "Sorry, Dad. No Ragnarok today." She turned and looked back at the ranks of the Einherjar who stood waiting, and spotted Taggert Overlea where he stood, his letterman jacket exchanged for leather and iron. "Hope that's not too much of a disappointment for you, Tag."

He shrugged and said. "No, I'm cool."

"I thought you might be."

"You don't know what you've done," her father rasped. "You don't—"

"I know *exactly* what I've done," she said, her voice cracking like a whip. "You can hardly call me a chooser if the choice isn't mine to make. I made it. You can live with it. Or not. That's *your* choice."

Laughter drifted down from above them, rich and musical.

Mason looked up to see Loki standing on one end of the Bronx Kill Bridge span, his face stretched wide in mirth, and Heimdall standing on the other, a thundercloud frown on his brow. In between the two of them, the Norns stood like statues, painted faces impassive.

"Better luck next time, Guardian!" Loki called to Heimdall, his eternal nemesis. "Or probably not. Not if these mortal wonders stay so fierce. Ye gods, they're more beautiful every time. And more entertaining!"

Heimdall's fist closed around the horn that hung from his belt, but Loki's smile disappeared, replaced with a warning scowl that made even Mason take a step back.

"Go back to Asgard, Watcher," he said in a voice like thunder. "Go back to your brooding and your scheming and leave these children to their world. You and I will meet again on another Valgrind. And maybe *then* we will end each other. Or the next time, or the next." He turned to address the Norns. "And go you with him, twisted fates. I'll join you soon enough and then we can all sit and toast to our departed brothers and sisters and wait for the next ending of the world!"

Heimdall shifted his gaze to Mason, and she returned his stare, unblinking.

As he faded from sight, along with Loki and the Norns, she wondered if she would ever see the Guardian of Bifrost again. And she knew that he'd better hope that day never came to pass.

XXV

"**I** still owe you a debt," Mason said as Rafe crossed the field to meet them.

The ancient god nodded once. "I haven't forgotten."

Mason bit her lip. She wished he had, but she knew that wasn't how this kind of thing worked. "My life?"

"That would do it," he said with grim reluctance.

"How about mine instead?" Toby said from right behind her.

Mason turned to see her fencing master standing there, bent with age, gray and weathered. "Toby?" She put a hand on his arm.

He ignored her, speaking directly to the god of death. "A lot more folks in this city are going to be finding their way into the Nether Realms after this day."

Rafe's dark gaze narrowed.

"And you're down one ferryman."

Mason shook her head in alarm. "Toby—"

"I can handle a boat," he said.

Rafe's mouth quirked in a half smile. "I know that."

"And I have more than a passing acquaintance with death."

"Your soul will belong to me," Rafe said quietly.

Toby shrugged. "You can have it. I've already gotten enough good use out of it."

"You will be at my beck and call."

"I've worked on a clock before."

"And you'll pay your bar tab on time." Rafe pulled a flask out of the breast pocket of his suit jacket and handed it to the fencing master.

Toby took a long swig and Mason watched the color flood back into his seamed, sunken cheeks. His rheumy eyes grew brighter and he stood taller. The gray began to fade from his beard.

"Are you sure about this?" She put a hand on his arm.

He nodded. "Oh yeah. It's the first thing I've been sure of in a long time. Other than *you*. Mason Starling, I pledge my life and soul to you to do with what you will."

She nodded, flooded with such overwhelming gratitude and affection for her coach that she could barely speak. But she managed to swallow the knot of tears gathering in her throat and said, "And I give that life and soul over into the keeping of Anubis, Lord of the Dead, as payment in full of a debt owed." She watched as Rafe's eyes flashed and he grinned. "He'd better take good care of you, if he knows what's good for him."

"The best, Lady." Rafe gracefully inclined his head.

"You can take that to the bank."

"That's it?" she asked looking around. Fennrys had dropped to one knee on the trampled ground and she needed to go to him. She needed to hold him in her arms and make sure everything was all right between them. "Are we done?"

"Yeah. We're done," Toby said. "It's over, Mason. We won."

They really had won. Mason only wished that she hadn't had to lose so much. But the field of Valgrind began to slowly sink back into the sea. The draugr, back into the soil. And the Dragon Warriors, at a word from their summoner, Daria Aristarchos, marched back into the gap in the earth they'd crawled out of. It was over.

Almost.

From beneath the shadow of the Bronx Kill Bridge, Mason's father staggered forward. He looked so unlike his usual elegant self, she barely recognized him.

"Are you proud, both of you?" Gunnar turned a baleful, poisonous gaze on Mason and Roth. "Are you proud of your betrayal of me? Of our family?"

Roth shook his head in weary disgust. "The only betrayal here is yours," he said. "It always has been. You knew. You've always known what I did. What Daria made me do. You *let* her, didn't you? How could you do that to Mason? To me?"

"Because I thought it might be useful one day to have you in her power," Gunnar said. "And it was. You were . . . oh, son. We *almost* won!"

"You're a sick son of a bitch, Dad," Roth spat and turned his gaze away.

Gunnar shook his head wildly, the mane of his silver hair hanging lank in front of his face. "No! I just know my place in the universe. My purpose. The Gosforth families all serve higher ends." He grinned madly. "Just because ours didn't win this time doesn't mean it wasn't worth the fight."

He stalked toward Roth, hands balled into fists, until Roth brought up the hunting knife he held to keep him at bay. Gunnar leaned into the point of the blade and nodded, his face going slack, serene.

"Now," he said. "Make an end of this. Of me . . ."

Mason held her breath. Silence descended and time seemed to stand still. Then . . .

"No." Roth shook his head. "You can go to hell, old man. But find your own way there. I've killed enough family members already."

Mason felt her heart swell with pride for Roth, even as she watched her father's impassive expression twist with sudden, incandescent fury.

"Coward!" he screamed.

His eyes went wild and dark, the glittering gold thread in his left eye turned scarlet and his mouth opened wide as he hurled invective at his eldest son. Mason bit her lip to keep from weeping in the face of her father's insanity. And then, from the corner of her eye, she saw the dark, cloaked shape of her mother gliding silently across the field. For a moment, Gunnar didn't notice, too consumed by his rage. But then, he saw her. And it was as if someone reached down and pulled the stopper from a drain. All of the rage flowed out of him. The mad light dimmed in his eyes and a hint of the man that

Mason had known and loved all her life flickered back into existence.

"Yelena . . . ?" Gunnar's deep voice was a bare whisper of sound.

He took a faltering step toward the vision of his beloved wife, as she pushed the hood back all the way from her face.

"I am Hel," she said. "I am what you made me."

"Take me." Gunnar held out his hands. "Take me with you!"

Yelena shook her head sadly. And in that moment, everything changed about Gunnar Starling. The savage sense of purpose evaporated and a frantic desperate need seemed to overtake him. The need to die and be reunited with the love of his soul.

"What of you?" He lurched across the field toward where Fennrys still crouched on one knee, holding his side. "Isn't it your destiny to make an end of me?"

Mason saw Fenn's fingers clench on the hilt of the long knife strapped to his leg. She held her breath as he drew the weapon from its sheath. And then the whiteness left Fenn's knuckles and he threw the blade to the ground.

"Like Roth said." He grinned coldly. "You want an end so bad? Make it your own damned self." Then he climbed to his feet and turned his back, walking away from her father, his steps halting, but his head high.

"No. NO!" Gunnar cried, desperate. He even looked to Daria Aristarchos, his eyes pleading and desperate, and Mason thought how this was the tragic last act of the strangest love triangle ever playing out in front of her. Yelena, Daria, and

Gunnar Starling. The two women exchanged a long glance, and smiles that were so full of sorrow. There was even forgiveness there—some, not all—for what Daria had done. She would spend the rest of her days making amends for those vile acts of vengeance. The rest of her life and beyond, Mason suspected, if the look in her mother's eyes was any indication. But there would be no help for Gunnar Starling.

No hand to speed him on his way to Helheim except his own . . .

"I will be with you again, my love," he murmured. And then picked up Fennrys's blade and drove it up under his rib cage with barely a whispered gasp.

As the light began to fade from his eyes, Hel whispered, "No. You won't."

And in a final act of cold retribution, Mason saw what it was that her mother truly had become. What her father had made her. She nodded once to Daria, who raised her face skyward and closed her eyes. Mere moments later, three shadows appeared in the sunless sky and the Harpies fell from high above to claim their suicide.

Mason turned away as the three goddesses descended on Gunnar Starling where he lay on the ground, Fennrys's sword in his guts by his own hand and his twisting, gold-filled gaze slowly fading to black.

When she turned back a moment later, he was gone.

"I think you dropped this . . . ," Fennrys said, as he walked haltingly toward Mason, holding out the Odin spear.

"Yeah . . ." She was trying so hard to smile through the

rivers of tears that poured from her eyes. "I'm kind of a but-terfingers. Thanks . . ."

Her fingertips brushed his as she wrapped her hand around the spear haft. Their eyes locked and Mason felt like she was falling into a cool spring hidden deep in a forest somewhere far away from anywhere. Fennrys suddenly went rigid with pain. He was so pale. Mason put an arm around him and turned to Rafe, whose own wounds were already healing—no more than fresh, fading scars.

"The Wolf in him is gone, Mase. But the Wolf's strength left with it," Rafe said. He put a hand on Fennrys's chest. "He's badly hurt. Broken bones, internal bleeding . . ."

"Perhaps I can help," Daria said, sharing a glance with her son. "One of the greatest of our gods was Apollo. The Healer. There are those in my family who still practice those magicks. I will do what I can. *We* will do what we can."

Rafe stepped back.

"Get him on the boat," he said.

Cal stepped forward and, before Mason had a chance to protest, got a shoulder under Fennrys's arm and half carried him in the direction of his father's yacht. Heather stepped forward and offered Mason a steadying hand, but after a moment she shook her head and lurched away from the gathered group of her friends, the Odin spear clutched in her fist.

She broke the spear in two over her knee.

EPILOGUE

The late winter cold bit at Mason's cheeks and forehead and drew diamond-bright spangles of tears to her lashes as she walked the few blocks back to the Gosforth dorm from the Columbia University hall where the awards banquet had been held. The fencing trophy in her hand was heavy enough to be a weapon in itself and she smiled, proud of the achievement.

Prouder still that she'd done it on her own.

Her return to the world of competition fencing had been hard without Toby there to coach her—harder still without Fennrys there to . . . well, to just *be* there—but she'd been determined to do it. The gala that night had been mostly on the sweet end of bittersweet and she was getting used to the loneliness. She hitched the collar up on her long coat and let the sounds of the city wash over her as she walked. New York had mostly recovered from its brush with Ragnarok. Recovered, and replanted, and rebuilt. The city and its inhabitants had shaken off the weirdness and the horror and, even if no one could quite explain just exactly what had happened, they had soldiered on in the way that New Yorkers did.

Gosforth Academy had seen a quiet, thorough administrative restructuring, with Daria Aristarchos taking up the position as headmistress—guided by a great deal of student council input—and with Roth Starling as acting chair of the school board. Classes had resumed only a few weeks after the city had been declared safe again by the authorities. In the intervening days, Mason had spent most of her time practicing in the university gym, along with Cal and Heather.

The three of them didn't talk much—they didn't seem to need to—but Mason knew that Heather had sent her parents a letter telling them she wasn't ever coming home again and they could send her stuff to storage. She'd collect it after she graduated, maybe. Cal had offered her a room in his mom's house for when summer came around again, and Mason was glad to see them growing closer. The fact that Heather hadn't used the golden bolt on him when she could have seemed to have opened Cal's eyes, Mason thought, and might just have the same end result, if only it took a little longer.

She was happy for her friends. Happy for herself that night.

The melancholy that she wore like a cloak those days had lifted a little.

Still. When she got back to her room and placed the trophy on her shelf, she felt a twist in her heart. It had been more than six months and nothing. Not a word. She knew it was because wherever they'd taken Fennrys, it wasn't anywhere with cell phone service. But it was hard. Mason sighed and shrugged out of her coat, catching sight of her reflection in the closed, darkened window of her room. She looked like an elegant phantom, with her hair pulled back from her face and the shimmer of the evening gown she wore lending her an ethereal quality. She went to pull the curtains shut . . .

And something hit her windowpane.

Something small . . . like a pebble.

The breath stopped in Mason's throat. She was imagining things—

Tink.

In an eye blink she had the window thrown wide. She stuck her head outside, gasping at the rush of cold, but she could see nothing. Everything was dark and still . . . and then he stepped out of the shadows under the trees and smiled up at her. That weird, wonderful smile.

And Fennrys said, "Are you ready for our date?"

Mason's mouth opened, but no sound came out.

Fennrys . . .

"I know you don't graduate until next year so it's not exactly prom, but that dress would still go awfully nice with this orchid." He held out a little box wrapped with a ribbon.

"Are . . . you wearing a tux?" Mason managed to ask.

"Not good?"

"No! Good!" Her heart was going to burst with joy. "*Fantastic!* Don't move . . ."

She ducked back inside and ran out of her room, not bothering with her coat or purse. She just needed to make sure he didn't disappear. And he didn't. He was still waiting there when she ran out the door and into his arms.

"Hey, sweetheart," he whispered into her hair. "I've missed you."

She reached up and pulled his head down and kissed him.

And the whole world and all the months that had passed just . . . fell away.

Behind them, Mason heard the throaty purr of a car engine and turned to see the dark shape of a Bentley pull to the curb. It looked like the one her dad used to own and she held her breath for a moment. But then the driver's window slid down and Toby Fortier's grinning face appeared.

"Where to, kids?" he asked as Fennrys opened the door and Mason climbed into the backseat.

"How about a Safe Harbor," Fennrys said with a laugh.

Toby raised an eyebrow in the rearview mirror. "Got an address for that?"

Fennrys looked down at Mason, nestled against him. "Take us to the High Line," he said. "And don't spare the horses."

ACKNOWLEDGMENTS

Ah, Ragnarok . . .

Well, I guess, first and foremost, as this series comes to an end, I should acknowledge the fine and fabulous city of New York—a place I've been cheerfully trying to destroy since the early days of the Wondrous Strange books. Er, sorry about that, NYC . . . I really *do* love and treasure your streets and parks and buildings and bridges and, without you, these stories would have been impossible to write. Thanks for every bit of sparkling inspiration you gave me.

Thank you, once again, to Jessica Regel, my agent, who gleefully encouraged me in my quest to unleash mayhem and monsters on her city. And to Tara Hart, likewise enabler of mystical ka-booming. You two, and the fantastic staffs of JVNLA and Foundry Literary + Media, have a lot to answer for. Thankfully!

Thanks, also, to my editor, Karen Chaplin, and all of the industrious, creative (wrecking) crew at HarperCollins:

editorial director Rosemary Brosnan; Maggie Herold and Alexei Esikoff, my production editors; and Cara Petrus and Heather Daugherty, my designers. Thanks, also, to Hadley Dyer and everyone at HarperCollins Canada for cheering on the literary destruction.

My mom and my wonderful family, as always, deserve all of the love, gratitude, and epic battles I can give them—and then some. So does my awesome collection of friends.

And I hope he never gets tired of reading this kind of thing, but I really do owe the biggest mythologically apocalyptic ka-boom of all to my partner in (occasionally fictional) crime, John.

As always, endless thank-yous to my wreckage-craving readers! You guys simply are the best.

Ragnarok-n-roll!

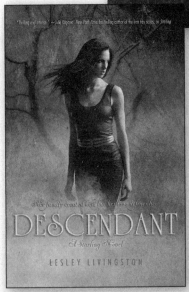